THE UNFINISHED

"This was such a refreshing read! Different from anything I've read recently and I just could not put it down until I was finished. Worth every penny!" – J. Stockett

"Absolutely loved this book. Different than any book I usually read. Just when you think you understand the plot you turn the page and it takes another turn, one you least expected. At some points it got my heart pumping so fast I had to put it down and come back. Loved the ending...sequel maybe? You won't regret buying this one." – L. Moreland

This is unlike anything I have ever read, so I was a bit skeptical at first. As I read chapter after chapter, though, I found myself drawn into the characters' worlds needing to know what would happen next. Just when I thought I had the book figured out, twists and turns would keep me guessing! I'm very impressed with Cameron's first book and am eager to see what comes next! – C. Meyer

WHILE YOU WERE IN AFGHANISTAN

"While reading this book I could feel every word written. The writing has a way of making you feel like you are there. The loneliness, the hurt, the tears, the love, the sharing of your soul. Good job!" – L. Moreland

INNUENDO

"They say that when people write songs the words come to them through life's experiences. I believe this holds true when it comes to Tory's book of poetry, Innuendo. Her words relate a young soul that has experienced so much more than most older persons. You feel the pain, the happiness, the good, the bad, the worry, the love, and every other emotion in the spectrum that she suggests in her writings - hence I think the name Innuendo. She is an excellent writer and expresses herself very well. She makes you feel life. This is the third book I have read of Tory's and I always leave them with deeper thoughts of myself and my surroundings." –L. Moreland

D1606194

Also by Tory Cameron

While You Were in Afghanistan
Innuendo

THE UNFINISHED

TORY CAMERON

DEDICATION

You inspired me to include my experiences at Tilden Lawn Nursery in this book; giving a character I have little in common with a very special part of me: you. And our connection, our bond, has inspired me to help animals with special needs, and to encourage others to adopt and save animals that would otherwise be destroyed for simple birth defects like deafness. You will always be my "hearing dog," my Goobie. You are forever immortalized in text, as well as in my heart.

To Yogi Bear "Goober" Van Lunen
Deaf Argentino Dogo Mastiff
2006 – 2014

ACKNOWLEDGEMENTS

It is hard for any author to name every single person out of thanks or inspiration. So if I forget to mention you, shoot me a line and I will rectify the mistake.

First off, a huge thanks goes to my mom, dad, and brother, for whom this talent of mine would not have germinated and flowered. Our family motto is never, ever give up. Mom, you gave me the tools to help create my dreams and then fight for them, and you've been my biggest cheerleader ever since I was born. And thank you for embarrassing both English teachers, in public, who said that I wouldn't get anywhere with my writing. Dad, thank you for every hug, smile, and small encouragements. Even though you butcher the English language, I get the message loud and clear. O.J., thank you for giving me lots of great material for writing little brothers (wink, wink).

To my Joshua, for being there for me when I needed you the most, and for giving me that perfectly planned birthday wish. For always being interested in my creative endeavors and giving me ideas. For helping me chill out when I get too serious. For encouraging me in anything I want to do. Muah to you, always.

To my amazing Aunt Marlene and Uncle Bobby, who took the time to show me around their home of Cumberland and gave me many bits of town gossip to play with. And for being a part of so many of my big life changes. I can't thank you enough!

To my Auntie Liz and Uncle Brian, for being there not only for my family in times of need, but for also being great role models for me growing up. Thank you for every bit of advice, every recommendation, and for supporting everything I've wanted to do in life.

To everyone at Tilden Lawn Nursery: Mark, Debbie, Clyde, Mary, and Karen. Thank you for all of the good times at work, and for all the inspiration (even if you don't remember those moments!). Thank you Mark and Debbie for all of those moments with your animals. Who would have thought they'd change my life?

I must also thank the English teachers who encouraged my writing and editing skills: Gail Snyder, Susan Cohen, Brandy Whitlock, Steven Canaday, Jaque Lyman, and Martha Nell Smith. Without you, I would not have been able to hone my skills as a writer. Thank you for believing in me!

To Burt Dall, for being a dedicated *Amaranth* assistant, a knowledgeable and talented writing workshopper, a generous hand with greenbacks, and a spiritual friend.

To Amanda and Stewart, for playing dress-up as the main characters for the book cover. And for almost being taken out by a falling tree branch for the sake of art.

To my 2008 college fiction workshop class, for giving me great feedback on the first two chapters of this book, and for encouraging me to write better. I hope you all are doing well!

To all of the people who have helped me in some way: Aunt Jeannie, Ruth & Matt, Casey, Andre, Josh & Lisa, Ryan, Lynn (aka Lynnrd), Jessica, the Taylor family, the Ball family, the White family, the Friedman family, the Pisano family, and the Third Eye Comics family.

And, finally, to those who are reading this book. You are the ones who will make this long, hard, and painful endeavor matter. Always follow your dreams no matter what, and enjoy this mystery ride!

THE UNFINISHED

To be
"In the arms of Morpheus"
is to be asleep.

1

MORPHEUS

"You are not alive," Morpheus argued with himself in the tall mirror on the back of her door. He tried to ignore the soft, delicate smell only *she* had, but couldn't resist watching her nose wrinkle as she dreamt. Her mirror had caught his self-esteem battles on several occasions and it was only a matter of time before his mirror self became bored with the nightly arguments.

Pacing back and forth, his footsteps echoed on the hardwood floor, but the girl sound asleep in her bed never stirred. The ceiling fan ruffled her blond hair, tickling her eyelashes as he stared at her. She was beautiful and kind and couldn't see him.

His tan, slender fingers grabbed short strands of his black hair and pulled. "Why torture yourself like this?"

"Yes, why?"

Closing his eyes, Morpheus let go of his hair. "Leave me be."

Narelle walked out from behind the girl's dresser, hips swaying with a natural seduction. Her red hair was pulled back in a mess of curls, falling over the thin white cotton of her dress. He'd seen her evocative entrance thousands of times, but every single instance he thought her looks striking.

"Alphaeus sent me to collect you," she sang, with an accent that wasn't quite British and wasn't entirely hers. She glanced at the girl softly snoring in the bed and then looked back to Morpheus. "You should stay away from her."

"Advice from Alphaeus?"

She shook her head. "He knows nothing of you coming here and I do not intend to advise him of it." She took his arm, carefully wrapping her long, thin fingers around his bicep. "You know humans cannot see us, and even if they could, she would not understand what you are."

He shut his eyes and pulled away from her.

She sighed and dropped her hand. "I will wait for you on the other side. Take your time."

"I plan to."

With a sad smile, she turned and walked back toward the dresser and disappeared before she reached it. She was beautiful, but the beauty wasn't hers. Everything about her was borrowed from lives lost, sold, or forfeited. When he was newly made, he'd fallen in love with her. She was good to him, almost too good. But he'd found over the century that she was the same as all of the females of his kind.

His attention instantly flew back to the sleeping girl. She'd turned onto her back, her hands resting on her rising stomach while she sighed in her sleep. He smiled despite the ache he felt inside. He knew all too well that the affection he had for her was the only thing he'd ever have.

"You are too good for me anyway," he reasoned, and disappeared from her room.

Instead of meeting Narelle, he decided to sit downstairs with the girl's father, Jairus. Even though it was well after midnight, the man was sitting up on the couch, wide awake, talking on the phone. The gray in his dark hair was highlighted by the glow of the television. He was still wearing the torn up blue jeans and plaid flannel shirt he'd worn to work that day.

"What do you want me to say, Alice?" he whispered loudly. He paused, listening to something Alice was saying. He apparently didn't like it, because his eyebrows swooped together as his lips curled in disgust. "I can't believe you'd even suggest that. No, I'm not going through with it. Forget it."

Running fingers through his hair, Jairus let his head rest in the palm of his hand. He didn't even notice Morpheus sitting on the couch or the sudden warning growls the mastiff at his feet was spitting.

Morpheus watched the actors on the mute television say their lines, touch each other, and laugh at something said. He looked at his own hands and then reached out toward Jairus as if he were going to touch him. The dog growled and then let out a deep throated bark before Morpheus could touch the man.

"Thorburn, *enough*," Jairus scolded before returning to his phone call.

Morpheus sat for a while longer, listening to Jairus talk and watching the dog at his feet stare at him. He wanted to pet the large animal, but knew his hands wouldn't feel the coarse hair or the warmth from its body that Brigh and her father always mentioned. Again he looked at his hands; saw the lines in the skin, still stretching, still growing. They were like the hands of any human being, but until he was finished he would not be able to touch anything in the human world. And that could take years.

"I cannot have her," Morpheus growled and vanished from the human dimension.

BRIGH

"Which color do you think I should wear?" Felicity asked, holding up two tubes of lipstick. "Red or mauve?"

Brigh twirled a tube of mascara between her fingers as she rolled onto her stomach. Lying in Felicity's bed felt like floating in a pool; her arms, legs, and torso held relaxed in their positions without something forcing them upright. And since the start of senior year was only a weekend away, relaxation was key.

"Do you want to be cute and friendly, or sexy and seductive?"

Felicity studied both tubes, looking back and forth from one to the other. Her dark brown hair slid from her shoulders, hiding her heart shape face and brown eyes. The mauve would've gone perfect with her rosy cheeks and pale complexion, but Brigh knew her best friend would be looking for her next conquest tonight, and that would mean—

"If there's any chance that Liam will be at Jake's party, I'm going full out siren."

Brigh laughed, throwing the mascara toward her friend. "Then red it is. And smoke your eyes a bit."

Felicity grinned and then swung around on her stool to face her vanity mirror. "So, are we excited to see Benji again?"

"There's not much to get excited over," Brigh replied. She picked up the closest copy of *Lucky* magazine and flipped to page forty three. Apparently Nordstrom was having a shoe sale for Labor Day weekend. *I won't be able to avoid it, but I will be able to afford it.* Her new job at the nursery was working out fine and she was getting paid more per hour than her classmates.

Felicity eyed Brigh in the mirror. "What about that kiss at the game last year? You two looked pretty cozy."

Brigh sighed and closed the magazine. Felicity never let up. If she wanted something she made sure she got it. Then again, she always got what she wanted. Where Brigh was the bright blonde who searched for answers on a test, Felicity was the dark brunette who searched for answers in life. Always dramatic and loud, she made sure people noticed her. They balanced each other out in every aspect.

"That was last year, Fee. We've both changed since then." She flipped another page and tucked stray hairs behind her ear. "Besides, he's been at his dad's house in Colorado—I haven't seen him since the last day of junior year."

"Lighten up," Felicity said between smacking her red-painted lips. "It's not like you're dating anyone else."

Swinging back toward Brigh, Felicity unbuttoned her shirt and squirted perfume at the hollow of her throat. A mix of lavender and vanilla tickled Brigh's nose. Felicity had a deadly obsession with Victoria's Secret that would undoubtedly damage her brain some day. But with a look at her vast collection of perfumes that kept growing, Brigh knew there wasn't much she could, or wanted, to do. Perfume collection was just a quirky hobby of Fee's.

"I'm just saying." Felicity crossed her legs underneath her and leaned back against the vanity table. "It's senior year. Homecoming, prom, graduation. You haven't had a serious boyfriend in years."

Brigh eyed Felicity with a grin twitching her lips. "I thought you said being single and flirty would draw attention from the male population."

"And it has," Felicity said proudly with a quick roll of her eyes. "I'm a *genius*. But seriously. If you want a date you can kiss, you need to narrow down the list."

"I didn't know I had to make a list."

Felicity threw up her arms in defeat. "And we're going to do something about that tonight. Maybe I can get Amelia and Chandra to hold you down while I line up eligible bachelors."

Jumping from her seat with a jolt of excitement, Felicity threw open her closet doors and turned to Brigh. "Come on, sexy mama—we're gonna dress you like a goddess."

Brigh couldn't help but laugh and throw a penguin-shaped pillow at her boy-crazed best friend.

R

The soft purr of the old BMW was the only sound on Prospect Court. A mile long, the dirt and gravel road took local teens all the way to Lover's Leap where an abandoned mansion all the local teens called The Gateway sat rotting away. Brigh and Felicity had been going to the mansion every other weekend for the last four years, dodging overgrown weeds and poison ivy to dance and meet guys. It was the only abandoned building in Cumberland, Maryland that wasn't patrolled nightly by cops.

"What do you have this thing in?" Felicity asked in annoyance. "Second gear won't get us there by ten."

Brigh laughed and shifted the car into third. "You worry too much. We're almost there. Plenty of time for you to make your grand entrance."

"*Our* grand entrance," Felicity corrected. "I'm starting to wonder if I shouldn't have worn the Nicole Miller, and driven my beetle. It's older, but it'll go faster than this piece of crap."

"Don't worry, Fee," Brigh said, keeping her eyes on the road. "I'm the one who has competition."

Felicity blew the last comment off. "Puh-lease. You're cheerleading Captain, President of the senior class, and head honcho for several clubs." She turned to look at Brigh with a bored expression. "I get the lead roles for the theatre productions. I've got nothing on you."

"You do better than the old theatre club president ever did."

Felicity threw her a look that said, *that doesn't make me feel any better.*

"Let's just get there." Felicity sighed. "Maybe the guys will get really drunk so we can paint their fingernails again."

Brigh crossed her fingers and grinned. "Here's hoping."

The mansion windows were already lit with flickering candlelight, silhouettes gyrating back and forth behind the curtains. Cars were parked as close to the mansion as possible, so others could park as far away from the cliff as they could. Concern about cops or curious parents showing up wasn't a thought in anyone's mind—no one traveled down that rocky road for anything.

Brigh parked her mom's old BMW next to someone's truck and sat for a minute, her foot still pressing in the clutch and brake. After tapping the brake nervously, she turned off the engine and popped the emergency brake.

She got that tingly spiders-crawling-up-the-spine feeling she always seemed to get around the mansion. And it wasn't because of its age and how much it looked like a horror movie set. Something itched at the back of her brain, trying to squirm through her thick memories. Fresh anxiety set in that had nothing to do with facing a boy she'd kissed last year. She didn't want to go into the house.

"What's wrong?" Felicity asked. She was halfway out of her seat, the door hanging open with her boot propped on the handle.

Brigh shook her head, feeling herself start to hyperventilate. She wished the feeling would go away. "I can't."

Felicity shifted back into her seat and shut the door. She rubbed Brigh's arm and held her hand. "Everything's going to be okay. Nothing's going to happen."

"What if it does?" Brigh asked, a primitive wildness in her voice that, even after a year, she still wasn't accustomed to.

Felicity only smiled and pulled Brigh into a hug. "I promise you. I won't let anything happen."

"Do you think Benji will be here?"

Felicity pulled away with a smirk slowly coming into place on her face. "If he's back in town, he'll be here. There's nothing else to do here except lust after you, of course."

Brigh smiled. Felicity always knew how she was feeling and knew just what to say. She was a goddess when it came to dealing with men, because she'd dated pretty much the whole senior class. Brigh, though admired by many, only had two letters of the alphabet crossed off, whereas Felicity had gone out with every single letter, even doubling and tripling some.

"Come on," Felicity said with a smile, as she unbuckled Brigh's seatbelt and opened her door. "I hear beer calling us."

Felicity linked arms with her nervous best friend and pulled her toward the mansion.

MORPHEUS

"Your self-deprecation makes me wish I could vomit," Narelle said through her hazy fog of boredom, as she watched Morpheus pace back and forth.

He wanted to rip every last strand of borrowed hair out of his borrowed skull. He'd never questioned his existence, never wondered why he, specifically, had been made. Not until he met *her*.

The cavernous walls were lit neither by candlelight nor electricity, but by the essence of the souls of which the two of them had been comprised. An old wooden desk sat in the center of the room, a large leather chair sitting behind it. Papers and books cluttered the desktop, as fountain and feather pens littered the floor around the desk.

"I don't know what it is about this girl that haunts me so." And he didn't know. Every night for the past year he'd spent watching her, listening to her whimper and smile in her sleep. Every day he watched her get ready for school, raise her hand to answer every question in math and history class, and delegate among her fellow students in the organizations she headed. And most nights, especially lately, he followed her to the old mansion on the eastside of town, to watch her dance, yearning to hold her in his arms as she swayed her hips to the music of her time. Particularly when she danced did he wish with all his being to be real, to exist.

He'd sifted through all of his memories from those who'd become a part of him to find something, some link to him and the girl. He knew it was a lost cause, the memories blurred together, hardly comprehensible. It was the first thing they learned upon creation, that the memories would not be theirs until they were finished. They developed as humans did, from child to adult, but the process was slow, taking as long as a hundred years to half a millennium or more. Some, like Narelle and Alphaeus, had been developing for hundreds of years. Until recently, Morpheus was only mildly anxious of existence among humans. Now he craved for the need to breathe, to feel his chest expand, to feel his face heat with embarrassment at dense things he'd said. He wanted the sun to soak into his skin, the rain to wash away the day's dirt, and the wind to tousle his hair. To feel her fingers roving through his hair, her eyes gazing into his with longing and love, and her lips searing his with a kiss, he would give anything.

"Do not beat yourself up about it," Narelle said. She stood in front of him, reached up, and gently ran her fingers through the front of his hair. He closed his eyes, leaning into her massaging touch. She was more like a mother to him sometimes and sometimes he could see the unconditional love for him in her eyes, a love that went deeper than he wished it to.

"Do not let the mortal interfere with your transformation," she continued, and kissed his cheek.

Morpheus backed away from her touch and combed his own fingers through his hair, mussing up the styling her fingers had made. For a second he'd fantasized that it was Brigh holding and kissing him. And he'd almost given in to Narelle's temptation, given in to the mirage, the fantasy. He shook his head and pinched the bridge of his nose. "She is at the mansion. I will be back."

"Be careful," Narelle said, as Morpheus called forth the door to other worlds and disappeared from their plane of existence.

Morpheus could've sworn that he'd heard the undertones of distaste echoing off the walls of his study as he left. But he shook off Narelle's anger as he went in search of the girl.

BRIGH

Ever since the fall of '84, there had been a big bash the weekend before Halloween. The place was falling apart, with creaking floor boards, holes in the walls, and cobwebs hiding every corner and curve in the ceiling. To combat the mildew and rotting wood smell, candles of all scents lingered on tables and in corners of the floor.

"You're late," Chandra announced as Brigh and Felicity came into the kitchen. The girl's creamy mocha skin glistened with sweat as she leaned on the back of a lawn chair. A yellow headband held back her retro afro, the long ends of it resting on her shoulders.

"Talk to Brigh," Felicity threw over her shoulder. She rooted through a cooler by the sink, sloshing ice and water all over the floor. "Damn. Who the hell filled this thing up?"

"That would be Kyle." Amelia came up behind Chandra and wrapped her arms around the other girl's waist. "You look sexy tonight, Fee."

"Thanks." Felicity smiled, even though Brigh knew the lesbian thing between Amelia and Chandra kind of creeped her out. She took a quick sip of her Coors Light, swished it around in her mouth, and then swallowed. "Let's mingle."

Chandra pulled her and Amelia next to Brigh, handing her a Bud Light. "We weren't sure you were coming."

"Yeah," Amelia piped in. "We know Halloween weirds out your family."

Chandra elbowed her girlfriend. "Shh. What did I tell you?"

"Sorry."

"What are they talking about?" Brigh asked, trying to ignore the subject.

"I didn't hear anything." Felicity played along.

As Brigh and Felicity broke apart from Amelia and Chandra, and moved from one cluster of people to another, they noticed a new group standing off to the side of the others in the living room of the house. They were the incoming freshman, huddled together with beer bottles grasped tightly in their hands. Brigh and Felicity had never been that anxious and obvious as the group of newbies. They'd always blended in with everyone else's drinking tendencies, but stood out when it came to dancing and mingling.

"Check out the new girls," Kyle said to his friends. "That one in the tight pink top is hot. Think I can score?"

One of the guys punched his shoulder. "I bet you five bucks you can get her into bed."

"Five?" another guy scoffed. "I bet *twenty*."

Felicity rolled her eyes. "You're pathetic, Kyle."

Kyle shrugged his shoulders. "I gotta do something while I wait for you to change your mind." He ran his hand across his chest. "Wanna go at this?"

Felicity put her hand out between them. "Talk to the hand, 'cause the brain's not interested."

"It's not your brain I need," Kyle said as he handed his buddy his beer.

"Calm down, Kyle," Brigh said, standing in front of Felicity.

All the guys acted like they were scared and then laughed. Brigh knew the beer was making them assholes, and she really couldn't do anything about their crudity. But she knew Kyle could be broken easily. He really could be a sweetheart when he wanted to.

"What's up, Brigh?" Kyle asked, grabbing his beer from his friend and taking a sip. "I didn't think you'd be here tonight."

"I'd never miss a night of seeing you guys get shit-faced and stupid."

Kyle laughed. "I missed you, Breen."

Brigh smiled. "I missed you too, Lazarus."

"Enough with the last names you two, let's party!" Jake yelled.

The music rose to an earsplitting level and everyone stopped talking and started dancing right where they were. Brigh and Felicity were lost in a crowd of football players as they all surged around them to have their dance with the two most popular girls at Fort Hill High. Liam found Felicity and the two of them broke out of the wall of guys to dance on the outside with everyone else. Amelia and Chandra waved at Brigh, grinning as they danced together, gathering attention from the freshmen guys.

Brigh lost herself to the music and gave each guy a chance to dance with her. Unlike with Felicity, the guys didn't crowd Brigh and her partner; they all waited patiently for their turn, knowing she had no favorites. She loved to dance, loved how the music made her body move and made her true self come out. She could've danced by herself, but she liked the energy that coursed between her and another person as they bumped to the beat.

As one guy stepped back, another guy took his place, following Brigh's moves as she twirled and dipped. As her next partner came up to her, she turned, facing away from him, and raised her arms above her head, shaking her hips and tapping her feet. She imagined she was a cloud, weightless and free of emotion. She cleared her mind and let her body move on its own. Her head slowly fell back and there were warm lips at her ear.

"I want to kiss you," the lips whispered, with a voice that echoed as if thousands of people all spoke at once.

Brigh lost her balance on that cloud of calm and swung around to face the person with the voice that made her heart slow in its rhythm. She expected to see so many different things—a tall monster bent over so he could face her at her five-foot-six frame, a floating torso with thousands of heads, etc. But none of them were even close.

Instinctively, she pushed him, forcing out every frustration she had. "What did you say?" she demanded, her words forced out between each frantic intake of breath.

"I said I've missed you," Benji repeated angrily, rubbing his chest where she'd pushed.

Brigh looked around her. No longer dancing, everyone stared at her like she'd gone insane. Someone turned off the music and an awkward, embarrassing silence followed. The hard thump of Brigh's rapid heartbeat replaced the intense pounding of the music in her ears to the point where that was all she heard.

Felicity stepped in front of Benji. "Brigh, you okay?" She felt the shaking girl's forehead and rubbed her back. "Need some air?"

"Yeah," Brigh whispered, and followed Felicity through the dark hallways to the front porch.

As the whispers of the others followed her and Felicity out of the house, Brigh hysterically asked herself, *what was that?*

MORPHEUS

He couldn't believe what he had done. How was it possible? There were no accounts in their history of any of them being able to reach humans in anyway. He'd searched his library dozens of times, even venturing into the section that wasn't open to anyone but mentors and teachers. And not once had he ever come across anything that went against what his people had preached for as long as they'd been created.

He didn't even remember deciding to reach out to her. He'd watched as her dance partner stepped back to allow the next guy his chance, and he'd walked behind her, in front of the next eager guy, just to be close to her. And then what?

"What the hell was that all about?"

A guy in a letterman's jacket strutted over to the drink table where the girl who had spoken was standing. His naturally highlighted brown hair was standing up in short spikes, causing his ears to appear larger in the dark than they were. The light from a nearby candle flickered, making the green in his eyes look black.

"Maybe it was a ghost," he said, mimicking a ghostly voice.

Morpheus turned toward the small group gathering around the two, and eavesdropped to relieve his mind of its questions for a minute. Everyone looked skeptical and full of gossip, but the person who most interested Morpheus was the one by the fireplace mantel.

"Ghosts aren't real," the girl said.

The guy in the jacket loomed closer, crouched with his hands out as if to grab her. "Are you sure? You know why this place is called the Gateway, don't you?"

The girl looked a little scared, but held her place and folded her arms across her chest. "No."

"Freshmen," the guy mumbled and shook his head. "Take it away, Jake-man." Jacket guy backed off of the girl and leaned against the wall by the lit fireplace.

Jake stepped away from the mantel, the flames throwing a wall of warm light around him. He was clearly good-looking, with hair a soft brown that curled around his ears and temples. Morpheus could tell by his squared jaw that Jake thought himself to be a leader. He looked like every man Morpheus had seen who'd taken a leadership role. The air around Jake was thick and strong. He was good at being a leader. But he, himself, was not good.

"They say this place is haunted," Jake began, stuffing his hands in the front pockets of his jeans. This small action made him look normal, like he was on the same level as everyone else in the room. But Morpheus knew the teenager thought himself above everyone. It was in his hazel eyes.

"They say," he continued, "that each year on the night of Halloween, the windows of this place light up so bright it's hard to see the rest of the house. That there are shadows of people passing back and forth in front of the light and soft music can be heard a mile away.

"Legend has it that a white man fell in love with a Native American woman," Jake went on, grabbing more and more people's attention—the crowd was a few people thick—as he spun his tale. "Unable to be together, they threw themselves over the cliff, plunging into a watery grave.

"That's how this land got its name, Lovers Leap." Jake took a sip from a beer bottle nestled on the fireplace mantle. "A lot of dumbasses have killed themselves over love just outside this house. Centuries on top of centuries of really fucked up people committing suicide. No wonder the 'accident' happened."

"What?" asked someone in the crowd.

Jakes eyes glistened as he smiled. "The cops are still calling it a suicide, but everyone knows this dude killed his wife. He did it on Halloween, people! That's the date when spirits from the grave come back to walk the earth again, when the veil between worlds thins." He pointed at the window behind him. "The family cemetery is out back; acres of people lost long ago. What spirit wouldn't want a night to party and live again?

"The guy who killed his wife was possessed," Jake finished.

Whispers erupted throughout the crowd. They were all obviously on edge. If Morpheus was capable of it, he would've scared them all by moving something or making some sort of sound. But he wasn't capable of it. Disappointment set into his shoulders and the dreamy smile on his face disappeared. Narelle and the others all thought he had a great sense of humor when he wasn't brooding. But he couldn't act on it most of the time, because his jokes and little pranks involved the living. And they could neither hear nor see him.

"So," Jake said, with a clap to his hands. "Who's interested in planning the Halloween shindig?"

Morpheus thought of all the creepy and funny things he could cause on that big night and sighed when the seventh heaven effect quickly wore off.

"Damnit," he muttered and disappeared to find Brigh.

2

MORPHEUS

She was sitting on the top step with her head between her knees while Felicity held back her hair. He sat on the same step as the two girls, not wanting to stand in front of them, to look them straight in the face and not be seen.

"I think I'm going to be sick," Brigh whispered. She took in another deep breath and stared out into the yard.

Following Brigh's stare, Morpheus saw only the bare land before the sharp drop of the cliff. He wondered why she would stare at something that could cause anxiety and nausea in a normal person to keep her mind off of vomiting. Trying to rationalize the short distance from the house to the steep cliff made even him a little dizzy, and he couldn't physically get sick.

"Are you cold?" Felicity asked.

"No, why?"

"Because you're shaking."

Morpheus finally noticed it himself—the shudders running down her spine, the little twitches to her fingers as they gripped her dress. He could even hear her teeth chattering. He raised his arm as if to wrap it around Brigh's shoulders and flinched when Felicity did the same and their elbows almost crossed. Well, they would have crossed had he been corporeal. He glared at Felicity's arm wrapped tightly around Brigh's shoulders, as he tucked his own against his side.

"I'm not really cold," Brigh said with a smile. "Just a little freaked, is all."

Felicity scooted away from Brigh on the top step of the porch, and turned toward her. The wind picked up and blew wisps of her chestnut hair across her face, her red painted lips catching strands. "What happened in there?"

"I think I had a panic attack." As she said it, Morpheus couldn't help but feel like she'd dropped something extremely heavy on his chest. He gripped his white shirt, pulling at the woven material as if to relieve the pressure.

"I don't think so," Felicity said with a shake to her head, folding her hands in her lap. "Brigh," she continued carefully, "did Benji say something to you?" She looked concerned and tucked a stray golden hair behind Brigh's ear. "Did he do something?"

"No, no he didn't do anything," she said slowly, as if putting several thoughts together. "I thought…"

"You thought what?" Felicity asked impatiently.

Brigh looked up at Felicity with an emotionless face that'd gone white. "I thought I heard something."

Felicity cocked her head to the side and licked her bottom lip. "Well yeah, you heard the music and Benji saying something to you—"

"No," Brigh interrupted, her words rattling out of her mouth. "I heard something else. Someone whispered something in my ear. But it sounded like there was more than one voice, like more than one person was talking at the same time."

Felicity looked away from Brigh, her foot bouncing off the porch step. When she looked back to her friend, her face had turned from impatient to serious. This was a look on Felicity that Morpheus couldn't process. He knew the girl was flirtatious, immature, and self-absorbed. The serious expression and set to her shoulders made him wonder what he'd missed on his assessment of Brigh's best friend.

"What did they say to you?" she asked Brigh.

Brigh shivered, tucking the short skirt of her dress under her thighs. "'I want to kiss you.'"

Felicity thought for a moment and then an amused expression pushed the seriousness away. "Well, if you're connecting with a ghost it better be a hot one."

"Thanks for your concern," Brigh said with a laugh. Her shoulders visibly relaxed as she leaned into Felicity, resting her head on the girl's shoulder. The smile eased a little when she closed her eyes, but it was still there, causing her lips to twitch every time they started to relax.

"Only the best for my best friend," Felicity replied with a contented tone.

But before Morpheus disappeared from beside the girls, he saw the worried expression on Felicity's face and wished he knew what it was he'd been missing.

ᚱ

"You were not gone long," Narelle replied to the loud entrance Morpheus made.

Walking down the hall of their rooms, he'd thrown everything out of his way, upending desks, shoving documents onto the floor and books off of shelves, and kicking a chair across the hall. His anger echoed off the walls as he yelled, his throat burning with the force of it.

"Get out," he growled. He picked up his desk chair with one hand and hurled it at the wall, grinning as it splintered into several pieces.

"That was unnecessary," Narelle said. She lounged on the edge of the table against the left wall from the door. "Have you gone daft?"

Out of the corner of his eye, Morpheus saw blonde hair and big green eyes that held desire. Shaking the image from his head, he turned around to face Narelle, the red haired beauty all of his friends lusted after. "I told you to get out."

"I am assuming tonight's visit did not go well." Dropping away from the table, Narelle sauntered over to Morpheus. She reached out to touch his shoulder and jerked back her hand as if he'd bitten her when he stepped out of reach.

"You try my patience," he said through his teeth.

"And what about mine?" She turned on him, glaring accusingly. "I have felt the sting of Alphaeus's anger far too many times because of your recklessness and selfish behavior. I cannot imagine what he would do to either of us if I were to inform him of your mortal lover."

"Nothing can become of it," Morpheus whispered. He walked to his desk, leaned down, and let his elbows hit the desktop as he cradled his head between his arms. The fire in him was suffocating in the smoke of Narelle's words. "You have said it before and so have all of our volumes: no one from our world has ever interacted with humanity. Therefore, there is nothing."

"I know," Narelle said sadly. "However, do you believe that? Do you, with all that you are, believe there is nothing you can do for or with this girl?"

Morpheus tightened his jaw, but did not look up at her. "I have to believe there is a chance."

BRIGH

When Brigh walked through the front door of her house, she assumed her father and brother were asleep. Quietly, she hung up her coat by the door and set her keys down on the table. She then searched for any lights left on for her to turn off before going to bed. Rich and her dad were always leaving on the lights, even after a high electricity bill.

"Just because I work around loud power tools," Jairus said, "doesn't mean I can't still hear you sneaking in at two on a work night."

Brigh let out a deep breath. Busted. She slipped off her heels and went into the living room. The television was on mute, and the only light source in the room. Her father sat on the couch, Thorburn at his feet. Brigh smiled at her big puppy and laughed when the poor thing tried to get up fast to see her, his feet sliding out from under him on the old hardwood floor.

"Thorburn, take it easy," she whispered. She knelt on the floor and let the dog tackle her and cover her face with big sloppy kisses.

"Thorburn, heel." The dog reluctantly obeyed Jairus, but licked Brigh before he moved.

With a smile brightening her face, Brigh walked around the couch and leaned down to hug her father, giving him a kiss on the cheek before settling next to him.

"Is Richard asleep?" she asked.

Without looking at her, Jairus replied, "He's at Tom Wilkin's house; won't be home 'till tomorrow afternoon, I think. How was the party?"

"Fine," she lied. "Felicity and I didn't get to paint anyone's fingernails, but we got to see Jake get rejected by a freshman."

Her father smiled. "Jake still thinks he's God's gift to women. So much like his father, it's frightening."

"Speaking of him," Brigh said, slowly, carefully, "are you coming to football tryouts next week?"

"Only if you're brother's interested in playing."

"Fair enough." She didn't have the heart to mention that the reason she'd brought up the tryouts was so he would come see her cheer. Brigh stared at the television screen with her father, until she got up enough courage to ask him something that'd been bothering her since the incident at the Gateway.

"Has anyone in the family ever—" She cut herself off before she could finish, and then thought herself a coward because of it. "Is there a history of, I don't know, schizophrenia or Bipolar in the family?"

Or maybe it's just me and my PTSD.

Jairus looked at Brigh for the first time since she'd come home. There were dark circles under his eyes and his skin looked pale. His always clean and smooth cheeks were taken over by a shadow of hair that made him look twice his age. "Why you asking?"

Brigh shrugged. "A sudden curiosity."

Jairus went back to watching the program on the History Channel, acting as if Brigh hadn't said anything at all. In his left hand was the remote control with his thumb resting on the channel button. To the casual observer he looked relaxed. But Brigh could see how tense and stiff his shoulders were, and how tightly his hand clutched the remote.

"I'm off to bed," Brigh said suddenly, getting up slowly from the couch. She leaned over and kissed her dad's left cheek. "Good night."

"Good night," her father responded mechanically.

Brigh felt tears gather in her eyes, but closed them and walked through the hall to the stairs from memory. Turning on the light, she caught her reflection in the hall mirror before she could escape past it. Her eyes were turning pink and her forehead creased with tension. Her hair was mussed where she'd bunched it up in her hands to hold it away from her face; a face that hurt her father to look at.

"Everything will be alright," she recited, and then headed up the stairs to her room.

$$R$$

Brigh woke five minutes before her alarm went off, and after lying in bed until it finally sounded at six, she stripped out of her long pajamas and climbed into the shower. Glad that Richard wasn't home to bang on the door and complain about her taking too long, she took her time lathering her body with soap and her hair with conditioner. The warm water relaxed her tight shoulder muscles and helped clear her mind. For once she didn't feel like she was being watched; the bathroom was the only place she found peace.

Downstairs, her father sat at the dining room table, reading the newspaper and drinking his second cup of coffee. Brigh walked past the coffee pot to the stove, taking the kettle to the sink to fill with water.

"There's no more oatmeal," her father called. "Rich ate the last pack."

"I keep telling him to leave my food alone." She filled the kettle anyway, for hot chocolate instead of the brown sugar oatmeal she'd been hoping to have. "He knows milk upsets my stomach. And I bought that box, too."

"Start hiding them in your room, then," Jairus said, and slurped down more coffee.

Brigh blew that suggestion off. If Richard didn't see the box in the pantry, he'd look elsewhere, and she really didn't want him snooping through her things. Her locked trunk kept a lot of her secrets safe, but she'd forget she put the oatmeal in there if she did.

"Who won the poker game?" Brigh asked, opening the packet of hot chocolate and shaking it into a coffee mug.

"Billy," he mumbled. Brigh heard the newspaper crackle and knew he'd turned two pages.

"Is old Mr. Squire mentioned in the obituaries?"

He didn't disappoint, because she heard him bring the paper closer to his face and then he replied, "Not yet. Any day now, I'm sure."

Grinning, Brigh listened as the kettle started to whistle. The kitchen filled with the sweet smell of hot chocolate as the boiling water swirled around the powder in the mug. She took in a deep breath and sighed.

"What time do you have work?" asked her father.

She glanced at the clock on the stove. "Eight. I'll leave in a couple minutes."

"Cutting it close?"

"It only takes fifteen minutes to get there, remember?"

There was no answer. The awkward silence started choking Brigh; she had to get out. Instead of waiting for the hot chocolate to cool, Brigh grabbed a travel mug from the cabinet over the coffee maker, transferred the hot chocolate from its ceramic mug to the travel one, and set the unneeded mug in the sink.

Holding the mug in her left hand, she scooped up her purse and sketchbook on the steps, and headed for the front door. "Bye, dad!"

"Have a good day at work," he called back. "Don't let those guys push you around."

"I think I can hold my own," she said with a devilish grin.

3

MORPHEUS

His hands were tightly fisted as he held himself back from trying to touch her; veins beginning to itch and burn with the battling of commands. Her blonde hair was highlighted by the sun coming in through the counter window, causing a pale yellow halo hovering above her brow. The man she was helping kept staring at her when she was working on the computer, and would give her the biggest smile when she looked back at him.

The man was handsome, but old enough to be her father, and when Morpheus glanced out the window at him he caught sight of a gold band hugging his ring finger. Though disgusted with the man for looking at Brigh like he owned her when he had a woman at home, Morpheus wished he could be him, especially when she smiled at the man.

"Okay," Brigh said, her eyes scanning her computer screen. "You're getting one pallet of wall stone—grey—

and one box of large adhesive. Did you need anything else, Mr. Ortiz?"

The man shook his head and gave Brigh another one of his smiles. "No, that's all today."

Brigh's smile in return was genuine, but not as strong as the ones she gave her friends and family. Morpheus took this as a good sign. He'd spent a century observing and mimicking people, but some things still bewildered him.

The smell of Brigh's skin, a cross between October air and summer flowers, made Morpheus dizzy, even though he didn't need to breathe. Her scent made him warm, even though he couldn't feel temperatures.

Brigh turned to put away the receipt in her cash drawer and looked up in Morpheus's direction. Air caught in his throat as her eyes focused in on him directly and a smile pulled at her lips. It wasn't like the smile she'd given her customer, but a real, heartfelt smile she gave to those she loved.

Jumping off her chair with a bounce in her step, Brigh walked past Morpheus to the door. "Yogurt, get down from there, you little goofball!"

Morpheus turned and found the dog peering through the high window in the door, with his paws pressed against the glass on either side of his long nose. Brigh let in the white dog and allowed the creature to lick her hand before he gave her his paw.

"That dog is in love with you," Arnold, her boss, said, standing in the doorway of the sales booth.

Brigh laughed and closed her mouth just before the dog's long pink tongue swiped across her chin. She hugged the animal, and Morpheus noticed for the first time how large and muscular it was, and how small Brigh looked next to it. And when she kissed the large black spots around its eyes, Morpheus felt his chest ache.

"You are the cutest Argentinean Dogo ever!" she gushed, grabbing the dog's massive face and planting a big kiss on its nose.

Morpheus couldn't believe he was jealous of an animal, and not just any animal, but a dog. His want of becoming real was starting to pluck at his sanity. He wondered if human males felt this way; surely they had to. He wished he could be in the dog's place more than the men, because this animal was getting more love and attention than anyone she came into contact with. If men didn't feel the same way as Morpheus about women and animals, then they were insane.

If only he could run his hands across her skin, to see if it was as soft as it looked. He wanted to know the texture of her hair, the warmth of her breath, and the intensity of her passion.

He'd toyed with the idea of pushing to reach her, by trying something new or extending his energy further. But where would these experiments get him? What if they did not work? For the last year he'd held onto some kind of hope that there was a way of getting to her, or that his time would come up and he would be finished, able to walk, talk, and eat among humans—among Brigh. If he tried…and failed…

"Failure is not an option," he ordered, and vanished from the nursery.

BRIGH

Arnold was the best employer anyone could ask for. Not only did he make sure everyone got half an hour of little breaks in the air conditioned office, he also let everyone take time to play with the animals. The nursery wasn't exactly a farm, having most of the property stocked full of rocks, pavers, and mulches, but there were a couple acres for the creatures to run around. Apple, the cream colored Icelandic horse, always stood face first in the far right corner of the field, chomping away at grass patches. His stocky, almost fat, frame made the children smile and the parents want to take a break from staring at rocks all day. Even the employees couldn't hide the fact that they, too, enjoyed the horses' company after a hard day at work.

There were also the dogs and the cats and the lonely pig. Bach, the pig, created more of a fuss and drama than the other animals, much to Arnold's chagrin. Every now and then Brigh would get the customer who'd spotted Bach and be asked similar questions. "What *is* that?" some would ask. Her favorite statement, full of astonishment and wonder, had been from a middle aged man who'd been covered with plaster and topsoil. "That is one ugly dog." The best part of that day had been trying to convince the guy that the ugly dog was really a thin potbelly pig.

Her favorite animal was the white monstrosity, Yogurt. He was smaller than her own mastiff, but twice as cute and full of kisses. He'd been a rescue from a breeder because he was deaf, Arnold's wife falling in love with him immediately. The first day Brigh started working, she'd been walking up the pathway to the sales counter when around the corner came this large white dog, muscles fit to bust. As he charged so fast he couldn't stop, he ran straight into her and knocked her off her feet, licking her face before she knew she was on the ground. They'd both been inseparable since. She'd taken him home, played with him out in the yard at work, and shared her French fries. Sometimes she'd look into his eyes and see intelligence staring back, as if he knew they were meant to be friends.

"Brigh," Arnold called from his office.

She stepped over the other dogs—a Saint Bernard, a Sheltie puppy, and a husky mix—with Yogurt on her heels, and turned into the room to face her boss. He was tall enough that he had to bend a little to get through a doorway, but about the same height as her father. A mustache that Magnum PI's Tom Selleck would be proud of hovered over his lips; one could only see his expression through his eyes.

"Yes, sir?" she asked, folding her arms behind her.

Arnold looked up from the solitaire game he was in the middle of and turned in his chair to face her. "I see Yogurt's infatuation with you hasn't ended."

Brigh grinned, grabbing one of the dog's ears and giving it a little tug. "I hope it doesn't. He's the best friend any girl could ask for."

"I'd say he is indeed," he agreed. "I—"

The door swung open, banging against the tall filing cabinet behind it, and the Sheltie charged into the room.

Anna, Arnold's wife, peaked around the door. The light glinted off of her glasses as they slid down her nose from the pointed look at Brigh.

"Brigh, are you doing anything this Thursday?"

Brigh opened her mouth to say something, but was cut off before she could answer.

"Good," Anna said with a business grin. "Some of the girls are coming over to make dog cookies and we need some young blood."

"Okay," Brigh said.

"Great!" Anna exclaimed, and then shut the door behind her. The Sheltie sat in front of the door, whining a little for someone to let him out.

Brigh turned back to her boss. "You were saying?"

With a sigh, he folded his hands in his lap. "I called you in about hours."

Brigh stood up straight. "Yes."

"What with the economy going downhill," he said uncomfortably—the words slow, the sentence broken, "we're not going to need you as often."

Her throat tightened. "I still have a job, right?"

He laughed, still uncomfortable with the conversation. "Of course. We just need to cut back so we can afford to keep you guys. You do a great job. And the animals love you."

She felt uneasy, no matter what his words. The animals adored a lot of people. Sure, Yogurt wouldn't eat until she'd petted him and let him lick her face a gazillion times, but that didn't mean he wouldn't attach himself to someone else. She took what he said and made sure that every single thing she did from then on would be carried out to the best of her ability and with a radiant smile. The way he'd said things made it sound like being laid off might be a possibility.

MORPHEUS

As Morpheus walked through the door of his study, he caught sight of a shadow inside his doorway, and got ready to yell at Narelle to leave him alone, but Narelle wasn't the one lounging against his desk.

His whitish blonde hair and brilliant blue eyes glowed softly in the shadows of the room. The white cotton shirt was too tight in the shoulders and arms, but no matter how many times Morpheus teased him about getting a larger size, Darius always shook his head and said the ladies loved an exhibit of muscle.

"Were you with her again?" he asked.

"Does *everyone* know?" Morpheus asked in annoyance.

Darius shook his head. "Only Narelle and I know of her. Though, I must admit, I am not as medieval in my thinking of the situation as Narelle. Ah, sweet Narelle…"

If Morpheus could've suffocated himself he would've done it right there in front of his love-struck friend. "How did you find out?"

"Narelle pulled me aside some time ago." He moved away from his perch on the desk and walked behind it. Fingering pages of Morpheus's journal, Darius continued, "She informed me of the situation and then expressed her concern. She does care for you, you know."

"Anything else?" Morpheus grumbled. He was tired of hearing how much his mentor felt for him. The idea of it was beginning to make him sick.

Darius's eyes narrowed, but he continued. "She asked for me to convince you not to see the human—"

"Brigh," Morpheus growled. "Her name is Brigh."

"—since you will not heed her advice."

Though Morpheus was used to cutting other people off, and then being ignored by them, he still wanted to strike his friend to the ground. Darius must've felt this, because, while he'd talked he'd taken several steps away from Morpheus.

"Then do what you came here to do," Morpheus challenged. "Convince me."

"Oh, I will not be doing that." The study filled with Darius' laughter, his chuckles interrupted as he snorted once and then twice. "Even if I tried, nothing I say will ever convince you to change your mind. Your skull is thicker than my own."

"Then if what you say is true, why do I feel like there is more?"

The smile left Darius' face as he cleared his throat and folded his arms behind his back. "May I meet her?"

Morpheus was stunned, and it must've really shown on his face, because Darius hurriedly went on, "I promise I am not reporting back to Narelle. I just…I would like to meet her. At least see what has captured your attention, and if I approve, being your friend and all."

Morpheus shook his head. The more Darius developed, the more Morpheus noticed a resemblance of Felicity in him. If Darius completed his transformation soon, the two of them together would be terrifying but fascinating.

Morpheus rolled his eyes, but nodded. "Follow my current. I am not responsible for you if you get lost."

Darius bounced on the balls of his feet, stretching his arms and punching at the air like a boxer. "I am not the one you should be worried about."

Morpheus grinned, already picturing endless lines of blues and greens speeding under him, and launched himself into the stream that flowed between worlds. It was like nothing in the human world, close to a fast flowing river but not, made of a watery substance, but dry. Slick and fast, the stream moved beings between worlds, coursing through different channels and passageways. They traveled in separate cylindrical tubes, each one stretching out from other worlds. All around them a system of passageways spread infinitely outward.

Others were using the stream, gliding through the channels with ease and agile grace. Some skied through the watery substance sitting down, some standing. It was easiest for your legs, if you had them, if you sat. Morpheus had begun coasting the channels standing up, and quickly found out that upon landing at his destination, his legs were wobbly and uncontrollable for a few moments, for the sudden stillness shocked his muscles. So sitting had become a necessary part of the journey to the human world.

Morpheus didn't have a name for any of the others coasting around them and didn't spend any time musing over what they might be. Once in the stream, it was vital to think of nothing but where one wished to go, otherwise you never knew where you'd end up. He always thought of Brigh, how comforting her room felt with its pale blue walls and soft yellow curtains and the sound of her subtle snores and mumbling in her dreams.

Before either of them knew it, they were deposited in front of a door, landing on their feet. Morpheus landed gracefully, whereas Darius stood for a second and then fell forward onto his knees. Unfazed, Morpheus walked toward the door with his arm extended and turned the knob.

"*Raido*," he said aloud. The rune carved into the dark wood flamed a bright, bluish green, before the door unlocked and swung open into Brigh's bedroom. The R-shaped design burned brightly, awaiting their entrance.

Darius wobbled behind him, his legs twisting sideways as he tried to keep upright. Morpheus kept his lips pressed tightly together so as not to embarrass his friend, but after watching Darius hop and skip to get his legs right, he could no longer hold in the laugh. He grabbed at the sleeves of his shirt, holding his arms against his stomach as his throat grew tight and sore.

"You could have warned me," Darius grumbled.

"Would you have believed me?"

After a pause, Darius sighed. "Not in the slightest."

"Then you should not have skipped the class on traveling."

Darius ducked his head, trying to hide a blush that didn't yet exist. "I was preoccupied."

Morpheus shook his head. "I fear for the women you come into contact with once you exist."

"Oh, they will love me."

"That is what I am afraid of," Morpheus said with a chuckle. Grinning, he stepped inside Brigh's room. The floor in front of the door and beside her bed were clean, but a pile of clothes and books littered the rug by her desk. Morpheus wanted to go to her bedside, to watch her chest rise and fall with each breath, but the idea of it felt too intimate to share with his friend.

Darius stood next to him at the foot of her bed, watching her roll onto her side and curl into a ball. "She is so small," he commented, crossing his arms over his chest.

Morpheus nodded, and crossed his arms as well. "She looks so peaceful, so alive, even in sleep."

"You really have watched her closely."

Morpheus closed his eyes. "I will have eternity to do just that."

Darius's arm snaked around Morpheus's shoulders. "I am sure the Elders will have narrowed down the date of your ascension. They are just slow in their ways. You will know soon enough."

"I hope you are right."

Darius must have noticed the intensity of Morpheus' gaze upon the sleeping girl, for he squeezed his shoulder and mumbled, "I will take my leave of you."

"I appreciate your understanding, Darius," Morpheus said. "You do not understand how much."

Darius smiled and backed up. "I promise not to get lost."

"Best not," Morpheus said. "I will not be there to follow and save you if you do."

Darius looked at the girl one last time and then disappeared from the room. Morpheus felt peace after his friend left, for he no longer had to put on the charade of happiness, though Darius did chase him out of his sour moods very quickly. Though older than Morpheus by a century, Darius acted like a stuck up ten year old. His tendency to follow the rules often made him boring, but he'd break away from them with a little influence and guidance from a troublemaker like Morpheus.

Without further thought of the outside world, he climbed onto the mattress slowly as if afraid he'd wake her. He closed his mind off from everything that wasn't her, concentrating on the sweet smell of her hair and pillow. Lying on his back, he closed his eyes and imagined her hands sliding across his naked chest, her fingers twirling in the dark hair around his nipples. Her breath would fan out across his ear as she settled into the curve of his body, sighing contentedly as she fell back to sleep. And then she would—

4

BRIGH

Brigh knew right away that she was dreaming. Which was odd, because never in her dreams could she figure out if she was awake or not. But this time it was clear. The woods she stood in smelled of pine and wet, rotting leaves as the cold rain soaked her pajamas. The soupy mud slurping up her feet felt sticky and warm. She had to have been awake. But how had she gotten here? Hence the dream of confusion.

Through the *slap-tapping* noises the rain made as it struck leaves, she thought she heard movement through the brush. When she turned around to follow the noise, a shock went through her system and for a second she couldn't breathe.

Behind her stood a man, his white shirt and black pants drenched with water. His black hair matted to his temples, raindrops racing each other across his cheeks and nose. Those dark brown eyes staring at her made him look older than he was. She could see intelligence in them and a deep, clinging sorrow.

"Who are you?" Brigh asked.

His eyes widened as if she'd scared him, but words fell
out of his mouth as he gaped at her. "I can be whomever
you like."

Brigh eyed the stranger warily. This was a dream, but
the realness to everything, the smell of the trees, the
tightness of the mud, and the sound of the rain, was
starting to freak her out. "Okaaay...then what can I call
you?"

As if shaking himself out of a dream, the man bowed
and said, "My friends call me Morpheus."

"I think I'm going insane," Brigh whispered, looking at
the hand he extended toward her. "First the voices and
then this totally realistic dream that I'm not so sure is a
dream in the first place. Yeah, I'm going crazy."

Morpheus took back his hand. "I beg your pardon?"

"No wonder people with disorders never want to leave
their world," Brigh continued speaking her thoughts as if
Morpheus wasn't standing five feet away. "They're
sharing it with unbelievably handsome men. Or women,
depending on their preference."

Morpheus ran his hand through his hair, unintentionally
spiking it up and scratching his scalp as he did so. "I
imagined this going in a completely different direction."

Brigh shook herself from her thoughts and looked at the
man. "What?"

Looking unsure of himself, Morpheus took four slow
steps forward. But Brigh was still lost in her mass of
questions. She tried to place his features with any of the
men in town, but couldn't think of a single person, local or
tourist. Every time she attempted to focus on a certain part
of his face, her vision became blurry and she had to blink
furiously to see straight. She knew he had black hair—that
was easy. He was tall, but not monstrously so, and his skin

was a shade slightly darker than her own. But his eyes...his lips...those she couldn't put a color or shape to.

"This is not a dream and I am not an apparition," he said gently, rocking Brigh completely out of her thoughts. He looked down at himself, his hands running over his stomach. "Well, not right now I am not."

"So you're not a ghost."

Morpheus shook his head. "I am something entirely different."

"Then what are you?" A small headache was starting to form between her brows, and she pinched the skin between them to alleviate the strain. Then she froze and thought, *a headache in a dream?*

"We have several names," Morpheus began. He looked confused as to where to place his hands, because first he folded them over his chest and then placed them on his hips. In the end, he let them hang at his sides, looking uncomfortable as he did so.

"But most call us The Unfinished. We are created from the energies—the souls—of humans who have passed. We are made with some of their traits, their talents, and even physical aspects. Our transformation can take centuries, but once every last piece of us has been sewn together, we are human."

The logical part of Brigh's brain kicked into overdrive. She was having a real hard time believing any of this, but she couldn't dismiss the fact that this was not a normal dream. Or the fact that this fit with the theory of reincarnation.

"Aha!" she called to him. "I'm having a dream about reincarnation. It makes perfect sense. Who knew a stupid documentary Fee made me watch would cook up such a crazy dream?"

Morpheus sighed, closed his eyes, and shook his head. "This isn't a normal dream. We're in an in-between."

That migraine was starting to feel like a possible brain tumor. "Okay, let's not talk about any more new things, okay? My brain is still having a hard time processing that I can feel pain while I'm asleep, let alone that there are aliens who break into said dreams."

"We're not—" Morpheus began.

"So what happens to you when *you* die? Do you get recycled?"

Another sigh escaped him. "I do not know."

One perfect blond eyebrow shot up to Brigh's hairline. "Seriously? Okay, I'm trying to understand this as best I can, even though when I wake up it's not going to matter, but I can't do that if I don't get some answers. How can you *not* know? This is about *you*."

Morpheus shrugged. "I have not gotten to that point in my training."

"Training?" she asked in confusion. Then she found the question she wanted to ask most of all. "How old are you?"

"In human years, I am past one hundred."

Her eyes growing wide, she started nodding to herself as if she cracked the code of his existence. "One hundred. Okay…So, what else can you tell me?"

"Are you sure you want to know?"

"Yes." *Not really. It's time to wake up now.*

"Well, our past, our achievements, and even our families are all created, rooted into the system of society at the very second we are made flesh. I do not doubt that you have seen some of us."

"I don't think so," Brigh said. She was nearing a total dream meltdown. For a dream man, he certainly had a lot to say. But something was off, and not just what he was talking about. She had to admit that he looked too perfect, speaking with an absolutely beautiful voice that sounded like bees in the hive, vibrating through the earth and echoing in her ears.

A smile twitched Morpheus' lips. "Ronald Regan. Marilyn Monroe. Bill Gates. John Wayne. Most of our kind tends to go for the spotlight of films and music, and even the electronic; we strive to succeed."

Brigh shook her head, holding her face between her hands. "This has gotta be a dream. None of this is true. People don't become something else when they die; they either go to heaven or hell." The voice of her devout Christian grandmother was reciting quotes from the bible in her mind just to prove that fact alone.

"The one who wrote the bible was one of us, the scribe of the man you call Jesus, and the being known as God." His eyes had gone cold, distant, but he didn't move toward her. "We have had major roles all throughout history. We are not all kind of heart; some choose the path of evil. But most strive to better this world."

"We are not impersonators," he promised, walking closer, "or ghosts, or what you call aliens. When we are finished, we are human."

"And until you're done being put together, you're leeches?"

Morpheus looked as if she'd slapped him, his eyes wide and a blank expression on his face. "We take from no one. What we are made of is given to us."

Brigh pinched the bridge of her nose and quickly realized what she was doing and whispered to herself, "I'm turning into dad. Okay, say I believe any of this. You said you guys are all over the place, right?"

"Yes."

"Then how come I've never heard of you? How come you guys are never mentioned? There aren't even fairytales about you.

"Tell me." Brigh walked right up to Morpheus, craning her neck to look up at his face. Raindrops slid down his lips, circling before dropping onto her own. A kiss of rain that made her lips tingle and her hands cold. "Why has no one ever mentioned *something* like you?"

His jaw clenched as his eyes narrowed. He didn't look friendly or safe anymore. "Humans cannot see us. They cannot hear or touch us. We are invisible in your world because, technically, we do not exist. We move through silently, watching all of your mistakes, seeing who you really are when no one else is around, following you as you go about your day, not appreciating everything you have, everything you have been given. And even when you think you have everything, it still is not enough. You waste your days until someone you love dies and your eyes are finally opened."

Brigh blinked back tears as she straightened and held her place in front of him. "If you hate us so much, why do you want to be human?"

Morpheus tore his gaze away from her and rubbed his eyes. "I do not hate…I want…to make a difference. I want to say that I have done something. I created something with my own two hands. I made someone happy and I made this world a better place to live in." He laughed to himself and closed his eyes. "Your world is more productive and alive than my own."

Brigh watched his face fall slowly, the smile lines around his mouth and across his forehead smoothing out until it looked as if he'd never had them. Staring at the waterlogged ground with a look of confusion, he seemed so lost and disoriented. She could feel his anger, his anxiety, and his depression because she felt that way too. She felt the rope between them, tying them together with all that they held in common, pull tighter. Whether she was going crazy or just stuck in a bizarre dream, Brigh felt she had to help this man find solace and maybe in the process find some for herself.

"Your world," she began, catching his attention. "Is it beautiful?"

He looked into her eyes, searching back and forth for something. Then he looked away, his eyes still racing under his lashes as he stared out into the woods. A minute passed until finally he looked back at her, a small smile creeping onto his face. It wasn't really the smile that made her uneasy, but the hopeful and desperate look in his eyes as he extended his hand out between them.

"Would you like to see it?"

5

BRIGH

Brigh's eyes felt heavy as she slowly opened them. She was on her back, the sheets pulled up to her chin, her hands shaking as she curled in on herself. It felt as if something was wrapped around her brain, tightening painfully.

Slowly sitting up, she took a deep breath and coughed dryly. She felt like she hadn't slept. In a week. As she held her head, trying to massage away the pain, she started shivering, her teeth clacking together stiffly. She yawned, long and hard, her lips stinging the further she opened her mouth. Tears collected in her eyes and she wasn't sure if it was from the headache or the yawn.

And then she remembered.

Wildly, she looked around the room, leaning forward, losing her hands in the folds of her comforter. Even as her eyes finally adjusted to the dark, she couldn't see anything in the room that resembled a human shape.

"Morpheus?" she whispered, for her throat was too dry and raw to speak louder.

She felt almost mad. Had she imagined everything? Was it just a vivid dream and nothing more? She wasn't sure. She couldn't be sure. Though, she could fall back to sleep and wait to be sucked into that forest. She remembered the cold rain pelting down around them, and when she fell back into the pillows the soft prickly smell of pine drifted around her nose. So she hadn't dreamt it. But that place couldn't be real.

Could it?

MORPHEUS

"How could you be such an idiot?" he growled. His hands found his hair and pulled the strands taut until his forehead burned with the force. But what he'd said and how he'd said it could not match his thoughts. He closed his eyes, trying to imagine the forest. But after seeing darkness behind his eyelids and her slightly lighter bedroom when he opened them once and then twice, his pictures of sodden woodland began to fade.

"Morpheus?" she called again, sleep suckling her voice until she was mumbling into her pillow.

He went to her bedside, careful not to touch the mattress with his knees. Dark circles curved under her eyes like cranberry half moons. Her lips were pale and shaking. She'd left the blanket around her waist, shivering on her side with her arms wrapped around her shoulders.

His first instinct was to wrap the blanket around her, tucking in the edges to keep in warmth. The next would be to kiss her just above the brow, slowly and gently so as not to wake her. As soon as he'd found himself back in her room, he'd known that invisible force field of impossibility had been put back into place. He didn't know how it was possible. He could still feel her warmth in between his fingers, could still smell her on his shirt. But he knew that if he tried to move the strand of blonde hair away from her eyes, his hand would swipe right through her and she'd shimmer out of focus as if she didn't exist.

He couldn't help himself from glaring at her bookshelf, the bed in which she slept in, or even the floor. Those he could touch. Though, when he'd tried to move a lamp or the remote control for the stereo system or even open a window, the object wouldn't budge, stuck, as if cemented to the spot. The objects were solid to him, but unyielding.

Trying to stamp out his anger, Morpheus turned to Brigh's nightstand and let himself memorize the objects it held. Her bubblegum pink alarm clock took up the corner of the brown wooden surface, the two dots in the middle mocking him with their rhythmic blinking of time. On the other corner sat the faded green lamp he'd tried so many times to turn on, and next to it, nestled between a vase with a dried rose and a mug with fuzzy pens, sat a silver picture frame. He'd stared at this picture many times before, always finding it fascinating for some reason. Posed within the photo were a man and a woman, both smiling in formalwear. The man was obviously a younger version of her father, his dark hair long and curling around his ears. The smile on his face reached his eyes, making him look younger than he must've been in the photograph.

Morpheus had never seen this smile on Jairus' face. Some days, when Jairus came home from work and went to the couch, Morpheus would sit next to him and tell him jokes. Although the man never heard him, it gave Morpheus comfort to sit there next to him and talk and laugh, even though he knew it wasn't real.

The woman in the picture wore a white dress and a white lace veil lost within the curls of her blonde hair. Her green eyes stared at Morpheus, the smile lines around her lips reminding him of the girl fast asleep in the bed. He assumed this woman was her mother, for the blonde hair and green eyes were almost identical. This was her parents on their wedding day, enjoying each other and the new adventure they were embarking on. But how long had the happiness lasted? What happened to the pair that had jostled them apart? Neither Jairus nor Brigh spoke about her, and Richard was always jabbering on about something new he'd gotten himself into.

If Morpheus saw Brigh again, he'd ask her what had happened. But until then, he'd enjoy her quiet ramblings in her sleep and wonder what would have happened had she answered him.

ᚱ

Brigh's alarm sounded at 6:30 on Monday, and instead of getting up right when she turned it off, she fell back to sleep. She flung the comforter over her head with a groan as the light trickling in through the blinds passed over her face.

Morpheus had lain next to her all through the night, randomly getting up to look at things around her room. After talking to her, he was overcome with this manic curiosity to see what it was that made her Brigh, even though he'd already quickly glanced through her things once or twice before.

As he ran his fingers over her small collection of books, CDs, and movies, he felt energized and impatient. He wanted to run, dance, and sing—though he knew he couldn't carry a tune. Every step he took seemed too slow, too awkward; he wanted to skip and climb a tree, things he'd never had an interest in until now. His thick brows slammed together in confusion. Though the feelings running through his core were hot and cold at the same time, making him dizzy with pleasure, he wasn't sure what had brought them on.

He was fetched out of his thoughts when Brigh's door swung open and in came Richard with a big grin on his face. The boy was only a year younger than Brigh, but his face was still a little round, his cheeks mildly plump. His eyes were the same green as his sister's, his lashes longer and darker. The green Hollister t-shirt was thrown over a long-sleeved white shirt, meeting the blue jeans belted snugly at his waist.

"Wake up!" Richard yelled, shaking his sister.

Brigh groaned, but didn't move. Richard shook her harder and when she didn't move again, he licked his finger and snuck it into her ear.

"You rat!" she shouted, wiping her ear.

She was out of her bed before Richard reached the door and pounced on his back, hanging on by his shoulders. He was a good five inches taller than her, but she took him down just fine as if they'd done this every day. Their bodies landed on the hardwood floor with a loud smack as they wrestled and called each other names.

"*What the hell is going on?*" Jairus yelled, stumbling out of his bedroom. He'd thrown on a wrinkled blue t-shirt and flannel pajama pants, tripping over a dog toy in his haste to see what the ruckus was about.

"Brigh wasn't up yet," Richard screeched as Brigh landed another harmless punch to his arm.

She gave a short battle cry. "He gave me a wet willy."

Jairus rolled his eyes, turned on his heel, and headed back to his bedroom. "Cool it, guys. Go to school, it's almost seven!"

That broke up the fight. Brigh pushed herself away from Richard and slammed the bathroom door shut. The exhaust fan came on just after the lock clicked.

Richard was still on the floor chuckling to himself when the shower started up and Jairus reemerged from his bedroom buttoning up a dark green shirt over a pair of unbuttoned faded blue jeans with a rip in the knee. Morpheus followed the two down into the kitchen where Richard raided the pantry and Jairus started making coffee.

"Whatcha up to today, dad?" Richard asked around bites of his bagel. He was still standing inside the pantry, taking stock of what else he wanted to eat.

Morpheus sat at the opposite end of the dining room table from Jairus who was now flipping through the newspaper. He was reading the sports section, the front page covered with pictures of varsity football and a questioning headline asking how the Sentinels would lead them this year. Morpheus was in the process of reading the article when Jairus folded the paper in half and picked up another section.

"Off to another job site," Jairus said, his voice sounding as scratchy as the stubble on his chin. "Peter MacRae's building a monster out near Accident."

"What's it supposed to be?" Richard asked, walking into the dining room from the kitchen with a piece of bagel hanging between his lips as he chewed.

Jairus shrugged with his gaze still on the paper. "Some two-point-five million dollar home, most likely." He shook the paper and then flipped the page. "I can only imagine what the building insurance is gonna cost him."

Richard tore off a piece of his bagel and stuffed it into his mouth. "You're not still holding that grudge, are you, dad?"

Jairus pulled the paper away from his admonished face. "I aint holding no grudge, Rich, for the last time."

"Sure." Richard took another bite of his bagel. "Liar."

"What?" Jairus asked incredulously.

But Richard didn't have a chance to answer, because Brigh was running down the steps, hauling on a light jacket while she flew into the kitchen. "Rich, grab your bag, we're leaving in five minutes."

Richard leaned on the back of his chair, watching his flustered sister grab a banana and a bottle of water from the fridge. "We're not going to be late."

"We are so," she argued. "Did you eat breakfast?"

"Yeah."

Brigh gave her brother a very stern and unbelieving look.

"I did," he said. "I'd show you, but you wouldn't like how it looks right now."

Brigh's nose scrunched up in disgust and Morpheus couldn't help but laugh. "Whatever. Get your stuff and start the car."

Richard rolled his eyes but obeyed his sister's directions. "See ya, dad."

"Don't terrorize your sister," Jairus grumbled, back to reading the newspaper.

Once Richard was out of earshot, Brigh stepped into the dining room, her hand holding onto the doorway for support. Jairus didn't even notice her staring until she cleared her throat. He looked up expectantly, but a little confused. He hadn't slept much, and there were faint creases on his cheek from the stitching of his blankets.

"Dad." Brigh took in a deep breath, looked at the floor, and then back to her father. "Do you think mom will be at graduation?"

Jairus was holding his breath and his face started turning a little red. To respond, though, he let it out and swallowed. He didn't answer right away and Brigh looked like she wanted to be anywhere but where she was standing. Finally Jairus came out of his thoughts and smiled at his daughter.

"She wouldn't miss it for the world," was all he said.

Brigh smiled sadly and left her father to his thoughts.

ᚱ

Morpheus had followed Brigh through her school several times when she was finishing junior year, but nothing he'd witnessed then was enough to prepare him for what he saw now. The halls were full of balloons, students having to push the long white strings aside to get to their lockers. Boys ran around people spraying each other with different colored silly string, the girls near them screaming and shielding their hair. Lockers were decorated by parents with the school colors and football designs. Some of the guys blushed at notes their moms had left on their locker door, others laughing and taking pictures.

Morpheus couldn't help but chuckle, even as people ran through him, unable to share laughter at the crude jokes he was making. Walking among the students made him feel an inch closer to humanity, even though they were a little more immature than he.

"Hey, Breen!" Kyle yelled over the crowd, a notepad and calculator clutched in his large hands.

Brigh turned with a tired smile. "Lazarus. What's up?"

"Ah, nothing," he said with a grin. "What's your first class?"

Brigh shrugged. "History."

His grin grew wider. "With Panatelli?"

"Yep."

"We have the same class."

She yawned. "Cool."

Morpheus eyed Kyle Lazarus with curiosity. The boy was almost drooling on Brigh's arm. Sure, he was handsome, and being a varsity football player didn't hurt him any. But he wasn't right for Brigh. He was too tall; his nose too long, and his clothing choice was more frightening than Richard's. Morpheus wasn't a mind reader, but Kyle definitely seemed interested in Brigh. Whether properly interested as a gentleman or scandalously as a prick, he wasn't sure. But he was determined to find out which.

"Hand over your backpack," Kyle said, still with that smile plastered on his face.

"I can carry my own stuff."

Kyle shook his head and stood behind her, carefully extracting the straps of her backpack. "I know. But you look like you haven't slept."

"And you did?" Brigh smiled.

Kyle laughed. "Slept all weekend."

Morpheus shook his head, but followed the two up the stairs and into the classroom where Felicity caught up with the pair just as the bell rang.

"You're late," Brigh whispered as Felicity ran over to the empty seat behind her.

Felicity shrugged. "Senioritis has kicked in."

Once everyone settled down, Mrs. Panatelli introduced herself, the course, handed out a syllabus, and started her lecture. They were covering foreign wars, everything from the Middle East, to France, through the United Kingdom, and America. Though Morpheus wasn't in the class, and had already covered most of this subject in his own studies, he sat in the back of the class, interested in what the teacher had to offer.

She apparently had a quiz, handing out blank pieces of white paper to each row. Some of the boys in the class rolled their eyes while most of the girls were leaning over their desks, gossiping with their friends. The teacher gave the talkers an unfriendly look and the chatting ended abruptly.

"Name six nineteenth century wars," Mrs. Panatelli said as the last of the blank papers were passed around. "Also, write down the years of the revolutionary War, the beginning of World War II, the second Jacobite Rising of Scotland, and Vietnam."

She smiled. "Let's see how good you are."

Pencils and pens hit the blank papers either with force, timid uncertainty, or blankly. Some students peered out of the corners of their eyes, passed notes, and even whispered a question to their neighbor. Mrs. Panatelli, though gray haired and a little shriveled, didn't show her age when she swung around to face the cheaters with a smile.

"You may look up for inspiration," she informed, "down in desperation, but you may not look around for information."

Kyle chuckled to himself as Felicity rolled her eyes.

Suddenly curious, Morpheus walked up the aisles, taking a quick look at everyone's papers. The girl in the second row, third seat, wasn't sure about a fourth war, busily chewing her rubber eraser. The third row seemed to either be satisfied with their answers, or desperately wishing they knew them, for their papers were turned over with their writing utensils on top. So far, six students had a quarter of their answers correct.

When he reached Brigh's seat, she was just finishing up her last answer, and before she could flip over her paper, Morpheus scanned her answers and smiled, satisfied, that she had every one correct. She and Felicity loved their movies and a share of television shows, but none of them had anything to do with history. He bet no one knew how much she loved history.

Mrs. Panatelli stopped everyone and asked for them to send up their papers. Since the class wasn't so large, she went through each sheet, quickly grading them while everyone chatted amongst themselves.

"Alright, settle down," Mrs. Panatelli said loudly.

With all the papers passed back out, Brigh was the only student who hadn't received hers; it was clutched in the old paws of her teacher who had a smile on her face.

"Brianna Breen?" she asked.

Brigh's hand rose confidently in the air, a small smile twitching her lips. "I'm here."

"Well, you're the only student who answered every question correctly." Mrs. Panatelli looked satisfied, but also a little angry. "Since most of you answered incorrectly, I will read aloud the correct answers as Miss Breen has listed them—"

"Why do you insist on following this girl around?" Narelle asked.

Morpheus was startled, his dreamy thoughts turning to those of anger. He'd been aware of nothing but the surrounding bodies and his girl. Had Narelle not said anything, he'd have continued on in ignorant bliss. Try as he might though, he couldn't ignore his mentor. She wasn't as tall as him, or as wide, but the obnoxious click to her fake British tongue was enough to wary any man.

"Why do you insist on following *me* around?" he asked in return. He'd wanted to say so many other things, but held his tongue. The only courtesy she was giving him was not blabbing his interest in Brigh to Alphaeus and the Elders. He could give her a smile and share a few laughs.

She snorted and walked around him, her hand running sensually down his arm. "It is my duty to keep you in my sight. Who knows what kinds of horrible nasties you are getting yourself into?"

He couldn't help but laugh. "True."

"Have you met with the Elders about your ascension?"

He glanced at Brigh, very briefly, and unnoticeable. He'd been with her almost every moment for the past few weeks; he'd forgotten about the Elders. That wasn't like him. Before he'd met Brigh, he'd inquired about his time of change only half serious and once in a while. Post Brigh, he'd been practically knocking down their doors with questions. His change in character was surely to be noticed by those above him and he didn't want them to even wonder.

"No," he said. "I will go to them now."

Narelle nodded in approval and walked out of the room. With one last look at Brigh, Morpheus followed Narelle out the door that led them home.

BRIGH

"That woman is nuts," Felicity shouted as everyone shuffled out of the classroom.

Holding her hand in front of her mouth, Brigh pushed Felicity away from the door where the teacher hovered. "You're nuts for saying that so close to her. She could give you detention!"

"First amendment, Brigh," Felicity said while shaking her head. "Besides, everyone thinks I have a mild form of Tourette's."

Brigh threw her head back and laughed, the small ball of anxiety in her stomach dissipating. She turned around to walk backward and talk to Felicity at the same time. "I still can't believe you and your mouth. You curse like a sailor."

"Aye, matey," Felicity gurgled like a drunken sailor, saluting Brigh as she walked backward. "And it's me own diabolical plan."

"I don't think a pirate would know a word that large."

Felicity shrugged. "I'm sure the women had larger vocabularies."

Brigh giggled. "Yeah, but—"

Brigh gasped at the sudden stop in her step as she backed into something. Grabbing her chest, she turned to see Benji behind her with his hands out to steady them. A nervous laugh left Brigh's lips as she tried fixing her hair.

"Hey, Benji."

"Hi," was all he said. He seemed nervous and like he didn't want to be there.

"I haven't heard from you since the Gateway." She readjusted her backpack, holding onto the right strap. "You been okay?"

"Yeah, fine," he mumbled, taking a small step back.

Brigh wrinkled her nose. "You sure? I thought we could do something. You know? Go see a movie."

Benji let out a breath and shook his head. "Look, Brigh, you're a very nice girl and all, but I'm not looking for a girlfriend right now."

"Oh."

Looking away and already heading down the hall, he called, "I'll see you later."

Brigh stood in the middle of the hallway, her hands grasping the straps of her backpack as though they were what kept her together. Felicity drew up on her right and she was sure Kyle stood directly behind her, there to catch her if she fell.

"Well, that little bastard," Felicity announced, looking after Benji as he rounded a corner down the hall.

Brigh shook her head. "It's fine. We didn't really have anything to begin with."

Felicity put her hand on Brigh's shoulder. "I know, but…that rat bastard. Would you like me to kill him?"

Brigh grinned deviously, but shook her head. "Nah, Fee. Save the energy and possible murder conviction for a guy who really deserves it."

As Brigh headed away, she looked over her shoulder to see Felicity pointing at Kyle's thick chest. Kyle had a good six inches on her and nearly one hundred pounds. But her best friend stood her ground, giving the varsity football jock the infamous Best Friend Dirty Look.

"That could be *you*," she said with a smile.

Kyle stepped back, holding out his hands. "Whoa, whoa. If all I have to look forward to is possibly losing my balls to a theatre nerd, then I'll take my business elsewhere."

Felicity laughed and wrapped her arm around his. "Just be cool and we won't have that problem."

Sometimes best friends were given too much power.

MORPHEUS

There was no wait to see the Elders, which in itself was odd. There was always a line of impatience and excitement. But never *nothing*.

Narelle walked Morpheus to the door, leaving a soft kiss upon his cheek before leaving him standing alone. He watched her glide down the long hallway, her voluptuous hips rising and falling with each step under her thin white dress. Her calves were small without any muscle at all and her ankles were thin and tempting.

He shook himself out of his daze, frowned, and walked inside the doors. Darkness greeted him, though once his eyes adjusted it wasn't as dark as he'd first thought. The Elders consisted of a group of beings far older than anything he could name. They were blind, shrunken little creatures who were shaped like men, but not men at all, lips sewn shut with manmade metal.

Stories of the Elders changed with each person he spoke with. Some said they were the ones who had created them. Some said they were once men, and when they died, they broke away from heaven to build their own race. Humans would have thought of them as faerie's exiled to another dimension. There were even rumors that the

Elders were demons forced from the world of man, shackled to this plane of existence to see all and not be able to do anything for themselves.

Morpheus had seen their group many times before and had always found a little truth to the demon rumors, for they sure looked and acted demonically. Seconds before he reached The Circle of Sight, their voices were swirling inside his head, not picking at his memories—he hoped, at least—but throwing their voices so that he could hear them speak.

Why have you come, young one? a sickly voice asked, his words scuttling through Morpheus's brain like mice.

Morpheus wanted to scratch his head, but instead turned to face the being from which the voice was coming. "I wish to know when I will become flesh."

Voices muttered to each other, but he couldn't make out the words. He wasn't sure whether that was because they spoke in another language, or because there were so many voices that they just blended together. His head began to ache from the pressure of their voices, but he didn't move to massage his temples.

We are having difficulty finding your date, another voice answered.

This is not unusual, as you should know, one answered from the left.

"Then how am I to know when to prepare?" Morpheus questioned angrily. "I have come to you several times and have been patiently satisfied with your answers. But my patience has run thin, and I am about to burst if I do not know the date."

Why the impatience? the first voice asked curiously.

Morpheus closed his lips. He was treading on dark waters and the Elders knew it. If he lied, they'd know. If he spoke the truth…well, he wasn't sure what they would do. He was the only one of their kind to make physical contact with humans. As far as he knew, there was no punishment for falling in love with a human, but it was frowned upon.

"I have seen their world," he began. "I have seen their humanity and their love and crave it with the unmade heart under my breast.

"I just wish to know," he went on, his voice lower with pain, "so that my waiting won't become obsession; I can do my studies without wondering when it will be my time."

One of the figures nodded approvingly. *We understand. Normally your time would appear to us, but there is something in the way. A mist in front of our eyes that we cannot part at this time. We will double our efforts and will have the date of your ascension soon. We appreciate your patience.*

Morpheus smiled. They didn't know how impatient he was, and what he was willing to do to get around it. Thank the stars they couldn't read minds.

6

BRIGH

"It's not the numbers that are confusing me," Felicity cried, flinging her pencil at the wall like it had something slimy on it. "What the hell's the point of all the letters—?"

"Variables," Brigh corrected.

"—whatever, they still don't make sense." Rolling her eyes, she huffed and got up to retrieve her pencil from under the dresser. "What're you wearing to homecoming?"

Brigh flipped a page in Felicity's Algebra book. "Actually, I was thinking of skipping it this year."

"*What*?"

Brigh looked up at the shocked open-mouthed expression on Felicity's face and wanted to smile, but was polite enough not to.

"It's not a crime if I don't go," Brigh explained.

"*Yes* it *is*." Felicity ran over and jumped on her bed. "It's wrong if the homecoming queen doesn't show up to the dance!"

"What makes you think I'll be homecoming queen?"

"Only that you've been in the homecoming court every year." She felt Brigh's head. "Are you getting sick?"

Brigh swatted her hand away. "No, I'm fine."

"You sure? You don't look so good. Are you using that eye cream I gave you?"

The laugh wound itself out of Brigh's stomach before she knew it was coming and suddenly found herself laughing uncontrollably, her face lost within Felicity's comforter.

"What the hell is so funny?"

Brigh shook her head, wiping the tears from under her eyes. "I'm sorry. I just—well, I couldn't help it. The conversation switched so quickly—we went from talking about homecoming to eye cream, *come on*."

The hard look in Felicity's eyes started to crack and then she was laughing too.

ᚱ

It looked like Brigh was going to the homecoming dance after all. Both Felicity and Kyle were making the rounds in the halls, grabbing people to the side for their signatures, nominating Brigh homecoming queen. What they were doing was nice, and Brigh felt grateful to have such caring friends. She just wasn't sure being in the spotlight around that night would do well for her nerves.

Leaning against the wall with her arms crossed, Brigh waited outside of her English class while her friends finished up their tasks. She couldn't help smiling and waving to those who came up to her wishing her luck. She wasn't running for President of the United States, but she knew that since it was her senior year, this year counted above all others. Plus, she didn't know who she was running up against.

Felicity seized one last signature before skipping over to Brigh. "You won't *believe* how many names I got!"

Brigh smiled, her anxiety rushing through her limbs at an alarming speed. Her heart rate spiked and she felt almost lightheaded. "How many?"

Felicity was already counting, most likely double checking an earlier total. "Two fifty. Damn, that's half our class!"

Brigh's smile widened, her heart slowing a little. But to slow the heart rate, she had to start picking at the skin around her nails. She had to do something before she felt so thin a wire could cut through her.

Kyle was still grabbing guys by their shirt sleeves and standing handsomely tall and obstructive in front of the girls. He was very charming. Though he was a bit big in the arms and taller than her by at least a foot, she admired his passionate and endearing smile and the way he looked at her. He understood just as much as Felicity did about her family, though he didn't express his thoughts in so many words like her best friend.

She was brought out of her thoughts when the guy she was filling her head with came rushing over to them. He was out of breath, light sparkling in his eyes as he smiled. He had really nice teeth, Brigh noticed for the first time.

"How many d'you get, Fee?" he asked, his shoulders rising and falling fast.

Felicity looked smug. "Two fifty. You?"

Kyle shrugged. "Three."

"Beat ya!" Felicity shouted.

"Woman," Kyle said with a shake to his head. "I meant three hundred, not three names total."

Felicity's face fell, and then she looked mad. "Yeah, well, this is just the beginning. We have a month to get names. I'll beat you, just you wait. And no double signing!"

"What the hell's going on?" Chandra asked, stopping in front of Felicity.

"They're seeing who can get the most names," Brigh answered before Felicity could open her mouth.

"For homecoming queen?" Amelia piped in.

Brigh nodded.

"Well, hell, let's get in on this!" Chandra grabbed Brigh's notebook and hurried down the hall. Amelia ran after her girlfriend, shrugging at Brigh's astonished expression as she passed.

"They're going to kick our asses," Kyle announced.

"*I'm* going to kick your ass," Felicity said.

Then the two were off, pushing through the throng of students racing to catch their classes. Brigh smiled despite the loneliness suddenly consuming her. She shrugged it off and turned to head into the classroom when someone bumped into her.

"Watch it!" Marissa McAllister yelled. She was one of those bottle blonde cheerleader look-alikes that were often on MTV and in horrible comedy films. And on her arm? Not a Paris Hilton Chihuahua, but the football team captain Jake MacRae. The only thing saving Jake from being compared to a Chihuahua was that his IQ ranged high, close to Brigh's.

"That sneer you got there's really attractive," Brigh said sarcastically. As sweetly as she could, of course.

Said sneer quickly disappeared, replaced by a dirty look and slanted hateful eyes. "I'd be careful if I were you, Breen."

Brigh smiled sweetly. "And if not, you'll trap my finger in your Prada compact?"

Jake smiled while Marissa's attention was locked on Brigh, his hand lightly covering his mouth to stifle a possible laugh.

"No," Marissa hissed. "Be careful what you say and do around competition."

"Comp—" Brigh stopped dead, her lips pursed in shock. "You're running for homecoming queen?"

"And prom." Marissa fanned herself with her class schedule. "I'd worry if I were you. You and your phantom date are no match for Pookie and me."

Pookie? Brigh mouthed to Jake. She wasn't particularly fond of the MacRae family, but she felt a little bit sorry for Jake at the moment.

He looked up at the ceiling, closed his eyes, and with a tightly clenched jaw, nodded.

"Good luck to you both, then," was all Brigh said before walking into the classroom and ignoring the glare she felt on her back. She leaned back in her chair and tried to relax through the minute before class. She'd heard bad things about Dr. Bob Allaby. Hopefully he wasn't as bad as the seniors before her made him out to be.

ᚱ

"Alright, people," Mr. Orloff shouted with his arms raised in the air. "As some of you know—by rumor I'm sure—all the art classes are holding a fieldtrip to Swallow Falls in little more than a month."

Whispers erupted throughout the crowd of seated painters, sketch artists, and those who had mixed talents in computer design and other Medias. Gossip was ripe at Fort

Hill High as it was at any high school. Brigh would smile at the words others brought her, but didn't feel right spreading them. After last fall, there'd been plenty of rumors about her, all untrue, proliferating through the town like a sickness, and she hadn't appreciated it. So she didn't participate.

"Settle down—quiet, children!" Orloff was a pushover and very badly needed a significant other. He reminded Brigh of Stanford from *Sex and the City*, but was definitely straight. He often switched from contacts to his black framed glasses when dealing with computers and today he had them hanging from his shirt pocket. Everything about what he wore and how he looked screamed *former/present nerd*, but Brigh thought it sweet.

"As I was saying," he continued, wiping his sweaty palms over his shirt. "All art classes will travel to Swallow Falls to take pictures and/or construct some sort of piece from something they see. Please bring jackets and high boots. It may rain."

Then just like any other class period, people stood to grab their art pieces, extra materials, and sat softly conversing with their table partner or listening to music on their iPods and cell phones. Brigh always brought her iPod, stuffing the little ear buds uncomfortably in her ear to blast her music. A lot of the details in her art depended on the different beats of the music she listened to. Her piece that hung in the school gallery had distorted figures and lines all over the place, the colors bleeding together. The song she'd kept replaying while constructing it was by Dream Theater.

This piece wasn't much different, though the music artist had changed. Alien Ant Farm raged in her ears, as her paint brush fox-trotted across her canvas. This piece wasn't going to take very long, the finished product already a picture in her mind. She just hoped this one would win Orloff's approval as did the one still hung in the gallery, even though it brought bad images to mind and worse nightmares.

R

After classes, Brigh donned her cheerleading uniform for the first time since last fall. A shaky breath escaped her trembling lips as she pulled it over her head; the memory of that first season game making her a little dizzy. Her pompoms took up space in the bottom of her gym locker, the red and white strings covered in a layer of dust. The memory of the fabric brushing against her hands, and the sound of them crunching under her feet as she'd rushed toward her brother's terrified expression, made her slam the locker door shut to silence her mind.

Richard hadn't known until that night. A piece of gossip caught in the air. He'd deserved better than to be told by some freshmen jock, but she hadn't thought to tell him the truth, or what she'd thought as the truth. Sometimes she thought that he still hadn't forgiven her, but she tried to act as though nothing had happened. Last year had been a colossal mistake.

She took a deep breath and turned the corner, running right into her coach. The taller woman staggered back, a laugh escaping her shiny Chap Stick lips. Her dark hair was pulled back in a low ponytail, swinging back and forth as she shook her head and smiled at Brigh. Her brown eyes were always unperturbed and kind. Brigh had never thought of eyes showing a person's true nature. But maybe there was something to the saying that eyes were the gateway to a person's soul.

"That excited to start tryouts?" Her Kentucky accent was softened by her relaxed tone, but a tinge of concern was there, left over from last year.

Brigh tried smiling to put her coach's questions at ease. "I'm just a little flustered with school. But I'm good. Let's get going."

Her coach smiled in return, but Brigh knew her coach would be keeping an eye on her for the rest of the season. Hence why she put exhaustion and nerves aside during tryouts, even allowing her coach to step in once or twice when the other team members got out of hand. Brigh just hoped the woman would keep her feelings to herself and not bring up that horrible night.

MORPHEUS

Morpheus hadn't had any time to even think of Brigh. Narelle was dragging him all over the place, quizzing him about certain things, but skirting around the girl with which he was infatuated. Everyone he passed gave him an apologetic smile and nod, walking around Narelle as they passed.

"Narelle," Morpheus said, as she pulled him along by his hand. "Do tell a fellow what it is you are doing."

She glanced at him briefly, snorted, and then tugged harder on his hand. The woman was fast. "I am taking you to your next lesson."

"What is it? Learning patience as well as exercise?"

She threw him a dirty look that he'd seen many times before, but said nothing more. They turned a corner and before Morpheus knew it, he was standing in front of an enormous door. Perhaps enormous wasn't the correct word, for this door was taller and wider than anything he'd ever seen, within his world and the human plane. Two golden sconces the size of his torso took over what wall space there was on either side of the wooden door. The handles, large gold hoops that were imprinted in the center from the many hands before him, could fit both his hands wrapped around the inside. The closer he got, the more he could see that the wood of the door wasn't smooth as he'd first thought, but prickly with tiny, splintery shards.

"What is in there?" Morpheus asked, not wanting to budge.

Narelle's diminutive hands were clutched around one bulky hoop as she turned to look at him over her shoulder. "Do not all of a sudden be a ponce. I am not telling, for what is a secret?"

"You know I do not appreciate secrets." He ran his fingers through the front of his hair. "Besides, why must I study today? I thought my classes were near ending."

"There is still much to know," she reasoned. "And since you are not advancing to human existence anytime soon, we should not forget your studies. Intelligence is important, you know."

"Any fool knows that," he muttered under his breath. Then, thinking upon the subject, Morpheus asked, "What happens to us when we die?"

Narelle looked put off by the question, releasing the gold ring to fully face Morpheus. "You know you will learn this in your final classes. Why do you wish to know now?"

Morpheus shrugged. "Curious."

Narelle eyed him for a minute before pulling the door open. Finally, reluctantly, he walked past the lioness and through the gates, wondering what the hell it was he had been thinking to make such a decision.

ᚱ

"So," Darius asked, chewing on Morpheus' quill. "How were your studies?"

"Horrible," Morpheus muttered from under his arm. He was lying across his cot, his knees hanging over the edge of the tiny thing, with his arm thrown over his eyes to shield the harsh lighting. Usually he kept his room shadowed, wearing the darkness like a comforting blanket. But Darius was all about light and attention, especially when he was snooping through Morpheus' things.

"'A bright and flaming halo,' hmm?" Darius leaned over the right arm of the desk chair, Morpheus' journal in his hands, thumbs coursing over the thick lettering. "I thought you were over your poetic stage."

"And I thought you were over your nagging and annoying stage. Can we please get over it?"

Darius laughed. "Touché. But I thought you were over this. Writing, I mean. There was a time when this book was only a quarter full. Now there are barely pages left. And all because of what? Her?"

"Do not start in on the lecture," Morpheus warned tightly. "I have Narelle for that."

"Sure, sure," Darius agreed. "I still do not think you give that woman enough credit."

"She is not a woman."

Darius turned on Morpheus with a confused, yet curious, look on his face. The two emotions were obviously battling it out on his face, his brows swooping and then parting, then swooping together again. Darius' face was like a circus of emotions; Morpheus could always tell what he was thinking.

"Is this about where she took you today?" Darius asked.

Morpheus shot up off the cot. "She told you?"

"Not exactly." Darius turned wary, looking back to the journal. "She just told me you were going to be busy with studies." He coughed; a very human reaction to nerves and very unlike Darius, Morpheus noted. "At the Crick."

"So she told you of where I was going *and* told you the name of it?"

Darius nodded fast. "I have not been there myself, but I have heard it can be quite nasty."

"Quite," Morpheus repeated, spitting out the word. "That is not *quite* the word I would use."

"So how is our girl, Brigh?" Darius asked.

Morpheus caught the smooth change in subject and realized that his friend was uncomfortable. Darius had no reason to feel uneasy; he was taller, broader, and possibly stronger than Morpheus could ever be in this world. If anyone, Morpheus should be the one to worry.

"I do not know," Morpheus choked out, feeling Darius' uneasiness creep in through his shoulders. "I have not seen her in two days."

"Ah," was all he said. He was back to reading Morpheus' journal, chasing sentences with the tip of his middle finger.

"Why did you bring her up?"

Darius' eyes flicked up at him and then quickly back to the page. "I was wondering. You have not spoken of her. My asking was plain curiosity."

"*Yours* or *hers?*" He'd never felt his brows so close to touching, or the little sting that came from stretching the skin.

"Do you honestly think I do everything for her? That I, I worship the ground upon which she walks?"

Morpheus raised a brow.

He folded his arms.

He felt intimidating, he must have looked it. The uncertainty was back in Darius' eyes. His shoulders slumped slightly. A tired and uncomfortable downward tilt to his lips. Darius could never lie.

"I am like a canine on a leash, am I not?"

Morpheus shrugged. "It is better than being a parrot in a cage."

Darius smiled. "Touché."

7

MORPHEUS

For the next couple of days, Morpheus trailed behind Brigh in the halls of her school and throughout her and Felicity's homes. Each day Brigh looked even more exhausted, the circles under her eyes darker and wider, a shadow under her makeup. He hadn't been able to watch her sleep, for Narelle would need him for something or some task would be set in front of him to accomplish.

Today at work she was vacuuming, the white dog chasing the light reflection of her bracelet on the wall. Morpheus watched Brigh's coworkers and customers laugh at the dog hopping around and wagging its tail. But he also noticed the same concern he was feeling show on her boss' face as he watched her and his dog.

She looked exhausted, tired in ways he couldn't conceive. Was she not sleeping? Were classes causing stress? As far as he knew, fall sports had yet to begin, so her role as cheerleading captain wasn't a stressor.

Watching her yawn and slowly roll the vacuum back and forth, he knew he'd see her tonight. He would dodge

Narelle and ignore Darius' questions, for he just knew that seeing Brigh tonight would ease the pain.

He just wasn't sure if the pain being eased would be hers or his.

BRIGH

Arnold and Anna lived in an apartment-style home above the garage on the nursery's property. Arnold's mother owned the two hundred year old house connected to the garage, kindly allowing her son and his wife to live on the property. The apartment wasn't very large as far as homes went, but it was big enough to house the two cats, four dogs, and their owners.

The dining table was a small flimsy wooden structure that most of the dogs could rest their chins upon. Yogurt was glued to Brigh's side as she rolled dough between her hands, his head resting heavily in her lap. Alex, the Saint Bernard, hadn't left Anna's seat at the table for anything, even when the woman would walk back and forth between the kitchen and dining room. In the living room by Arnold sat the Husky, who answered to both Airplane and Airen, and the Sheltie puppy whose name, Hanger, confused everyone who asked.

Lynda, thick blonde hair pulled up into a tiny bun, leaned over her freshly shaped peanut butter biscuits and winked at Brigh. "I was just thinking about you the other day, little muffin."

Brigh quirked her eyebrow and smiled. "I've thought of you, too. How do you like your new place?"

Lynda's rosy cheeks lifted up as her smile turned into a devilish smirk. Her voice was high, lilting with grace and a saintly soprano. But once she spoke, the recipient of her attention came to find out that only Lynda had the talent of sounding like an Angel while spilling the words of a sinner.

"It's pretty," Lynda explained, rolling her next piece of dough. "But it's a bitch to clean the goat shit off your shoes at the end of the day."

"She's joking," Anna said with a smile as she rushed back into the room with a clean cookie sheet ready for the oven. As she began stacking up the newest bone and initial shaped cookies onto the sheet, she smiled at Brigh. "How are classes going?"

"They're fine. Even my AP classes are easy."

"That's great, honey," Anna said before she disappeared back into the kitchen. "Are you seeing anyone?" she yelled, bent over in front of the hot, open oven.

Brigh was in the process of spelling out Thorburn's name in individual cookies when she sighed. "There's this guy I like, but I don't know if he's right for me."

"Don't you worry," Anna called from the kitchen. "You're young. You have plenty of time to find someone."

Lynda shook her head. "Yeah. Just don't inadvertently accept drinks from a drunk who might try to get into your pants. *Especially* while listening to Journey's *Anyway You Want It*."

Anna peaked around the corner and gave Lynda a look. All Lynda did in return was shrug and mutter, "It was the eighties. And Merryweather."

Brigh laughed, but cut it short as Arnold sauntered into the room. His evergreen nursery shirt was dark in patches from shoveling mulch and wet with dog drool. With his glasses set high on his nose, he scooped two dog cookies off of the tray Anna was bringing into the dining room. All three women stared after him as he continued walking into the adjacent "couch room" where most of the dogs slept. He stopped just short of reaching the plaid covered couch in front of the television and turned with a sour look on his face. Crumbs hung loosely from the hair of his mustache, his jaw cocked at an angle that suggested he'd been chewing and stopped mid-motion.

Lynda and Anna took in a breath as Brigh tried to hold back a laugh. "Something wrong?"

Arnold's bottom lip snuck up under his mustache as he frowned. "These cookies taste like shit."

Lynda was the first to crack even though Anna was giving her the death glare. Arnold still looked confused as Brigh straightened in her chair. "Well, I guess they will taste horrible…when there are dog hairs and saliva baked right into them."

His glasses magnified the roundness of his eyes as they widened. "What?"

Brigh shrugged and patted Yogurt's head. "When the dough got dry, I let the dog lick my hands. It's not my fault if a few white hairs got in there."

Arnold looked down at the cookie, swallowed, and then headed back into the living room without another word. Technically the cookies were edible for humans, but if

Brigh continued to moisten the dough with the dogs help, then none of the batches would be human friendly.

With that thought, a wicked smile curled her lips.

ᚱ

As Brigh rested her head on the pillow, the fear and uncertainty that came before sleep crashed over her, almost drowning. The heat from the hair falling over her cheeks didn't warm her, nor could the comforter and wool blankets.

She hadn't seen Morpheus in three nights. She'd been back to that forest, though, more than once. But when she had stood out in the middle of the endless trees, ungodly howls and eerie shrieks were heard all around her.

After the first dream, thinking of Morpheus as a good thing would have made Brigh laugh with insane hilarity. Having been faced with the other possibility in that eerie forest land with nothing but silence, her imagination, and the infrequent noises of predators in the shadows, she began to see Morpheus as almost a savior. She knew it was insane to think of him as anything more than a figment of a very overactive imagination, inside the subconscious of a person in mourning, but there was still this need to feel protected. This need to have some part of her life make sense.

"Please," she whispered shakily.

And closed her eyes.

The forest unwrapped around her like origami, the edges dulled and mildly unfocused. Rain misted her brow as the mud collected her toes. She took a deep breath of cold air that sliced at her throat.

His back was to her as he plucked an orange leaf from a nearby branch. Drops of water splattered his arm, but he seemed unfazed as he reached for another. He stared at the dying leaves like he'd never seen them before. Maybe he hadn't; Brigh wasn't too clear on what Morpheus had or hadn't done or seen.

She was too scared to move. Catch his attention and open the possibility that he was a nightmare mirage, or, call out his name and seek comfort in his acknowledgement and/or embrace. Her fear of him not being her dream man kept her mouth shut.

"I can hear you breathing," he said without turning around.

Brigh didn't think it possible, but her heart stopped. Her breathing only continued when he turned around and his face was normal. No fangs, no boils, no flaming nostrils; a normal, human face.

"Are you unwell?"

Brigh shook her head. She wasn't sure how she was. But she sucked up whatever fed her emotions and smiled. "I'm fine, thanks."

"Mmhm." He nodded his head, a far off look on his face.

"How come you weren't here the last two nights?"

His eyes focused on her face, curiosity and hope wrapped up in a small smile. "Did you miss me?"

"No, I was just wondering how often I'm going to be sucked into this kind of dream."

His brows met unattractively and his lips curled downward. "If you do not wish to see me, I will go."

"No, please!" She stepped forward— her feet caught in the caking mud—and tripped. Before she could panic, he was there at her side, catching her arm and pulling her into his chest.

He smelled strongly of soil and trees, and something else that Brigh couldn't quite identify. The smell was sharp and made her head ache slightly, but being this close to him already made her head swim. The smell eventually didn't bother her so much.

There were little curls of black hair peaking out of his white shirt where the brown leather strings were tied into a neat bow. They were soft to the touch and cool. His skin radiated no heat, nor did his chest vibrate with the thump of a beating heart.

With a gasp, Brigh snapped back her hands, but didn't step away. "You're not—"

"Alive?" He was smiling when Brigh looked up into his face.

Brigh rolled her eyes. "I was going to say you're not *breathing.*"

"Well, those who are not alive do not breathe."

"You're serious?" She noticed he still held her by her arms, close to his chest. She wasn't sure if it creeped her out or comforted her.

"I would never lie to you, Brianna."

"No," she said, flustered. "I know dead people don't breathe. What I meant was you're honestly not alive?"

He smiled. "Well I am not dead."

"You're giving me a headache."

Closing his eyes, he let her arms go. "My apologies."

There was a pause between them; not awkward or even completely silent. The rain ricocheting off of the trees and leaves kept the silence between them comfortable, calming, and peaceful. Brigh imagined nights of silence in his arms. How easy it'd be to step back and feel his arms wrap around her waist and his chin atop her head. A perfect fairytale, if she'd ever imagined one. Prince charming infinitely caught in a romantically sodden world where she could be her true self.

She sighed heavily. "Why is it always raining?"

"I do not know," he replied. "Are you cold?" He held out his arms invitingly without thinking.

She shook her head harder than she'd meant to. Because, to be honest, she wanted nothing more than to be held like a child, coddled and cooed over. It wasn't that she knew he'd do it—she felt it, as if his arms were already cradling her head to his chest. The feeling was so strong; she remembered the last time her father had held her that way. He'd come to tell her—

"Walk with me?" he asked, holding out his hand. Relaxed, his arm extended out between them, palm up, hand tilted down. She noticed how the skin of his hand was only marred by a couple of lines, all short and straight. She wasn't sure if that meant he'd live a short life, or if the length of it had yet to be determined.

Again Brigh got that warning in her stomach, making her throat tight and her tongue slick. A short burst of vertigo captured her in its grasp, and she suddenly felt like she couldn't catch her breath. As far as she could remember, she'd never gotten sick in any of her dreams. Any hope of being in the dream world was slowly starting to slip away.

She took his hand, not because his smile was sweet and inviting or because he looked harmless at the moment. She wanted to feel the electric spark that jumped between them where their skin met. The way his fingers curved around her cold, clammy skin with that strike of fevered fire that held no warmth, but incited it with just a touch. When he held her hand it felt as if he were holding all of her.

They walked for a few minutes, hand in hand, inches away from each other but never touching anywhere else.

He never said a word or looked down at her, and she found the silence so peaceful she swayed in it without worry. Wet soggy leaves and mud foamed between her toes, but she couldn't bring herself to find it disgusting.

Brigh looked up at Morpheus with the kind of curiosity a child had when it came to something new and foreign. Though the rain had pasted her hair to her neck and cheeks, his short crop stood up in little spikes seemingly unaffected by the slow weight of the water. His discomfort and unease was only apparent in the way his hair stood. She glanced over at his other hand, leaning forward to catch sight of the swinging fingers with wonder if his skin would be glossy from the rain.

"What are you doing?" he asked, looking down at her. He hadn't sounded angry or confused, only scholarly curious.

"Are you nervous?"

A small smile formed and then he laughed. He brought his hand to his hair to feel the spiked strands, and then ran his fingers through again. "Narelle said I would grow out of such a nervous habit, but I guess it has stuck with me. I hardly notice my doing it."

Brigh smiled and pulled them both to a stop. With their hands still clasped, she stood in front of him with her head tilted back. She wasn't sure of his height; maybe shy of six and a half feet. Her hand came up before she knew what she was doing. He closed his eyes and bent his head while she played with the ends of his hair, curling the strands around her fingers and making bigger, fatter spikes hanging over his forehead.

Her pointer finger ended up getting caught mid-spike and he laughed, bending down to untie her finger. Their eyes met as he brought down their joined hands.

"Who's Narelle?" she asked.

The smile on his face smoothed out and his brows came closer to meeting. "She is my mentor."

He started walking again and Brigh had to hop over some tree roots to catch up. Once she fell into step with him, she grabbed his hand and jerked him to a stop. The look in his eyes wasn't entirely friendly, but he seemed calm and somewhat at ease.

"What's it like?" Brigh asked timidly, trying desperately to change the subject.

"What is what like?" he asked.

His nostrils flared and she couldn't tell if he was angry or uncomfortable.

MORPHEUS

"Your world," she said.

Morpheus looked at Brigh's fidgeting hands, watched her pick at the skin around her fingernails. He stepped forward and took those hands into his, holding tightly to her fingers. Her need to desecrate herself was palpable, stinging the hands he held her with.

"It is pale in comparison to your world," he began, not taking his eyes away from her hands. "It is made of structures without trees or water or food. There is no such thing as the internet, or cell phones, or television. Everything is devoid of color, personality, and love."

"Sounds horrible," she whispered. "I mean, I could live without the internet. But the rest…" She looked at their joined hands questioningly, but did not let go, and wiggled her fingers. Morpheus loosened his grip until her fingers weaved around his and they were holding hands.

Touching her, feeling the heat of her skin creep up his own, following the slow thump of her heartbeat pulsing through her fingers into his palm, made him feel complete. Stretching his fingers one by one, he wrapped them tighter around her hands, his thumb running across her knuckles.

They both looked up at the same time, staring into each other's eyes with fear and interest. As he watched her lower lip stick out invitingly, Morpheus felt something inside himself shift. He wasn't sure what to make of it. He'd never felt so alone in all his years. To have her in this moment, knowing in the back of his mind that he'd never really be able to hold her, to laugh at Felicity's jokes, or to watch television with Jairus. To have her, even for a moment, felt worse than never being able to have her at all.

"Sometimes the loneliness consumes us to the point where thoughts are hard to form. But we find ways of passing the time, like visiting your world and watching people experience life."

"Have you watched me?" Brigh asked.

"Every day."

Brigh's eyes widened.

"I do not watch you undress or relieve yourself," Morpheus hurried on. He'd never been more embarrassed in his whole existence. Come to think of it, he'd *never* been embarrassed. He was usually the teasing one, the one who noticed every little thing someone did or said. Never had he had to explain himself, tripping over words.

"I give you your privacy when it is needed," he finished awkwardly.

"How long?" She sounded close to tears as she stared at the ground.

Why did she keep asking if everything he told her made her want to cry? He'd seen this happen so many times over the century with different people. They kept asking questions that were attached to horrible answers. Why did they hurt themselves over simple curiosity? He didn't want to hurt Brigh anymore, not if he could help it.

"Only a few months," he said. "Three at the most."

Brigh visibly relaxed. The lie had crept slowly to the end of his tongue, timidly teasing the tip of it, and then diving off of the muscle so easily. He'd never been one to lie, never had a reason to.

"You said you guys are invisible to humans, right?" Brigh asked.

He nodded.

She bit her bottom lip. "Then how come I can see you?"

"I do not know."

When she'd first spoken to him he'd wondered how it could be possible. But after that he'd completely forgotten his confusion and fallen into their conversation. Of course, nothing was going like he'd planned. He'd written out a fictional first draft of what meeting Brigh in flesh would be like. He'd never thought the words *hopefully* or *maybe*. He'd been so certain everything would fall into place.

Beginning to wonder if some of his souls were unrealistic dreamers, he couldn't help but feel doomed before he started.

"I *am* a fool," he whispered.

"What? Are you talking to yourself again?"

"I do not—" He cut himself off. She'd only been around him twice. There was no way she could've noticed so much so quickly. "I do not talk to myself. I merely speak what is on my mind."

Brigh gave him a look. He'd never been given such a questioning, smart-alecky look in all his years. She had the audacity to stand there, arms folded over her chest, brow raised, and her hip comfortably cocked to the right. But by all the God's and Goddesses of the world, did she look beautiful. Her gorgeous face only added to his frustration.

"Do not do that," he said.

"Don't do what?"

"*Look* at you, woman."

"I don't have a mirror; I couldn't possibly look at myself."

Morpheus rolled his eyes. "Your beauty, girl. I cannot stay angry with you looking like that."

"You think I'm beautiful?" she asked, seeming a little shocked.

"Why would I not?"

She shrugged. "I don't know. I mean, there've been guys who have told me I'm *hot*, but..." She shrugged again, and Morpheus couldn't help but see her as a child: young, innocent, and unaware.

"I don't know why I asked," she said breathlessly.

"Do you not believe it?"

"What?"

"That you are beautiful." Morpheus sighed and suddenly felt like stuffing his hands in pant pockets, though he knew he didn't have them and wondered where the sudden feeling originated. "I do not understand this generation. Or the one before it, for that matter. Things used to be so much simpler."

"How?" Brigh asked, though she sounded a tad confused.

Morpheus began pacing. "Women are not paid their due. Men use meaningless words to woo them into their company. I have yet to hear one who told their woman that they are beautiful."

"My dad used to tell my mom she was." Her voice was so low, Morpheus had to strain to catch the last bit and then add words to make the sentence make sense.

"What happened?" he asked gently. He truly didn't wish to pry; he wanted to understand where she was coming from.

"I don't want to talk about it." She shook her head, her hair sticking to her cheeks in blonde streams. "Can we talk about something else?"

"Of course. What is your fancy?"

A laugh pushed at the barrier of her lips, but she managed to speak without giggling. "Your talk's so weird."

He smiled. "So is yours."

8

MORPHEUS

They walked through the forest a while more, silently, their hands close, but not twined. It seemed though, to Morpheus, that about every ten minutes Brigh asked a question about a certain tree they passed, or shrieked because she thought she'd stepped in more than just mud in her bare feet. He tried to keep quiet most of the time, only smiling or laughing when the occasion called for it.

The girl in question looked up at him as they stepped over a fallen log. "Do you have a last name?"

"No."

"Favorite car?"

"No."

"How about a favorite color?"

"Green," he said with a smile down at her.

She shrugged in answer to his smile, oblivious to the reason behind his favorite. "Mine's gray."

"Gray is nice."

"It's an in-between color." She spoke looking out ahead of them. "Anything and everything important is gray, or in-between. Unspoken words or things half said."

"Makes sense," he offered.

"Do you like to read?"

Morpheus smiled at her, even though she wasn't looking at him. She was trying to hide the force of her curiosity by making straightforward conversation. He couldn't help it, but he thought her trying adorable.

"I have exhausted our library," he began. "I have read over the shoulders of law students, medical students, librarians, children, and the elderly. If there is a book I have not read, I find some way to access it."

"So you guys have Shakespeare where you are?"

He nodded. "And Tennyson. And Poe. And even some of the silly new literature. We are not dead, Brianna, just—"

"Unfinished?"

"Exactly." He sighed.

"Does holding my hand make you feel more complete?"

He opened his mouth to say something, but was caught off guard by her words. He also couldn't say anything to ruin the moment of watching her cheeks grow red and a nervous smile cross her lips. She was hardly ever embarrassed; he decided to enjoy it while he could.

"It does."

BRIGH

She couldn't figure him out. She had no proof of him being real. She'd never heard of a schizophrenic seeing people in their dreams, but there was a first time for everything. Perhaps she had created him in her head. Maybe he was based off of several television shows she'd recently watched. Or maybe, just maybe, he really did exist and she was trying to make up excuses as to why he couldn't.

When she woke the next morning, her alarm rousing her out of a deep, yet restless sleep, she burned with the need to learn so hotly she had to throw the blankets off of her. He had said that no one could see them. But she could. There had to be someone else out there who'd seen or heard of the Unfinished. She just had to dig a little.

"*Briiigh!*" Richard yelled, her door practically rattling in its hinges with the intensity.

"Ugh," she huffed and threw the blankets back over her head.

ᚱ

"What are you singing?" Brigh asked Felicity as they walked from history class to astronomy.

"Manic Monday," Felicity replied before blowing a gum bubble.

"Spit out your gum," ordered a teacher in a doorway.

Felicity rolled her eyes, but didn't stop to oblige. "Jeez, I get the gum from one teacher and another tells me to throw it out."

"They don't like gum on their desks." Brigh shrugged.

"I got this from Schroeder."

"*No*," Brigh said with a gasp. "Sticky Schroeder? She hates gum with a passion. I think she ordered a protest against the manufacturing."

Felicity blew another gum bubble before replying. "Not today. She handed out gum on a plate. There weren't any wrappers, except the silver one. We had to sniff the pieces to find out the flavor."

"How many were there?"

"At least five. I stopped when I hit spearmint."

Brigh smiled and followed her friend into their astronomy class. All of the chairs were empty except for three, and the boys occupying them were playing some card game Brigh didn't recognize. They did, however, stop to say hi to Brigh before her and Felicity took their seats, which made her smile.

"Why are we taking this class?" Felicity asked. She'd broken out her compact and was applying a thin layer of lip gloss to her already moist and sparkly lips.

Brigh pulled the thick notebook from her satchel and opened to the appropriate class section. "Because we need another science credit to graduate."

Felicity sighed and continued to check her hair, mascara, and then nails. "I'm not going to be an astronaut; I don't see the point of this class."

"It's interesting," Brigh defended, readying her pen and reading what was scribbled on the chalkboard. "Haven't you ever looked at the stars and wondered if they're still alive? I mean, we see them, but they could've died several years ago and we won't know for a long time."

Felicity stopped playing with her bangs. "No, I haven't."

Brigh smiled but let the subject die. She suddenly felt eyes on her, but when she looked around, no one was even looking in her direction. Her smile twitched, caught between happiness and panic. But in the end curiosity won out, which is why she wrote on a piece of notebook paper and waited a few minutes before she ripped it out of her notebook and rolled it into a ball.

I'm one hundred percent, sign-me-in-doc, crazy now, she thought. *Writing to an invisible feeling, thinking about a guy I met in my dreams? I should just have dad commit me now.*

MORPHEUS

Morpheus grinned at her, his elation interrupted by the loud clapping noise that came from men's expensive dress shoes. He followed the teacher's long strides as he crossed the classroom to his desk. The man was of average height, hair beginning to gray and recede. His thick framed glasses were small and square, hugging the very end of his nose and causing him to squint and blink several times.

"Get out your books," the teacher spoke, his words fast and clipped. "Turn to chapter eight; we're covering the moon and its phases."

Everyone did as they were told, the sound of zippers and books slapping desks filling the classroom. Morpheus laughed along with the other students as someone pushed back from their desk and the chair rolled out from under them.

As the teacher wrote notes on the blackboard, Morpheus took one last look at Brigh, smiling at something Felicity said, and stepped out of her world.

I like poetry was what her note had read.

Morpheus exchanged salutations with those who passed in the hallways toward their rooms. The smile on his face didn't feel forced, the happiness warming his cheeks as he waved. Even the dull, gray walls didn't dim his happiness. Others noticed the spike in his mood, for they turned and stopped, opening and closing their eyes.

"Beautiful day," Morpheus called to one of the stunned.

"Absolutely," the man replied, laughing nervously.

Morpheus's grin widened as he turned the corner to their rooms, running straight into Darius. Their heads collided painfully, both falling back with grunts.

"Do watch where you are going, Darius."

Darius rubbed his forehead, checking his fingers for blood. "I did not think anyone was coming."

"That is the mysterious thing about corners," Morpheus replied, forgetting the pain and heading toward his room.

Darius gave him a dirty look. "Where are you heading to, anyway? You were coming at me pretty fast."

"I was not 'coming at you.' I was walking to my room."

Darius kept with Morpheus's fast pace stride for stride, pausing only to shake away the stars in front of his eyes. "Have you seen Narelle?"

"No."

Darius sighed. "She has her hair pulled back in a braid. I had thought before that her eyes were gorgeous, but now—breathtaking."

Morpheus, without stopping, pushed the door to his room open and headed right for his bookcases. "Obsession suits you."

"And it does not you?"

"What do you mean?" Morpheus asked as he thumbed through his collection of stories, novels, and poetry one after the other. Nothing seemed appropriate. He'd read them over so many times that he could recite each and every one from memory. Which made them dull and useless in a conversation, as far as he was concerned. He wanted to bring something new and interesting to his time with her. Something neither of them had been exposed to.

Darius shook his head. "Never mind. What are you looking for?"

"A poetry book." His finger followed with his eyes across titles.

"For?"

"Brigh likes poetry."

Darius sighed once more. "I do not understand your infatuation with this girl. Why not try *Poets of Maine?*"

Morpheus stopped searching and turned a questioning look to Darius. "I do not think I have that one."

Darius shrugged. "If not, I do. I will get it for you, if you answer me one question."

"Of course."

"What makes Brigh your obsession?"

Morpheus opened his mouth with answers to all sorts of questions he knew Darius capable of asking. But he wasn't prepared for this one; this inquisitive question he both did not wish to discuss and could not answer.

"I do not know," he settled with saying.

Darius nodded, understanding or conforming, and left him to his thoughts. Thoughts, which he had an abundance of, but could never tether down for more than ten minutes, escaped him for the moment and were replaced by the usual and unusual questions he had or hadn't been asking himself lately.

"Why am I drawn to you?" he asked the silence. "I know there is something…something pertinent…to something." Morpheus shook his head at the words coming out of his mouth that were both stunning and embarrassing him. He let his head fall heavily into his hands and wondered what his purpose in life was supposed to be.

BRIGH

As president of the senior class, Brigh stood alone in front of the thirty people gossiping in the auditorium seats. She knew nearly all of their names, but knew none of them personally except for Kyle and Amelia. Both her friends sat in the front row, smiling encouragingly. Brigh wished Felicity was a part of student life functions, but she had abstained from anything considered pride for attending a high school. Brigh guessed the slightly rebellious attitude Felicity had harvested for two years was in part due to being in theatre.

"Okay, guys," Brigh began. In the middle of taking a breath to continue, she noticed that the noise level hadn't abated as she'd thought it would.

She scanned the crowd to see who was at the heart of the conversation and glared at Marissa as the girl let out an overly dramatic giggle. Her dark blonde waves bounced as she leaned forward, giving the group of guys around her a clear view of her push-up bra cleavage.

Instead of calling the girl out, Brigh tried again to quiet the group, but to no avail. Ms. McCormick, the senior class advisor, smiled with the intention to let her know she had backup, but the woman said not a word.

Kyle jumped out of his seat, arms swinging enthusiastically. "Guys! Shut it for a minute. Brigh's got something to say."

As Kyle took his seat with a pleased smile on his face at the sudden deafening silence, Brigh grinned and mouthed *thank you* to him.

"Okay," she began, pacing from one side of the seats to the other. "As you all know, the senior class voted on a retro-themed homecoming float. It—"

Marissa thrust her arm into the air. "Excuse me, but didn't we all agree to overthrow that decision?"

Brigh folded her tongue behind her teeth. "No, Marissa, I don't remember discussing that."

"That's because no one *discussed* it with *you.*" Marissa stood, hands on her hips, looking like a prominent model for *Cosmopolitan.*

"What are you saying?"

Marissa crossed her arms. "No one trusts your judgment. And how can we when your own mother couldn't?"

Hands fisted, Brigh stood her ground, gritting her teeth. "Does everyone need to know about you and your mom in California two years ago?" Brigh's challenge was met with a glassy glare, but Ms. McCormick ended the fast approaching fight just as Marissa opened her mouth with a retort.

"Alright, alright," Ms. McCormick clucked. "Settle down, Miss McAllister—back on subject. Go ahead, Miss Breen."

Brigh tried to ignore the whispers amongst those who hardly knew her and the speculative looks from those who didn't at all. She struggled to regain her leadership pose and follow the rest of the meeting objectives, but after seeing the pity cross Ms. McCormick's face and a shadow of the same on both Kyle and Amelia's faces, she'd had enough.

"Cover for me," she said to Amelia as she walked past her.

"Okay," Amelia said to the group, "the float. Can I hear some ideas for a theme?"

There were footsteps behind Brigh that echoed in her ears as Richard's had that night last year. He'd been disappointed and in tears. For a second she imagined the footsteps belonging to Ms. McCormick running out to take her to the nurse's office, but the deep bass of the sound didn't match the *click clacking* of her high heels.

"Brigh, wait up," said Kyle as he rushed up behind her, "I can't go into the girls room."

She let out a humorless laugh as she stopped. "You should go back."

"And listen to Marissa's bullshit? No thanks."

"Look, you don't have to bad mouth her. She's got her own problems."

Pointing at the auditorium doors, he said, "*She* has no excuse to be a bitch. *You* do. And do you exercise that right? No. Because you're not like her. Don't let her push you around. She's just trying to get a rise out of you."

"I know," she said with a sigh. "I thought all of this was behind me. I didn't think it would come back up."

"What happened is not your fault."

She shrugged, said, "Tell my father that," and walked into the bathroom.

ᚱ

"So, are we going to the Gateway tonight?" Felicity asked, as her and Brigh maneuvered through the throng of seniors searching for their cars. The parking lot wasn't that big, but with everyone on their cell phones or talking to their friends, finding the right car turned into a mission.

"I don't know," Brigh said, pushing past a guy struggling with all of his football equipment. "I'll have to see how much homework I get done."

Felicity rolled her eyes. "I swear the day will come when all of your time's spent studying and you stop worrying whether or not your hair looks right."

"What's wrong with my hair?" Brigh asked.

"Thank god!" Felicity cried. "Oh, my car."

Felicity ran to her old vixen red beetle and hugged the hood. "Oh, my poor baby's been out here all this time. You want mommy to drive you, don't you?"

"You might want to establish what kind of driving you want to do," Brigh called with a laugh, unlocking her BMW two spaces down. "You don't want to disappoint the poor thing. It may leave you stranded." She waved to Chandra and Amelia across the parking lot before the two girls proceeded to kiss each other.

"Screw you," Felicity said, trying to get the stuck driver-side door unlocked.

"It's jealous."

"Is not."

"Hey," Kyle said, appearing at Brigh's side.

Brigh grabbed her shirt over her heart and took a deep breath. "Jeez, Kyle, where'd you come from?"

"School," he said, with a smile on his face. "Where you came from. And to answer the question you're about to ask—I see your lips moving—I'm here because my car's right next to yours."

Brigh shut her mouth and looked around Kyle's wide chest. She could see the nose of his RX-8 R3 Mazda, a car many of his football buddies coveted and drooled over. Of course, this wasn't any competition to Jake's car. Brigh searched for the Acura RL speeding through the parking lot, but the overpriced Honda was still parked with Jake and Marissa making out on the hood. The sight made Brigh cough, choking on air.

Kyle apparently hadn't seen the duo several rows in front of them for he didn't notice Brigh had looked away. He watched her, still smiling.

"Did you say something?" Brigh asked him.

Kyle blinked and the smile turned nervous. "No, I didn't. Should I've said something?"

Brigh shook her head, smiling herself. "Nah, that's fine."

"Okay, good," Kyle said. "Because I want to *ask* you something."

"Sure." Brigh turned to open her car door and get the windows rolled down. When she looked up, she saw Felicity grinning like the devil and giving her a thumb up. Brigh closed her eyes. Felicity had set this up. Whatever Kyle was about to ask her had to do with homecoming. Probably a question planted by her love guru friend.

"Will you go to homecoming with me?"

Brigh smiled nonetheless. Her heart gave a little summersault. The sudden excitement startled her, causing her to frown and laugh at the same time.

"I take that as a yes?" Kyle asked.

Brigh nodded. "Sure. But don't you think it's a tad bit early?"

Kyle shook his head. "Nah. Right on time, actually. I wanted to be the first one to ask you. Guys kinda drool over you."

Brigh smiled timidly, knowing that he wasn't wrong. "Well, I gotta get to work. I'll see you later?"

"Sure," Kyle said with a smile. "And don't worry about what Marissa said."

Brigh nodded with a sad smile and was glad Kyle knew it still bothered her, even through her shield.

As Kyle left to get into his car, Brigh turned around to see Felicity miming sex with her fingers. Brigh rolled her eyes, gasping at Felicity's crudity. The girl's brain was always in the gutter. And now that Brigh was going to the homecoming dance with Kyle, a very handsome and charming guy, she felt the beginning worry of *her* mind falling into the gutter.

9

MORPHEUS

Impatiently, Morpheus waited for Brigh in the woods. She normally appeared after a few minutes, for she went to bed the same time every night.

He held the book in his hands as if it were a bouquet of roses. A dozen red roses was tradition; he'd watched the exchange several times during his existence. He didn't want to admit it, but standing there grasping a book instead of roses made him feel inadequate. Worse, he felt like a man who had nothing to give, and technically that was true; until he could parade around town, he had nothing for her.

His shoulders slumped, the hand holding the book falling worthlessly to his side. How could she make him feel this way? Impatient, impotent, and infatuated; never had he felt any of these until he'd met her. He thought things would be better once they saw each other, could talk and touch. But everything was worse. He waited, wanting to sit and read her poetry, to discuss the ideas behind the words, to caress her head as she curled against his side.

"Where are you, Brianna?" he whispered to himself.

He had a feeling. Where and who she was with. His lips curled into a snarl and he dropped the book into the soaked moss.

BRIGH

The music pounded in Brigh's ears, so loud a headache formed behind her eyes. She found herself dipping and swaying her hips to the beat nonetheless, letting her mind fall into the numbing abyss dancing created. No one around her noticed anything off; the guys surrounding her all had smiles of anticipation on their faces. Felicity had given her several questioning looks, leaving whether or not she wanted to talk up to Brigh.

She wasn't sure what was bothering her, for something surely was. She'd felt...off ever since her forest dream. Concentration in both classes and clubs was becoming an issue; she couldn't seem to stay focused on anything for more than a minute. Her mind wandered, but never settled on anything. Felicity thought she was a late bloomer, ADHD being her main suspect to the changes. But Brigh didn't think so. Something was up and she wanted answers.

"Mind if I cut in?" Kyle shouted.

Brigh smiled, her dance partner backing away to let Kyle step in his place. The smile on Brigh's face grew wider as Kyle took both of her hips in his large hands and pulled her closer. The song changed. Instead of pounding bass a sensual beat took over. Whistles and catcalls erupted around the two, but neither of them broke apart in embarrassment. They never looked away from each other. For all Brigh knew the partygoers had vanished, and all that stood in the main room of the house were her and him.

She wasn't sure if the close proximity and intimate eye contact felt comfortable because they'd known each other since birth, or because she actually enjoyed Kyle's presence in a more-than-friends way.

She was the first to break the trance, turning to face away from him to shake her hips, arms raised above her head. Dancing she understood, so she gave herself over to it. Kyle's grip returned and tightened on her hips as she rolled them back and forth in slow, circular motions. Once she established a rhythm, he pulled her closer, following it himself, and she found she liked the close contact.

Kyle nuzzled into the curve of her neck, taking in a deep breath of her. "Have I told you you're an amazing dancer?"

"You just did." Brigh rubbed cheeks with him without thinking, her skin tingling from the buds of hair along his jaw. Kyle radiated life and heat. Never had she felt such need coiling around her and another person. She felt like she could fly.

"I don't want to stop dancing," Kyle admitted.

"Me neither," Brigh confessed herself.

The crowd around them had backed away, thinned somewhat, the slow sensual song over some time ago. Brigh pulled away from Kyle enough to curl her arms around his as he held her waist, her fingers grabbing his arms. Kyle cradled her with his body and she felt like he could protect her from anything, even the things they couldn't see or touch.

"I've wanted this a long time," Kyle breathed into her ear.

The vibration of his voice, combined with the heat of his breath, made a chill escape down her spine. Brigh found herself turning her face so that her lips were inches away from his. "Have you wanted me?"

"Yes," he said, turning to bring their lips together.

The floor shook with sudden fury and then gave out from under them.

ᚱ

She knew in an instant that this was not a dream. No, the forest she seemed to find herself in every night or so was a dreamland. This was a nightmare. A room full of quiet, sniffling people wrapped around her like an itchy wool blanket. Women hugged, men grabbed each other's shoulders, and little children looked up in confusion at their elders.

The carpet was a sickly teal color, dotted with golden fleur delis in the corner of thin gold squares. All four walls were covered with light golden wall paper marred by art pieces that were supposed to fill the person with joy instead of grief.

Nothing in the room filled Brigh with anything. She felt empty. Her heart beat sluggishly, air slowly filling her lungs. How many signatures were in the guestbook didn't place a smile on her face, neither could the many times she heard *sorry* or *I understand* come from friends and relatives. No amount of hugs or kisses on the cheek could make her heart beat at its normal pace.

Tears glittered in her brother's eyes, but not one fell. He stood in a group of his friends; all once talkative and jokers. But none of them joked now. Her father sat in a chair in the corner, his head in his hands, as relative after relative tried to talk to him. Brigh's heart squeezed and the need for air got smaller.

She wore a simple black dress, one her mother would've called *tacky* if she'd seen her wearing it. But it was the only thing in her closet she could let go. Once this was over, she was going to burn it.

Felicity and Kyle came up behind her, Amelia and Chandra behind them. Felicity's hand found the thin bone of her shoulder. The two embraced, Felicity's shoulders shaking with muted tears. When Felicity pulled back, Kyle pulled Brigh into his chest, his large arms wrapping her in a protective cocoon. He'd always been an older brother to her, one to defend her in debates or when a guy tried to push his luck. In middle school, he'd even walked behind her all the way to the nurses' office, so others wouldn't see the red stain on her jeans that her period had left.

"Are you ready?" Felicity asked.

Brigh took a deep breath, but couldn't look. Amelia and Chandra oddly stood off to the side of their little group.

Was she ready?

Would she ever be ready?

She turned and walked between the two neat rows of uncomfortable wooden chairs. Those in the way parted, leaving her a clear view of what she'd been avoiding. A set of stairs waited for her to kneel and pray, or, say something nice. She wasn't sure what to do; she'd never been in this situation.

She closed her eyes as she took the last steps toward the casket. The air felt too cold, too dry. She suddenly couldn't breathe. Her hand shot out to grab the edge of the casket for balance. Trying to catch her breath, she opened her eyes to find the casket occupied by...her. Pale in a frozen, bluish state, her hands were cupped around a blank sketchpad over her unmoving chest.

An eerie chill skated down her spine and before she could take in a breath to scream, a hand clamped down on her shoulder, spinning her around.

"Don't trust the red," her mother said.

ᚱ

Brigh woke, felt herself being dragged out of the dream world and into reality, into a numbing cold she'd never felt before. At first she thought the world was dark, and she feared that her dream had been real and the darkness was from being inside the shiny white casket. But then she realized that her eyes were shut after slowly prying her eyelids open.

She heard voices, muffled, like her ears were clogged. She gave a short and shallow yawn, the noise level rising dramatically, popping her ears.

"I don't care what they do," a man yelled. "Just make sure it's leveled by tomorrow morning." There was a pause; no answer. "What do you mean we can't get crews out there? *A week*? Are you fucking kidding me? You know how much money I've pumped into this little shithole town?"

"Sir, no cell phones," Brigh heard a woman say.

"I can talk on a cell phone all I want, lady, I practically own this hospital."

There was no question as to who that rough and sharply clipped voice belonged to; Peter MacRae. He was slipperier than a snake and the richest man in the tri-state area. He was her father's boss, a man unkind and unwilling to help others who were not himself.

The door to her room shot open, and—*speak of the devil*, she thought—Peter MacRae, with a Bluetooth glued to his ear, and the iPhone clutched in his hand, continued yelling at the person on the other end of the phone, even though she was still presumably asleep.

"Do you know how much this is going to cost me if the families decide to pull their heads out of their asses and sue? We're talking *millions*. Not to mention *your* job and every fucking person I have out on sites. Now I want this problem fixed in two days. Not a week. *Two. Days.* If you can't handle that, then you'll be standing in line at the unemployment office downtown."

Peter took in a breath and plastered a fake smile on his face. Apparently the call had been dropped. "Sorry about that. Trying to tie up loose ends. So, how are we feeling today?"

"Where's my dad?" She wasn't happy that the Snake was in her room, no less having to talk to him.

The smile twitched. "He better be around here somewhere. Hasn't gone to work in a couple days, I know that."

If Brigh had the strength to, she would've slapped him across the face. But seeing as she was lying in a hospital bed with IV drips and a cast on her leg, she wasn't going anywhere anytime soon.

And, as it seemed, neither was the Snake.

"I hope they've made the room comfortable," he went on, the smile still stretched out falsely on his fake tanned face. "I made sure you're to get the best out of this hospital. Extra blankets, extra doctor visits, extra pain meds."

Brigh was about to say something nasty, but saw her father step through the door behind Peter, and decided to let him take care of it.

"Peter," Jairus said.

"Jair," Peter replied, clapping her father on the back. "Sure glad you're here. Poor Brianna's woken up and no one was here."

Jairus looked at Brigh and forgot his boss, rushing over to her the second he noticed her eyes were open. His hands were warm and sticky with sweat as he gripped her fragile hand in his. His eyes were red, dark circles underneath his lashes. He looked exhausted.

Brigh patted her father's hand. "You need sleep."

Jairus smiled. "What I need is for you to get better."

"What happened?"

Jairus looked over his shoulder at Peter, the other man raising his brows defensively. When Jairus looked back at her, he was no longer smiling.

"The floor in that old house collapsed." He kissed the back of her hand. "Took several of you kids down. The police say the floorboards were rotten. You're lucky you didn't break anything besides your leg, or worse."

Brigh closed her eyes and pinched the bridge of her nose. "How's everyone else? Who's here?"

"Kyle," he replied. "Some girls from Allegany. Couple football players. Don't know how they're going to play in a month."

Brigh sucked in a breath. "I won't be able to cheer!"

Jairus shook his head. "You can sit on the sidelines and cheer from a chair."

"Dad," Brigh said, "that's not how it works. I'm cheerleading captain; I have to be with them."

"I don't care," Jairus commanded. "You're not cheering, even if that cast comes off. It's much easier to break it the second time around."

"Listen to your father," Peter chimed in.

Jairus's jaw tightened. "We'll see how you're feeling in a month. Until then: *no cheering.*"

Brigh wanted to pout, but thinking about the energy it would take to do it made her change her mind. She also knew it took much longer than a month for a leg break to heal. But that bit of information wasn't going to be shared any time soon if she wanted to get on that football field. "Okay."

Jairus smiled, but the warmth in it was dwindling faster than he could keep it on his face. "I know how much you kids like that place. Your mother and I shook the rafters ourselves when we were your age, but it really isn't safe."

He really did look tired, exhausted beyond belief. Brigh couldn't help but feel like she'd been selfish, even though she'd been unconscious the whole time her dad had been worrying.

But the thing that was bothering her most, as her father and Peter talked in hushed tones across the room, was her dream. She wasn't sure what it meant; didn't even know where to begin. What had her mother meant by 'don't follow the red'? Red what?

Brigh wasn't in the mind or mood to ponder this question. Neither was she willing to wonder why she'd been thrust into that dream and not back into the forest where her unfinished man waited.

Too many questions, not enough brain power. And, just like that, it shut down.

MORPHEUS

The screaming was dull compared to the roar of his anger inside his ears, but ignoring the cry only made it louder. He'd taken two steps and suddenly was blind with pain; his eardrums screeching. Nothing he tried worked. He attempted plugging them with his fingers, but the noise seemed to be internal. Those around him stopped and stared. He thought to beg for help, but couldn't pry his teeth from his bottom lip.

He ran through the throng of gawking passersby, hands held to his ears. The screaming was so loud he couldn't tell if it was male or female. Then the noise shifted, the pitch of it increasing to a shrill opera.

He couldn't take it anymore. His legs gave out from under him, causing those around him to jump out of the way as he rolled to the floor. He felt the floor vibrate with running, steps taken, and yelling. He watched, paralyzed, as someone ran toward him, rolled him over, and leaned into his line of vision.

It was Darius. Morpheus watched his friend shake him, mouth his name, and ask others for their assistance. Before he blacked out—he didn't lose consciousness, because that was the only state he could be in—he thought he saw fiery red hair in the crowd of unfinished beings circling him and Darius, and a pair of satisfied eyes tinged with anger.

10

MORPHEUS

The next slap was caught in Morpheus's fist. He opened his eyes, confirming that the hard slaps against his cheek were coming from Darius. He should've known. Had anyone else offered to wake Morpheus from his frozen state, Darius would have thrown a tantrum and then forcefully knocked the good doer to the side to do the honors himself. Morpheus's lips slowly upturned with an amused, yet slightly agitated, smile.

"You knew I was present," Morpheus growled, the small pain in his cheek dulling.

Darius grinned, ignoring his friend's tight grip on his fingers. "Never can be too cautious."

Morpheus slowly sat up, rubbing his jaw. He'd heard this more than once, though not for something of this magnitude. He could have sworn he'd dreamt, though this for him was not possible. He could believe that the Elder's were wrong about humans and their kind and that the two sides couldn't communicate, however, dreaming was certainly not an option.

"Are you alright?" Darius asked, more amused than concerned.

Morpheus's brows drew tight together. "I am fine."

"You sure?" Darius pressed again. "To be honest, you look awful."

A buzzing began in Morpheus's head and no matter how much pressure he applied to his temples or his eyes, the throbbing continued to intensify. He sat in the middle of curious onlookers whispering around him and all he could think of was something he hoped he hadn't dreamt about.

Gnarled blonde hair streaked red with blood.

BRIGH

Brigh wasn't happy. But that wasn't entirely a surprise. The hospital had sent her home in a gruesome looking leg cast with a prescription for painkillers and demands of bed rest. By the looks the doctor and nurses had shot her, she knew her father had told them of her plan to get back to cheerleading. And knew the doctors had shared with her father the time period for a fracture to heal.

Brigh sighed. Being in bed when she should've been at school, and then practice, wasn't a total loss. Her dad had bought a copy of her favorite style magazine, a skinny latte from Starbucks, and a new sketchpad from Rite Aid. It was plain in comparison to her other one that was covered in taped-on sketches she'd done in middle school, but it suited her just fine.

Sitting up in bed, she tugged the blanket to pool around her waist, grabbed a sketch pencil from her nightstand, and started doodling. She didn't know what to draw, which was a first, but she hadn't sketched anything in weeks. After five minutes, her hand started cramping and a yawn escaped from her lips. Why she was drawing and not sleeping, or even reading her magazine, was beyond her. But she felt her hand being drawn across the large white page, shading and stippling as though something guided her.

Still, she couldn't get the dream out of her head. Whenever she stopped thinking about it she felt a mental nudge to revisit what her mother had said. Every time she went back to thinking about her words, the questions piled up more and more, and the headache behind her eyes was starting to grow.

Her cell phone rang next to her on the nightstand, causing her to jump and drop her pencil. With a sigh of frustration, she grabbed the tiny phone and flipped it open without looking at the caller ID.

"Hello."

"What do you mean, 'hello'?" Felicity said. "You never say that when I call you. Did the doctors tell you that you had brain damage, too?"

"Feeling the love," Brigh said sarcastically. "I haven't had a great couple of days, in case you forgot."

"Alright, I'm sorry." The line was silent for a minute. Brigh heard a sigh. "You know I can't handle this kind of thing."

Brigh focused on a painting of her mother's hanging on the wall above her door. "I know."

"So, how's the dad treating you?"

"Magazine. Latte. Sketch pad."

"Ah, the guilt gifts are already coming in. I was afraid of that; which is why I didn't buy you a copy of *Seventeen* myself."

Brigh smiled. Felicity knew her all too well. Her dad felt guilty for not paying attention and being an active parent.

"I won't even ask about Rich," Felicity went on. "How are *you* doing?"

The smile left Brigh's face. "I had a dream about my mom."

Brigh heard a car horn on the other end of the phone and then someone yelling. She should've known Felicity was on her phone while driving; the sudden noise in the background shouldn't have surprised her. But since she was laid up and trying to ignore that her pain medication was beginning to wear off, she wasn't exactly on line with Felicity's usual quirks.

Felicity coughed into the speaker. "Did you just say what I think you just said?"

"Yeah. Did you just almost get into a car accident?"

"No." She sounded guilty.

The static-y sound of wind rolling past the speaker of Felicity's phone stopped. She'd finally rolled her window up. "The last time you had a dream about your mom—"

"Something bad happened."

"Shit," Felicity said in a rush, "What happened?"

"Long or short version?"

"Medium."

Brigh rolled her eyes. "I was at a funeral. You and Kyle were there, Amelia, Chandra, my dad and Rich, too. But when I went up to the dais, I—the—I was in the casket."

"What color was it?"

"And you thought I was ADHD?"

Brigh knew she was shrugging right now. "Sorry if your bud's looking out for you."

"Touching."

"Thanks, now please continue." Her turn signal clicked in the background and Brigh wondered what road she was turning down.

"So I was standing by the casket—"

"I thought you were *in* the casket."

"I was, but I wasn't." Brigh took in a deep breath. Tried holding it in to ignore the pain, but found out quickly that it made it worse. "Look, I was walking around in my dream and saw myself in the casket. That's beside the point. Point is my mom was there."

"Did she say anything—do anything?" Felicity's voice was hushed as though she didn't want anyone else to hear. But by the sound of her turn signal, Brigh knew she was still on the road.

"She said, 'don't trust the red'."

Felicity paused. But only for a second. "That's it?"

"I woke up after it."

"Red what?"

"That's what I can't figure out." She flexed her toes without thinking and a tremor ran up her leg. When she continued, her teeth were gritted. "There're millions of things out there that are red. Red flowers, red cars, the obvious red fire trucks. I don't even want to attempt to look."

"I'm curious though."

Brigh raised a brow. "What?"

"Okay," Felicity said. "She said, 'don't trust the red', right?"

"Ye-ah," Brigh said slowly.

"Maybe she meant a person."

Her quick deduction of Brigh's dream made her a little angry because she hadn't thought of it first. "Or she meant your beetle."

"Don't be picking on my baby. You hardly ride in it anyway."

"I know," Brigh said with a sigh, the anger leaving her as quickly as it had come. "I'm just—who would she mean if she was talking about a person?"

"Hell if I know. Hence why a little search is in order."

"I thought you hated research."

Brigh heard Felicity's car come to a screeching halt as she knocked over one of her dads recycling bins by the garage, the crash echoing outside her window. "That's only for school. Now, I hope you're up for some history homework, 'cause I'm coming in! That and I'll need to hide from your dad."

"Blame it on Rich."

"He can't drive."

"Precisely."

The phone gave a click and the line went dead. Brigh shut the electronic nuisance and set it back on her nightstand where she hoped it would stay for the rest of the day. When she looked back to her sketch, the pain in her leg intensified as she jerked instinctively. Because, there on the page, was an unfinished detailed sketch of a man's face, one she hadn't seen in her dreams for the past several nights.

She only had a few seconds to catch her breath before Felicity flew into her room with a history book in one hand and a bag of Lindt chocolate in the other. Oh, and the expectant smile on her face that Brigh so wasn't looking forward to.

11

BRIGH

Though she'd stormed into the room looking chatty, Felicity sat across from Brigh on the bed staring at her history homework in silence. Besides the few short answers she gave to Brigh about classes, she hadn't said a word.

Felicity wasn't reading her history textbook. To her, anything that didn't have a brand name, a gorgeous face, or promises of a good and entertaining evening was a waste of time. So when Felicity turned the page, sighed, studiously rested her hand on her chin and pretended to scan the page, Brigh knew she was full of shit.

"Can the act, what's wrong?"

Without looking away from the page, Felicity replied, "Mel Gibson is way hotter than the real William Wallace."

Brigh reached across her bed. "Give me that."

She pulled the book out of Brigh's reach and still wouldn't look away from the page. "What for?"

"Because you're hogging a book you're not actually reading."

Giving Brigh the death glare, Felicity gripped the edges of the textbook tighter. "I am, too, reading."

"Don't be an idiot," Brigh said. "My leg's under the blanket—can't see a thing. Is that what's bothering you?"

Felicity went back to staring at the book. "Nothing's bothering me."

"Really." Brigh stifled a whimper. Her leg was starting to throb. "Then how come you've been staring at that book the entire time and are lying to me?"

"Look," Felicity spat. "I'm not lying and I *have* been reading. Just because you're not in the spotlight for five seconds doesn't mean I'm lying to you."

"And just because your sister died doesn't mean you can be all quiet and nasty to me."

Felicity's lips creased, her eyes looking away in guilt. "Sorry."

A deep breath rolled down Brigh's throat. She shouldn't have dug up an old grave. Felicity's older sister had died of Pneumonia when she was eight, but the loss obviously still bothered her. "Me too. I just don't want you freaking out about the cast and bruises. They're really not a big deal."

"Liar," Felicity whispered, flipping back a few pages in her history book.

Brigh smiled. "Then we're twins."

They both grinned at each other and laughed.

"Panatelli misses you," Felicity said after a while of silence and actual studying.

"That's nice."

"I think Marissa might miss you, too."

"Good for her," Brigh said absently, flipping the page to finish a sentence.

Felicity cleared her voice in annoyance. "Rumor has it Kyle's going to be a daddy."

"Huh?" Brigh snapped out of her trance and fixed Felicity with a look of doubt. "Who said that?"

"Finally," Felicity shouted. "You were so engrossed in that book I was scared you'd gotten lost in the eighteenth century."

"The seventeenth, actually," Brigh corrected, still a little confused. "Have you read any of that yet, honestly?"

"A few pages, why?"

Brigh pushed herself back up into a sitting position. "I'm trying to do a little research."

"About the 'red' thing?" Felicity sat up as well, interest coloring her cheeks.

Brigh shook her head. "Entirely different. Have you ever heard of something called the Unfinished?"

Now it was Felicity's turn to shake her head. "Fuck if I know. Are we supposed to be going over it in class?"

"No," Brigh said, drawing out the vowel. She wasn't sure how much she should tell her, or if she'd believe a word that came out of her mouth. "I've had some other weird dreams, not just the one with mom."

"Are they rated R?" Felicity asked innocently.

Brigh gave her a look. "You're so dirty."

"Don't sound so surprised," Felicity said. "You knew that when you signed on for this friendship."

Brigh couldn't help but smile. "I know."

"Good. You were saying?"

"Okay," Brigh said after clearing her throat. "I'm in this forest. I'm not sure where. But it's always raining, always cold. And there's this guy."

"What does he look like?"

Brigh closed her eyes, the image of Morpheus instantly accessible. "He's tall, really tall. Dark, handsome—kinda beautiful, actually. He always wears a white shirt, dark pants. He doesn't have a heartbeat."

"Sounds like Mr. Perfect to me," Felicity said after a minute. "More of an Angel than Spike though, and you know which one I love the most."

Brigh's lips curved upward at the *Buffy the Vampire Slayer* reference, despite the chill she got from thinking of Morpheus.

"But you don't think so?" Felicity asked in concern.

Brigh sighed. "At first I thought he was perfect. But, it's weird. Most of the time he's fine, and then out of the blue everything around him goes dark and his eyes...he looks murderous."

"So he's bipolar," Felicity said with a shrug. "And he's not real. Don't get so worked up about a dream. It's just a dream."

Brigh lowered her eyes so Felicity wouldn't see the uncertainty and fear in them. Her uncertainty was obvious, but her fear? Brigh didn't have the courage to tell her friend that she both loved and feared the man in her dreams, and that part of the fear was of loving him.

MORPHEUS

The book was where he left it, only now the pages were soaked and a little muddy. He knelt in the puddle by the tree and its giant unearthed roots and grasped the book by the cover. A sick suction sound followed the book as he pulled it into his hands. The pages were salvageable, thankfully. Morpheus already didn't want to explain the poor state of Darius' book, let alone having to give back his friend one that was no longer legible.

At this point he would've cried or cursed the opposite sex for all eternity, according to books he'd read and the few films he'd watched. But unlike his favorite characters, he didn't come with the option of tears, only the emptiness he felt inside. Like a shell without a center, a hollowed out tree trunk.

What would a heart feel like? Would he need to take in deep or shallow breaths after a run? How much would walking on hot rocks hurt the skin of his feet? Could his arms lift a car or bend metal? He knew a select few humans could bend certain metals and even lift a car in a time of great need. But could he?

"Morpheus?"

He looked over his shoulder to find Brigh leaning against a tree across the small clearing. He stood, absently brushed some mud off the book, and smiled at the girl; but his earlier annoyance with her dissolved when he noticed the cast hugging her leg and the bruises marring the skin around her eyes.

His smile fell. "What happened?" The ground threatened to trip him as he rushed over to where she stood. Closer up, the bruises and cuts were more menacing and harsh against her pale skin. He reached up to touch her face, but was afraid of hurting her, so he settled with taking her hands in his.

"I kind of fell," was her reply. A blush tinted her cheeks, turning the bruises a palette of colors. She smiled shyly. "I didn't know I'd fallen asleep. Felicity's going to kill me."

Morpheus wanted to smile, but the realization of how frail and fragile she really was made him sick with worry. "Are you going to be alright? Please tell me nothing else is wrong."

Brigh covered his cheek with her palm, lightly scratching the hair above his ear. "I'm fine. Just some bruises and a broken leg. It could've been worse."

He closed his eyes against the image he had of her blonde hair tattered and bloody. "Let's not think about that now."

Brigh's soft smile relaxed. "What's that in your hand?"

Morpheus held up the wet book and smiled. "Poets of Maine. Darius lent it to me."

"Is he your friend?"

Morpheus smiled. "Or as our teachers liked to calls us: 'partners in crime'."

A laugh escaped Brigh. "Felicity and I've been called that once or twice. Sounds like her and Darius would get along."

"I am sure they would," he agreed, hoping she thought the same thing of her and him.

BRIGH

"Would you like to sit and read?" he asked.

"In the mud?" She laughed as his brow rose in confusion. "There's nowhere to sit."

Morpheus closed his eyes and nodded. When he looked at her, his normally bark brown eyes were outlined with a bright shade of green. Brigh blinked several times to see if she'd imagined it, but the green ring around his iris was still there.

Maybe it's all the greenery and the rain reflecting... she wondered.

He held out his hand, and without giving it much thought, she gave him hers. He led her through the forest, dodging thick tree roots and holding up low branches so she could pass. His chivalry and gentlemanly gestures made a blush creep over her cheeks when she remembered how provocatively she'd been dancing with Kyle. And then, just for a second, she felt guilty for what she'd done with Kyle and for thinking of him while Morpheus was being so kind and generous.

Before she knew it, he'd led her into a smaller clearing where the central focal point was a weeping willow tree. Just a look and trusting smile was all she needed to know to let go of his hand and wait. He stepped aside, holding back a few branches for her to walk under the small canopy the tree provided.

Inside, the ground was near dry, the thick feathery needles of the tree protecting them from the rain. Besides being cold and her leg cast slowing her down, she'd have curled up in a ball on the ground and fallen asleep.

Morpheus walked past her, lightly sliding his hand across the small of her back so he could pass without knocking her aside. Or, at least that's what she told herself. She wasn't sure whether or not the shiver running down her back was from the cold or his touch.

"This should not be too terrible," he commented, plopping down so that his back pressed against the trunk of the tree. With the book clutched in his left hand, he held out his arms invitingly with the most sincere expression she'd ever seen on anyone's face.

She tried her best to hide the smile, but when her lips wouldn't cooperate she turned around. And before she could think of how to sit down, Morpheus took hold of her hips and slowly guided her into his lap. The setup, with his arm around her stomach, holding her to him, was awkward. But then he moved his hand to her hip and brought the other one around to place the book in her lap.

"I will hold this end if you will open it," he said.

Brigh swallowed the sudden monsoon forming in her throat and opened the book. The binding had broken some time ago, the flowery paper inside the cover wrinkled and brown. Two fancy signatures graced the first blank page, both of which seeming to be merely scrawls of past owners and having nothing to do with the book itself. The title page was stamped with the year of 1888.

She turned to the table of contributors, but was stilled in her page flipping by Morpheus's gentle hand.

"Page one hundred and thirty nine," he whispered, moving his hand aside. "Rufus Tukey."

Brigh turned the pages, careful not to rip the thick, yet delicate, paper. As she happened upon the page he'd wanted, she was about to read the words aloud when his voice filled her ear with soft and magical words before she could get a word out.

He recited from memory. She'd turned her head the moment she heard him speaking and found his eyes closed, head resting against the bark of the tree.

"'There is a mystery in the passing breeze—
In the deep music of the storm-lashed sea—
In woods and glens in birds and flowers and trees
But more than all, in that which lives in me."

She continued reading where he left off:

"The human mind—oh, in that mighty power
For good or ill, what fearful mysteries dwell;
Man counts the stars, dissects the simple flower,
But who the source of human thoughts can tell?"

They read the rest of the poem that way and several others after, each reciting a stanza and pausing for the other to continue. Throughout the poems, Brigh grew tired and chilly, and found herself in and out of consciousness several times. She hadn't known of her drowsiness until Morpheus had taken a gentle hold of her chin and slowly turned her face to him. She'd woken then, with sleep still caught in her lashes, and angled her body toward his. His brown eyes showed warmth where his body did not, as his arms wrapped around her shaking shoulders. A sudden burst of lust crawled over Brigh, and before she could shrug it off, Morpheus took her lips with his, a kiss that seared the cold between her shoulder blades.

Again, her list of admirers was lengthy, but the amount of those who'd actually kissed her could be counted on one hand with fingers left to spare. And this kiss had no comparison. His lips were soft and smooth, as was his tongue, yet the muscle remained dry no matter how many times hers wrapped around it. Shifting so she could touch him and keep her neck from cramping, she sat sideways in his lap. He held her face in his hands, her own lost within the thickness of his hair. He grabbed at her when she nipped his lip, but the tenderness of his touch only made her nip him again.

Slowly, he was the one who broke the kiss, leaving Brigh faraway and far from satisfied. When she opened her eyes he was smiling, his own eyes crinkled at the corners and lazy. His lips were dry despite her having licked them, looking like they had before he'd kissed her.

"You don't have any saliva?" she asked.

The smile was replaced with an *o* of confusion and a raised brow. "Of course not."

"That's so gross," she said with a laugh and a harmless punch to his shoulder.

He broke out into a laugh himself and rolled them both into the dirt.

12

BRIGH

Brigh woke to the disquieting sound of the doorbell chiming. A sound only her mother loved. Her father hadn't had the heart to change the annoying tone even though both she and Richard had begged him to. Not only did the sound rub her ears raw, but it woke her from the best dream she'd ever had, even if it hadn't been real.

A glance at the clock told her she'd been asleep for ten hours, though she didn't feel a bit rested. She sighed, stretched as much as she could, and lay in bed wishing she could go to school. She missed the routine of getting out of bed at an insane hour, dressing up in her favorite clothes, and seeing her friends at school. But the thing she missed the most were her classes.

"How many people can say that?" she whispered.

A knock made her door shake. "Can I come in?"

A smile broke out on Brigh's face as the door slowly opened. "Alice!"

"Don't look so surprised," her aunt said, dropping her purse in the desk chair. "I would've been here earlier, but Owen and I had a gig in Annapolis."

Brigh hugged her aunt as hard as she could, forgetting for a moment how bad the woman's back was. "I don't care. How *is* Owen?"

Alice shook her head, blowing a blonde perm curl from her vision. "Obsessing over his guitar. I told him he'd stay single for the rest of his life if he kept it up."

"Maybe you should help him with that."

With a laugh, Alice sat on the edge of Brigh's bed and patted her good knee. "We'd drive each other nuts. Being in a band together is already killing us."

Brigh grinned. "Did you see Rich?"

"Yeah," Alice said. "Your dad's at work—that's why I'm here."

Brigh admired her aunt Alice more so than any other of her relatives. Unlike her mother, whose natural thin frame seemed delicate and soft, Alice's slender body came from hitting the gym hard every day. The sisters both had the same platinum blonde hair, but Alice chose to go the curly route while her mother kept her locks straight. And they all had the same green eyes.

"So you heard about everything," Brigh said.

Alice took in a deep breath and stared at Brigh. "Bits and pieces. Your father's not a big talker."

"Sorry."

"Not your fault," Alice said. "But enough about that. I'm here to rock out with my favorite Niece."

"I'm your only niece," Brigh reminded her aunt for the gazillionth time.

"What're you up for?" Alice continued as if Brigh hadn't said anything. "Checkers? Trivial Pursuit, Eighties edition? A boring documentary on the Black Plague?"

"Actually," said Brigh with honest excitement, "the documentary sounds great."

Alice rolled her eyes. "You're so like your mother."

"Sorry about that, too."

MORPHEUS

Darius sat across from Morpheus, staring with determination at a chess piece. A few minutes had passed, and Morpheus started wondering if Darius thought that by staring at the Queen she'd move herself. He also wondered why they were playing such a game when neither one of them very much enjoyed it.

"It is your turn," Morpheus said.

"You have said that twice already, thank you," Darius replied, half amused, half annoyed.

Morpheus folded his arms. "One of us will be human by the time you move her."

"Shush up," Darius said with a glare. He held his arm out over the board, his fingers at the ready, eyes scanning for the best move. Closing his eyes, he picked up the

Queen, suspending her over the board for a minute and then set her down gently back in the square from where she came.

"Do you think it will be sunny or cloudy today?" Darius asked.

Morpheus rolled his eyes, leaning back in his chair. "I think it will be dull and lacking warmth as it always is."

Darius pursed his lips, shook his head. "Cloudy and cold, then."

"Why do you do that?"

Darius was still eyeing up the chess pieces. "Do what?"

"Pretend as though our world is the same as theirs."

"I do not pretend anything," Darius said. Giving up, he reclined in his chair, mirroring Morpheus's relaxed appearance. "Why must you question everything?"

Morpheus' jaw tightened. "And you do not question things?"

"Why should I?" Darius sighed and pushed himself up from the chair. He walked to his bookshelf and picked up a light blue volume, his back facing Morpheus. "I have known you a long time, Morpheus. You have always had an interest in the unknown. But lately it has turned into an addiction, one that is detrimental and sick, and as your friend I do not think it wise."

"Oh come out with it already, Darius," Morpheus criticized. "You do not approve of Brigh."

Darius turned to face Morpheus, the book clutched in his hands. "She is a wonderful girl, Morpheus, do not get me wrong." His expression changed. He no longer had the teasing lift of the eyebrows or smile hiding in the corners of his lips that were his trademark. "There is a great difference between the two of you as of right now, and as of right now it is not fair to either of you to continue this. You must see it."

Morpheus locked up, staring at the chess board like it was the door to freedom from this conversation. He'd dreaded this subject, but had never thought Darius would be the one to bring it up.

"Have you ever wondered what it would be like to be alive?" Morpheus asked aloud, still keeping his gaze on the board.

There was a long pause between them, one that straddled the line of awkwardness, but never fully crossed. Finally, as Morpheus was about to say something, Darius opened his mouth.

"I try to imagine what humanity feels like, yes."

"No," Morpheus said. He slid back in his chair, leaning forward to prop his elbows on the edge of his knees. "Not the physicality of existence. I mean the *being* piece. To have a soul. To feel past your fingertips. To need something more than just air and food and water." He looked at his friend, seeing the scholarly doubt fill Darius's face. They both were equal in many areas and shared a lot in common, but in that one moment Morpheus realized how different their views on the human world and existence were. He also realized that without Darius sharing his views, he was in the minority where beliefs were concerned. And in a society where majority ruled, he'd better begin keeping certain theories and thoughts to himself.

BRIGH

"Got any two's?" Alice asked.

Brigh shuffled through her cards, rearranging them as she looked. "Go fish."

"This game is so *lame*," Richard said dramatically.

Alice picked a card from the pile, stuffing it in with the rest of her colorful cards. "Then you shouldn't have come in looking to disrupt girl time."

"I thought you'd be painting each other's toenails or doing each other's hair."

Brigh grinned, looking up from her cards. "That can be arranged, you know."

Richard sighed. "I'm just going to pick from the pile. Neither of you have jack."

Brigh shrugged. "You shouldn't give up so easily."

"You got any fours?" Richard asked.

Brigh shook her head. So did Alice.

"Fine then," Richard said, "I already picked my card. Next."

"Rich, fives?" Brigh asked.

"Fuck," he said in reply, forking over a five.

"Don't curse," Alice chided.

"Sorry."

"You guys have anything exciting at school coming up?" Alice asked as Richard handed over another card to her.

"Homecoming," Brigh and Richard said in unison, the first with excitement and the second with dread.

Alice smiled, thumbing through her cards. "Brigh, any sixes? And have you found a dress yet?"

Brigh handed a six to her aunt with excitement. "Felicity and I've been looking through some magazines, but nothing's been promising. I want something yellow, though."

A blonde brow rose, but her aunt didn't look up. "Yellow?"

Brigh nodded. "I want something different. Everyone goes for black or blues, and sometimes purple. Honestly, I'm tired of these dances looking like a giant bruise."

"You've got that covered all on your own," Richard interjected helpfully.

"Quiet, Second Born," Brigh said.

"Sorry, First Born," he replied.

"I think yellow will be lovely," Alice said, ignoring the sibling spat. "How about I take you out dress shopping once you're able to stand by yourself?"

"That'd be awesome!" Brigh said with a smile, throwing her arm around her aunt.

"Brigh, got any eights?" Richard asked after the two pulled out of their embrace.

"You cheated," she accused, after checking that she had four eight cards.

Richard shrugged. "Hey, give a man an opportunity and he'll take it. Fork 'em over."

Brigh rolled her eyes, but obliged.

MORPHEUS

"Have you been avoiding me?" Narelle asked, accusation tightening her gaze.

Morpheus lazily rolled his shoulders back and shook his head. "I would never do such a thing."

"Liar," she said.

"You have not been around for me to avoid," he said defensively.

"Perhaps I have been too busy."

Or perhaps not busy enough, he thought to himself. To be honest, he hadn't missed his mentor's interjections at all; neither did he want her following him around wherever he went. He didn't know if she could access his forest dreamland, but he wasn't curious at all to find out.

"We have missed some of your schooling," Narelle announced, finally evacuating the doorway to his room and slinking in to sit on his cot.

"I am not revisiting the Crick," he said with finality.

Narelle gave him a look. "Do not be such a ninny. The Crick was not so bad."

"Not so bad?" Morpheus thundered. "You failed to mention *Cetus* awaited me by the shore's edge."

"How was I to know?" Narelle said innocently. "He is a human mythical beast."

Morpheus pinched the bridge of his nose. "You of all beings know from where human myths originate, Narelle. Medusa's severed head may have turned Cetus to stone, but his being came back to his dimension, and that door you took me to led me straight into the Bog of Tortured Souls. Do not shake your head at me, woman."

"You are so judgmental."

Morpheus blinked. "Excuse me?"

"Why must you insist that everyone is out to get you?"

"Why must you insist on driving me mad?"

"Wanker," she said with a sigh.

"Bloody bitch," he said with an attempted British accent, mimicking Narelle's facial expression of boredom and disgust.

"Do not get me started," she said authoritatively. "I apologize about the Crick, but for you stumbling upon the Bog of Tortured Souls and Cetus was not my doing. That door should not have led you anywhere but to the Crick. There you were supposed to observe the wildlife and plant growth."

"I studied the jaws of a mightily pissed off greyhound instead," was Morpheus's solemn reply, "slipping in a quagmire in my haste to escape."

Narelle's expression softened. She lifted her hand up to his face, curving her long fingers around his chin. "I am sorry for my anger. I did not mean for any of it."

Morpheus nodded, accepting her apology. He pulled back from her touch, gesturing to the hallway for them to walk.

He followed her out, ignoring her sultry sashay as they passed offices and the library. The cave-like walls weren't smooth, though they may have been long ago. The ceiling was low, forcing those who were tall to slouch and walk as though their body were disfigured in some way. Morpheus was one of those who bent over, pressing his face closer to Narelle's hair. A hint of cinnamon and calla lily embraced his nostrils, the smell almost soothing his tense shoulders.

"What would you like to study today?" Narelle asked without turning to look at him. "I will let you pick this time."

Morpheus nodded in response to someone passing by who smiled at him. "From what do I have to choose?"

Narelle bobbed her head back and forth in thought, tossing her hips so that her shirt twirled around her. "There is the review of basic human knowledge, statistics on lifespan and causes of death, a review on entertainment and entertainers. Honestly, the list goes on."

Morpheus gritted his teeth. "I would like to skip the lectures today, please."

Narelle shot him a look over her shoulder, but continued to skip ahead as he trudged behind her. "At the rate you are going, your human self will be clueless and ignorant."

"I take offense to that," he said.

She turned to look at him. "I only speak the truth."

Morpheus opened his mouth in reply, but was cut off when Narelle ran right into the large chest of Alphaeus. On reflex, Morpheus grabbed Narelle to steady her as she shook her head. He stepped back, giving room to the immense presence of their leader. Alphaeus was a large being, though he stood only a few inches taller than Morpheus. His thick shoulders and toned limbs were intimidating and large, his coarse, blonde hair just long enough to touch the tips of his ears in waves. His eyes blazed an icy aquamarine as he regarded Morpheus holding Narelle.

Hastily, Morpheus let Narelle go and bowed his head. "Alphaeus."

Narelle followed his actions, even repeating their leader's name.

Alphaeus nodded in return. "Doing well in our studies?" His Russian accent was broken, thick on certain letters and seeming nonexistent on others.

Morpheus shrugged. "As always."

An amused smile graced Alphaeus's lips for a second, but was quickly thinned out. "Do well to behave."

Morpheus suddenly felt the force of Alphaeus' probing stare. He studied Morpheus like a human studied an insect under a microscope, full of question, full of wonder, and full of interesting facts already discovered. Could Narelle have spilled his secret? Or Darius? How could either of them betray his trust like that?

"Always do," Morpheus said.

"Mmph," was Alphaeus's reply. "Be well and continue your hard work."

Narelle and Morpheus nodded, bowing their heads as Alphaeus passed. Several people behind them stopped Alphaeus in greeting, their voices hushed respectfully.

Narelle hit Morpheus in the gut. "Why must you be a smartass?"

Morpheus shrugged and continued walking. "I did not hear you object."

13

BRIGH

During the day for the next two weeks, Brigh sat up in bed sketching images of a soggy forest and painting portraits with watercolors and acrylics of the man whose features were burned into her memory. Thorburn stood guard on the floor at the foot of her bed; and by guarding, he was asleep half of the time or chewing on an old tennis shoe someone had left out. She'd had to call up her dad several times to spread out her drying pieces because her bed couldn't hold them all, forcing the shoe destroying dog to move from the floor to her bed, his legs dangling over the edge of the mattress as he snored.

"Where's all this coming from?" Jairus asked her one day, while staring at a painting full of trees in different shades of green and a dark figure facing away. Morpheus's white shirt was comprised of shadowy facial features, all grimacing or calling out in despair. She wasn't sure where that image came from, but when she'd painted it, the idea had just popped onto the page without much thought.

Brigh looked up from her sketchpad, her fingers tingling from sketching so long. "A dream I keep having."

Jairus took in a breath and raised a brow. "That's one hell of a dream you got there, kiddo. Who's this guy?"

Brigh felt her cheeks grow hot. "Just some guy."

"Uh-huh." Jairus arranged her art pieces neatly around her bed, making a little path leading to the door. After surveying the sea of green, white, and black, he turned to Brigh with a sigh. "Need anything from the kitchen?"

"Nah, I'm good for now," Brigh said, chewing on the end of her charcoal pencil. "How's the mansion on Prospect coming?"

The corners of his eyes crinkled as he smiled. "Still standing. Peter's fighting it out with the historical society and it looks like they're gonna win. Demolition was supposed to be a week ago, but the protestors are standing strong behind its age and value to the city."

"Do you think they're right?"

Jairus sighed. Carefully stepping around her artwork, he leaned on the edge of the bed, looking at his calloused and scarred hands. Thorburn gave a soft *whoof* and nudged Jairus's hand with his wet nose to be petted, but the man ignored it. "We're talking about my job, Brigh, so what we say here can't leave this room."

"Promise," she said breathlessly. At that moment she would've promised him anything. She'd waited so long for him to lean in close, to confide in her things he never shared with anyone. Though the small town didn't have many secrets, some things could be kept hidden if told to the right person. But he still had to be careful. Too many of his secrets had already been spread around town.

"Personally," he began, "I'd leave the place alone. Maybe restore it a little if it's possible. But honestly, the land's worth a lot—Peter's talking about putting up a hotel, one that could bring good money here."

Brigh looked back at her unfinished landscape, the mansion a detail-less foundation lost within all the vegetation. Would she miss it? The weekly partying would come to an end, as would the thrill of being a part of a secret only those in high school were in on. No more long drives on that empty road, able to pop her car into each gear and go as fast as she wanted without worry about tickets and pedestrians.

It really was just a house, with a cemetery whose history stood unmatched in their little town. Most of the windows were boarded up, the stairs rotten and mildewed and splayed with splinters. Holes in the ceiling the size of manholes threatened nasty falls, and now the floor where she fell through. Why no one had kept up the building was lost on her. The place had promise. But to be honest with herself, it'd seen better days. Still, it'd be a shame to see the place go.

"So you agree with him?" she asked quietly.

"I'm kind of stuck, Brianna," Jairus said defensively, a hint of anger deepening his voice. "If it weren't for our livelihood I'd be out there right now with one of your paintings strapped to a stick."

Brigh hugged her sketchbook. "Please don't."

"Wasn't going to."

"Thanks."

"I'm sorry," he continued quietly. "I know how much the place means to you kids, but it needs tearing down. It's not safe."

Brigh's lips thinned as she turned away from her father. The pencil was back in her hand, her fingers fast at work. Angry jagged lines cut across the front of the mansion— Brigh not caring about realistic resemblance. She'd started on the front porch by the time her father stood in silence and walked to her door.

"Is Alice still here?" she asked monotonously.

"Yes," her father growled. He rubbed his eyes and then stretched. "I'll pay you twenty bucks to convince her everything here's fine so she'll go home."

"Not a chance." Brigh laughed. "By the way, could you ask her to come here, please? Thanks! You're the best dad ever."

Jairus shook his head, and as he closed her bedroom door behind him, she heard him mutter, "This better get me a great Father's Day present."

Devilishly, Brigh chuckled before going back to drawing. The end result of her pieces was always a climactic experience, but the actual process of creating them filled her with peace and tranquility. The way the charcoal caught every impression in the page; the shine the paint left before drying; the way her tools glided across the paper, slowly dragging any and all stresses or anxious thoughts from her shoulders. This feeling of quiet and peace was stronger than that which she experienced while dancing, but the two of them combined drowned out everything negative within her, leaving her spent with nothing but optimistic sensations.

"Hey, Bree Bree—Whoa." Alice stood in the doorway, her fist hovering in front of the door about to knock. "What in Sam's hell's going on in here?"

"Painting."

Alice's eyes were wide as she surveyed the massacre of green all around her. "I was going to say Thorburn coughed up a family of geckos, but what do I know about art?"

Brigh smiled. "Thanks, auntie."

"Bleh," Alice said. She stuck out her tongue and pretended to gag. "What did I say about the aunt thing?"

"That it's 'traditional and decrepit-old-lady sounding'."

"Thank you," she said sweetly. "Now what do you want?"

"Jeez," Brigh said with a laugh. "What crawled up your butt and died?"

Alice puffed at a curl obstructing her sight. "I was tuning my guitar, smartass. Owen and I have a gig at the pub tomorrow night."

"So Owen's free tonight?" Brigh asked hopefully.

Alice narrowed one eye in question. "Why do you want to know?"

"He got a degree in parapsychology, right?"

"If Owen has a degree in something, I haven't been able to see it yet." Alice sat down on Brigh's bed with a yawn, scooting the partial sketch out of her way. "But I do think he took a class about that weird shit his junior year."

"Do you think he could help me with a little research?" Brigh's heart started pounding, her excitement hardly contained. Would he know? Could he help? What kind of questions would she ask? She didn't know much of anything on the subject, only the few vague details Morpheus gave her. And then she worried—would she have enough information to form a question? She wasn't sure; she'd never had that problem.

"I don't see why not," her aunt said with a shrug.

Brigh gave a girly shriek and threw her arms around Alice. "Thank you!"

Brigh hoped Owen wouldn't think she was insane. But then again, Owen himself was a peculiar guy, so the conversation would be odd on both ends. She did feel a little guilty for having Owen drive all the way out to her house, but her anticipation of learning anything about her dreams outweighed the guilt she had.

"Get some sleep," Alice said, her voice filled with affection and a motherly love that made Brigh's heart skip. "If your dad finds out I've been up here shooting the breeze instead of mothering you he'll have a conniption fit."

Brigh grinned. Her aunt was not wrong. "Go play something for me, please."

Alice nodded and leaned over to kiss Brigh's forehead. "Sweet dreams, Bree Bree."

As Alice left the room Brigh settled into the pillows and took in a deep breath of her lingering perfume. Her aunt's presence always reminded her of her mother, but Alice never carried sadness. She was always light and upbeat and kept her father on his toes. And more importantly, she loved art with a passion even though she had no talent in it.

Alice began playing downstairs, a soft strike to the strings, lulling Brigh to sleep instantaneously.

MORPHEUS

More than one thing surprised him about Kyle, and it wasn't the boy's choice of clothing or cologne. One, if it was possible, the boy's condition looked worse than Brigh's. Two, his home and his room were not at all what Morpheus had pictured: an old mansion-style house with white pillars and black shutters graced out front by a large driveway. Kyle lived on the street curving up and around a mountain overlooking the town; the houses larger than most of the buildings below them. The walls of his room were plastered with football and soccer posters, separated by pictures of Major League baseball players and patches of white paint. His blue carpeted floor was relatively clean and clear of clothing, but one corner was hidden by football gear.

"No, mom, I'm fine," he said into his cell phone. He winced as he tried to move his leg. Both were concealed under his comforter, but by the bulge of the blankets, it looked as though something bulky was holding his legs together; something larger than the cast helping set the broken bones in Brigh's leg.

Kyle heaved a sigh. "Mom, slow down. Gran's here, remember? Everything's good." His lips thinned and Morpheus could hear the loud vibrations of his mother's voice coming through the tiny cell phone. Kyle opened his mouth several times to say something but was cut off instantly before he could get a out word.

Listening to the struggle Kyle was having with his mouth and his mother, Morpheus took a look around the large room. A massive oak desk sat nestled between a window and the door to the room, the top of it cluttered with papers and school books. Atop the stack was a folded over printout from the internet paper clipped to two tickets for the homecoming dance.

Leaning on the desk, he pressed his palms into the wood, wishing it would creak. He looked over his shoulder. Kyle was in the same position as before, but the phone call had ended and now he lay in his bed. His eyes were closed, head turned toward the wall, softly snoring.

Morpheus shook his head, banishing the curious smile coming across his face. He wondered about the papers printed from the internet and why they were attached to the tickets. The only reason he knew they had something to do with the internet was because whatever link he'd used had printed out along the bottom of the page. Something about a Bed and Breakfast.

"What are your intentions, human?" he asked in a thoughtful daze.

"More importantly," Narelle said abruptly, causing Morpheus to jump away from the desk, "what are your intentions by being here?"

"Narelle," Morpheus said with a nervous smile, "how nice to see you."

She pushed him out of the way to see what it was he'd been looking at. She leaned over the same way Morpheus had to get a look inside the folded paper, her hair thrown over her shoulder, baring her neck. The pale skin of her slender neck appeared translucent, fragile. Something easily grabbed and held in submission. Something soft and smooth for lips to caress.

Narelle pulled back from the desk with a shrug to her shoulders, the movement breaking Morpheus's attention. A bored expression held her face from smiling or frowning, her lips relaxed and ready for words. Sometimes he wished her lips were immobilized by the same manmade metal silencing The Elders. But then again, he did owe a lot of his intelligence to her, so he immediately felt guilty.

"I will not ask you the obvious question," she said. "But what does this human have to do with anything?"

Morpheus pictured the boy asleep in his bed. "Truly nothing."

"You are sincerely a horrible liar."

"Thank you for the confidence," he murmured.

Narelle just stared at him, her fiery lion's mane still slung over one shoulder. He watched her struggle with herself not to fold her arms in agitation. Over the development process, their kind frequently experienced little ticks humans had, such as the crossing of arms, sighing, rolling of the eyes, and more. Narelle couldn't hold back the eye rolling—honestly, Morpheus thought her unaware of the action when she did it—but she despised the need to cross her arms. He would have laughed had he not experienced a mutual feeling of running his fingers through his hair.

"You could crush the boy," she said.

Morpheus blinked. "What makes you think I would want to?"

Narelle shook her head. "I implied that you could, given your larger body structure and muscle development. You are strong now and will be even more so once you are made."

"I suppose I will remember that," he said awkwardly.

"Very well," was all she'd say in return.

14

BRIGH

Owen wasn't very tall for a man, and he couldn't grow enough facial hair to make him look over thirty. The square wire-rimmed glasses and faded blue jeans with a rip in the knee added to the young musician look; his cowboy boots and black and white baseball tee with a seventies band printed on the front were the only things that seemed to age him.

Soft brown eyes set in a handsome tanned face met Brigh as he entered her bedroom with Alice trailing behind him. Standing next to each other, Brigh got a good look at the possibilities of Owen and Alice being a couple. She was a hair taller than him and her thinness was accentuated by his thick torso. The two made a handsome couple but she agreed with Alice—they would kill each other. Both competitive and strong willed, their fights as friends and band mates were already like going into battle. Upgrading their relationship only called for major disaster.

"Good to see ya, kid," Owen said. "Though I must admit, the setting isn't very fashionable."

Brigh had the urge to throw her stuffed animal at him. "Nice to see you too, Bugeye."

He grinned. What little bit of facial hair he did have sprouted over his top lip, curving with the force of his smile. "Uh, you—you wanted to see me?"

"Can I ask you some questions?" Brigh asked.

Unsure, Owen looked at Alice, rubbing his hands together. "Yeah…I guess so."

Alice smiled at Owen's awkward attempt at acting younger than his actual age. "I'll be downstairs tuning." She paused and held her hand out as if to touch Owen's shoulder and then thought better of it. "Don't scare her too much, O. She's the only niece I have."

"Duly noted," he said in response and saluted her.

"I'm right here, guys," Brigh huffed sarcastically.

Alice gave her an exaggerated smile and shut the door behind her.

"So…" Owen walked to Brigh's computer chair in a gauche dance and flopped, jumping at how the chair rocked back and banged against the desk. "Uh, what did you want to ask me?"

"Did you study anything called the Unfinished when you were in grad school?"

His eyebrows shot up, eyes wide and white. He let out a breath and then laughed. "I'd remember something that unoriginal." His eyebrows swooped together in a mesh of confusion. "Why do you ask?"

Brigh shrugged, feeling suddenly silly. She'd kind of hoped Owen would say yes and end this lonely feeling of madness. Now she wasn't so sure her sanity was as credible as it once had been. She shook her head, the loose wisps from her pony tail tickling her cheeks. "I don't know. I don't know where it came from. I've had dreams and they seem so real. I just…I don't know. I can't explain it."

Owen leaned forward in the chair, suddenly on edge. "What kind of dreams?"

Brigh looked Owen in the eyes and saw something she'd only seen in the eyes of one other. A newness, but also age. Something she'd never noticed before. She looked at him and it seemed to her that someone had torn a wrapper open around him and his eyes were what peaked over that tear. His eyes mirrored what she saw of him on a regular basis: a man of forty-two acting and feeling as though he were fifteen years younger. But the show he usually put on for everyone was lighter than what she was getting from his eyes now, vivid and filled with laughter. His eyes weren't laughing now.

Her heart hiccupped an unsteady beat. "Are you okay, Bugeye?"

He blinked and leaned back in his chair. "I'm fine. What's up?"

She wasn't sure she should say anything. She didn't know what she'd seen. Had she even seen anything in the first place? The pain coiling around the lobes of her brain made her clutch the side of her head.

"You okay, kid?" Owen asked, coming to the side of her bed. Brigh searched his face through heavy lidded eyes, the pain causing black spots everywhere she looked. He still looked new and old at the same time as though he'd cheated some sort of mystical timeline, but he was normal Owen, as normal as he could get.

Brigh shook her head. "I haven't been getting much sleep."

He ran a comforting hand across her back. "Dreams been keeping you up?"

"Not keeping me up. I sleep through the night. It's just I feel exhausted in the morning, is all."

He cocked his jaw, thinking. "I'll ask your aunt to get you some sleep aids. They should help kick out the dreams so you can get rest."

"Okay," she whispered.

"Get some sleep in the meantime." He smiled awkwardly. "Sorry I wasn't much help with your unfinished people. I'll do some searching for ya, though."

She smiled in return, the pain drawing her back into the pillows. "Thanks. And thank you for coming. You always make me feel better."

"Well, I just gave you a headache," he said. "Don't think I did anything good."

"It means a lot for you to come over." She snuggled under the blankets, drawing them up and under her chin. She closed her eyes. "Go rock the house with Alice."

"Sweet dreams, Princess."

She heard the door click and the soft clack of his cowboy boots down the hall. Seeing another person other than her family made a difference. She didn't feel like a prisoner in her own home anymore. Failure of accomplishing something still filled her with defeat. It wasn't something she experienced often, and when she did, she tried hard to make up for it. Owen hadn't known anything, but a part of her felt like that was all a lie. Deep down he knew something. He had to. She hadn't let him know the little slip he'd given her. Because he'd clearly said 'your unfinished people' and she hadn't said the *people* part.

ᚱ

Over the few weeks of meeting beneath the willow tree to read and talk, Brigh had began to wonder if Morpheus owned a poetry book other than *The Poets of Maine*. Not that she had any complaint; the words within moved her more than anything modern she'd ever read. But she felt contained, as though stuck in a tiny corked bottle. She decided to keep these musings to herself; Morpheus was easily embarrassed.

"You choose," he offered, running his fingers lightly across her hipbone.

Brigh sucked in a gasp but took the book from Morpheus' hand without a word. Over the course of their time together, Morpheus had slowly grown bolder with his feelings for her—holding her hand here, urging her forward with his hand at the small of her back there. She still sat in his lap, a custom he seemed insistent about without making a big deal out of the affair. The tips of his fingers continued to stroke the bit of bare flesh peaking out between her pajama shirt and shorts. The slight tickle comforted her more than the hugs she received daily from Kyle, and after a minute of following the lines his fingers made on her skin, she found the tickle traveling elsewhere.

He had been the one to choose the poems, sharing the reading with her. She wasn't sure who to look up or what subject to read. Suddenly she felt self-conscious, an emotion she hadn't experienced since that night at the game.

Her face flushed, and with a spark of irritation, she flipped open to a random page, jumping at the sound of ripping paper. Throat tightening and tears on the verge of swelling over her lashes, Brigh bit her lip and fought not to make a noise.

Morpheus' arm around her waist tightened slightly. "Something the matter?"

Brigh shook her head, taking in a breath. "Fine. Nothing. Annie Brown."

"Would you like me to—?"

"No," she firmly said, "I'll do it."

His arm relaxed a little, but his fingers slowly traced larger circles across her waist. The feeling calmed her again, but she still felt on the edge of crying, and that was something she didn't care for Morpheus to see. Men usually didn't know what to do with a crying woman; her father especially didn't. She didn't want to alienate Morpheus or scare him off, so she sucked up whatever had leaked into her well-walled control and blinked at the pages before her.

"'Will you love me when I'm old,'" she read the title, her throat suddenly dry on the words.

"'When these sunny days are vanished,
When the charm of youth is fled
When the rosy bloom is banished—
Age's frostiness, instead—'"

Morpheus continued, his deep voice adding another emotion that her soft and wavering one couldn't.

"'When the eye has lost its brilliance,
And the voice is weak and old,
Will I lose this heart-surveillance?
Will this love of thine grow cold?"

Brigh picked up the next stanza and the two began switching off, the tension falling away behind the words. She'd always found solace in poetry, but dancing and painting still cooled her off better. It'd been a long time since she'd cried, and she owed the lack of emotion to her passions. Her father had always told her to suck it up and move on, and on some level her mother had agreed. But instead of holding everything in, her mother had showed her the release such artistry could supply. She just wished her mother had showed her other things.

Morpheus whispered into her ear the final lines of the poem, his chin resting lightly upon her shoulder.

"'Safe, together may be ended
All our work on life's broad stage;
Safely may we sleep together
In the calm grave's quiet fold—
Then, ascending, dwell forever
Where no being e'er grows old.'"

"It's beautiful," she spoke softly. Felt the pages' edge with a fingertip. She wondered how something could survive so much time. How something so much more fragile than human beings could outlive them. How many years would these words outlive her? How many years would Morpheus?

Morpheus closed the book in her hands and set it on the ground. He turned his face toward her ear. "Something is on your mind."

The lack of breath on her ear sent a chill down her spine. She eased out of his embrace and stood, taking a few steps away from him. The air seemed colder now that she was standing, but that could've been a breeze stuck in the branches from outside. The cool air soothed the heat gathering in her face but not the tension in her shoulders. It made her shake.

"Have I done something?"

Brigh turned and saw he was still sitting. He seemed so innocent, gazing up at her with his legs parted, hands resting on the bent knees like a child. His eyes a darker green than they had been before.

"What are we doing?" she asked.

He blinked at her. "You mean, what am *I* doing."

He hadn't played stupid like a person usually would. That unnerved her, and she didn't understand the feeling. Normally she'd have wanted a person to cut the crap and get to the good part. But the way he easily did that, without a thought, made her uncomfortable. It wasn't natural.

"Yeah, maybe." She sighed and looked away. "I don't know."

Morpheus looked to the ground. "I know I am not a wise choice, nor am I a better candidate, but—" With this he stood, holding out his arms at his sides in surrender. She didn't like the look, didn't want the responsibility. Didn't know what his intentions were and wasn't sure about her own.

He stepped toward her, his arms relaxing at his sides, but still a symbol of his submission. "—would you have me?"

Her first reaction was to tell him yes. But was that what she truly wanted? The rain plummeting through the trees struck her bare forehead, insisting on an answer with a sickly tapping.

"I don't know what to say," she said honestly.

Her response didn't seem to thwart his mood any, neither did he seem wary as he moved toward her. She wanted to dance away, felt his nearness as a signal to flee and hide from him forever. But she couldn't take a step, couldn't make her heart slow in its beating.

"What're you doing?" she asked in a breathy whisper.

Morpheus searched her face, wiping away the rain droplets from her forehead. His eyes seemed greener the more she looked at them, shining with a warmth and gentleness she'd wanted for her own for so long.

"I do not know," he whispered back before leaning down and claiming her lips.

Any doubts she'd had about how she felt for Morpheus quickly dissolved as he held her. This was their second kiss, but it felt like they were kissing for the first time, touching for the first time. She suddenly had an image of him lying above her naked body. The image tore an animalistic growl from her throat, surprising her and shocking Morpheus.

He wrapped his arms around her and laid them both down on the grass, sliding her atop him. His fingertips snuck under her t-shirt, teasing the flesh above the waist of her pajama shorts. His kisses quickened and then slowed, those dry lips tasting her, tongue darting over her teeth.

Rolling them over so that he lay over her, his hands circled her shoulders, holding her to him. The weight of his body and the feel of his lips on hers made something twist low in her belly. The feeling and her wanton thoughts came crashing together in recognition of what lay ahead, and she rolled them back over so that she straddled him.

Her eyes opened. She couldn't breathe. Her lips stilled. Suddenly she couldn't find the calm to relax, wasn't sure what to do. Her heart raced, pounding with a nervous annoying tempo behind her ears. She tried letting her arms go lax, her legs wrap around his, locking them in place. But her hands still shook, her breathing becoming shallow and quick. What would he see when he pulled back her clothes; how would he feel seeing her bare curves?

He slowed, noticing her stillness. She felt him stiffen in her arms like a rock. Were these really her arms? Did she exist here? Was she about to hand over her virginity to a man who didn't exist?

"What has stilled you?" he asked.

"Why are you staring at me?"

Confusion clouded his eyes. "I am not ignorant, Brianna. Though I may be pigheaded and belligerent sometimes—alright, most of the time—does not mean I do not see your beauty. Or the fact that you are not happy."

Silence stretched between them, him allowing her to speak if she had the nerve to. Every time she wanted to say something the words didn't seem right, or how they'd sound wouldn't feel right. How he could render her speechless seemed illogical.

"Please," he asked again. Taking her hands in his, he brought them to his lips and kissed both of them, then held both to his chest. When he looked up at her, she finally recognized why his eye color had attracted her, but wasn't sure how she'd come to the conclusion.

"Please tell me what is wrong," he said. "I cannot help feeling incompetent as your..." He sighed. "Whatever it is I am to you."

She knew she'd have said anything, anything at all to get rid of the look on his face. Without thinking, she let her body say what words couldn't; allowed herself to be put on autopilot. Taking his face in the palms of her hands, she watched his surprise and confusion battle each other in his eyes. His hands covered hers, sliding between her knuckles before cupping them.

She took in a deep breath, held it, and let it out as her words. "I love you."

His reaction resembled an animal's usual response to curiosity; head slowly tilted to the left, eyes squinting in their search for the truth. Everything about his being was wrong; she knew it in her gut and heart. Feeling the way she did made her slightly sick, but she knew this was right.

She wasn't sure when those words had attached to Morpheus in her mind, but she knew that even though he was most likely a figment, he was definitely her dream man in every way possible.

His lips parted, pursed, and formed a line before he spoke. "I love you, as well."

His reply didn't comfort her as much as she'd thought it would, neither did it feel real—the words, just words. She laid her head on his shoulder, stretching out along him like a body pillow. He kissed her forehead and strung his fingers through her hair, massaging behind her ears. She wondered if he understood what had happened between them. On some level, he most likely did. She wondered if he had been on the same level as her, euphoria and fear twisting together throughout veins and muscles. She'd feared what might come instead of putting attention toward the present and riding that wave of adventure she'd only heard about. And now that she'd reached the possibility of being in that boat of pleasure, she wasn't sure the adventure was worth the heartache.

15

BRIGH

Orloff led the group of half-awake seniors through the ferns and logs on the way to the falls. Brigh had been to Swallow Falls a number of times, but the beauty of the water never ceased to amaze her; an extraordinary foundation for such a thing. All around her were flirty ferns, large fallen trees outlining the paths, and boulders that could hold a whole family for pictures. Small alcoves in the rock walls around the trails housed creatures from chipmunks to arachnids, foxes to beetles. The enormous boulders weaving through the water from one side to the other could be crossed by jumping. She and Richard had done so many times. Her father had even mastered many of the boulders and made it across the water several times because of his long legs. She'd read about the other wonders and sights of the world, but until she saw them for herself Swallow Falls was the greatest.

"Keep up, people!" Orloff called over the chattering of students. He waved everyone on and then resumed his leadership march ahead.

"That man's too damn happy this early," Felicity remarked. "Makes me want to puke."

"Be nice," Brigh said. "Would you rather have him or Panatelli on this trip?"

"Oh just shut up, will ya?"

Brigh laughed, locking arms with her friend. Felicity's shoulders sagged. They'd met at Brigh's house before five so they could drive over to school to make the bus. Brigh's crutch slowed them down, but at the rate Felicity was going, slowness was not a problem. She'd had two cups of coffee, but even caffeine was no match for a sleepless night and then an early rise. Felicity was the night person, Brigh was the morning one.

"You know," Felicity began, "I've never willingly taken an art class in my life. In fact, I'm not even in your art class."

"*Shh!*" Brigh exclaimed with a finger sliding to her lips. "I told Orloff you were working on some pieces and wanted to put them into the art show next month."

Felicity threw her a worried look. "Are you serious? You mean I have to parade around the fact that I can't even draw a stick figure to save my ass?"

"No," Brigh said with a laugh as the two of them awkwardly made their way down the handicap ramp toward the falls. Every wood plank on the property was wet. Dogs were permitted so long as they stayed on a leash. And that usually meant they ended up in the water and soaked everything around them. "I'll paint you something. Don't worry. I just needed someone to help me on this trip."

Her friend eyed her with question.

"What?" Brigh asked.

"Something's up," she said. "And it smells fishy."

"That might be the falls," Brigh pointed out.

Felicity shook her head. "You've been hog-ass-weird since the other night. What gives?"

Could she tell her? Felicity already knew of Morpheus, but she also thought of him as just a dream. Once upon a time Brigh had thought the same, but now she wasn't sure. She had felt—and acted—a little strange since the dream the other night; Felicity wasn't wrong on her observation.

She'd conjured a plan—an experiment—one she was hoping Felicity would agree to and, because of it, not think she was nuts.

"I have a favor to ask you," Brigh whispered.

Felicity, seeing the secrecy in her coming question, pulled the two of them behind a prickly evergreen. No one came up behind them; everyone was racing each other like three year olds to the falls. Brigh would have joined them had she not been disabled and had something this huge to ask of her friend.

"I need you to sleep over tonight," she said.

Felicity gave her that look again. The one where she knew whatever it was she was about to agree to couldn't be good. Something she was going to regret. "Okay…Now get to the part that you really need me to do."

Brigh blushed, the cool air racing across her cheeks. "I need to see if you enter that dreamland like me."

Felicity's head rolled back as her eyes did. She sighed, slapping her thighs in defeat. "Alright. But what makes you think I'll go to the same place you do?"

She wasn't sure if Felicity agreed out of curiosity or to amuse her. She didn't care either way.

"I don't," she said, "not exactly. But who knows. You might. And then we'll know for sure I'm not crazy."

"Or that I'm just as crazy," Felicity said.

"That's the spirit!" Brigh said with excitement.

They started walking again, tripping over exposed tree roots and thick ferns. The sound of water hitting rock raced to their ears, soothing the quiet in Brigh's mind. Even though the crutch impeded on their fun, her and Felicity still smiled at the nature around them and laughed and joked about memories.

"Children," Orloff sighed as Felicity and Brigh came around a curve in the rock wall. He had his hands on his hips. The bright orange and yellow neckerchief tied European style around his neck blew lightly in the wind. "I know you're disabled, Breen, but you can't keep the whole group waiting."

"We're coming," Felicity huffed, hurrying the two of them along. To Brigh she added, "You know, we'd be moving a lot faster if you gave me half your weight instead of using the crutch."

"I don't want to be any more of a burden than I already am." Brigh winced against a shooting pain up her leg as she brushed against a fallen log. "We're almost there anyway."

Felicity nodded and steered them toward the group milling around the edge of the larger of the water falls. Being up on that rock so many feet in the air brought memories to the forefront of her mind. All those times Richard had teased of throwing her over the cliff into the water, every family Christmas picture right there on the icy rocks, every smile her parents had shared with each other as they celebrated another anniversary there at the park.

She needed to change the subject before tears threatened to wash away her mascara and leave her looking like a gothic reject.

"How's Kyle?" she asked.

Felicity hopped over a large puddle in the rock, turning back to help Brigh swing over. "Bad. Worse off than you."

Brigh managed to make it over the puddle with only a little splash on her pants leg. "Have you talked to him?"

"No. The whole town knows he's fucked to hell. It's all his mom talks about now."

Brigh shook her head, her cheeks reddening as she imagined his obvious mortification. "She *is* the gossip queen."

"Doesn't matter what she is," Felicity fumed. "Shouldn't be jawing all damn day about how she has to help him to the bathroom or change his clothes like a baby."

"Oh my God."

"I mean," Felicity continued, not even looking at Brigh any longer. "If my mom were to talk about my business like that to the world, I'd kill her."

"No you wouldn't," Brigh interjected, hopping over to Felicity as she stopped at the tree line.

"Yes, I would," Felicity turned on Brigh. "Could you imagine all of your secrets, your privacy, being known by everyone in the town?"

Brigh's brow rose high as she leaned on the crutch to place her hands on her hips.

Felicity looked away. "Of course you would. Sorry. I just…" She shook her head. "Here comes Orloff."

Brigh looked over her shoulder as Orloff skipped around the many puddles her and Felicity had minutes ago, the two easels, canvases, and art supplies teetering dangerously between his arms. He looked annoyed and tired, like he always did. Her art class didn't take many fieldtrips. Orloff claimed that if they could paint things they couldn't physically see at the moment, sitting there in the dank little art classroom, then they could paint anything anytime.

"Miss LeBlanc, Miss Breen." Orloff nodded at them both. Awkwardly, the art supplies were set down before them, the paint and brush bucket dropped because he'd lost his grip. "We'll move further along the trail in an hour. Just paint as much of the landscape as you can before you hear my whistle. And please, add your own little touch."

Orloff turned his back on the girls, muttering, "Trees can become quite dull."

Felicity tried to hold back a snicker as they began setting up the easels and canvases. Felicity ran over to the cart holding the stools and grabbed three while Brigh laid her crutches down beside her station.

"What am I supposed to do now?" Felicity asked as she set down Brigh's chairs.

Brigh flopped onto the uncomfortable metal stool, propping her leg up on the extra one Felicity had snagged. "Just sit in front of your canvas and act like you don't know where to start."

"That won't be too hard to pull off," Felicity mumbled.

Brigh looked around her, squinting at the high sun as she took in her surroundings. Plenty of evergreen, rock, and wood. Her painting would be nothing but dark colors unless she looked harder and noticed the sun kissed leaves on some of the trees, or the puddles in the rock glistening with golden light. Any art form called for complete awareness of one's surroundings and the artist had to have a depthless imagination to pull any two objects together and make them one being. She'd never had problems with perception, imagination, or observation. It was the making everything fit together that gave her a hard time. Most of her paintings looked as though she'd pasted them all together at the last minute. Blending was the technique her mother hadn't fully taught her and it was something Orloff couldn't seem to enforce. He gave her perfect scores on everything, but Brigh suspected that an art teacher gave out A's like a crack dealer gave out drugs. It was their job and sometimes they got a high from it.

"How were tryouts?" Brigh asked as she picked out her paints and squirted them onto her palette.

Felicity cocked her head to the left, eyeing the canvas with doubt and curiosity. "They're called 'auditions' and they went perfect. Scored the lead role."

"As always," Brigh whispered.

"There's no more competition in theatre at Fort Hill." Felicity sighed and picked up a paint brush, fingering the hairs. "It's almost boring. I should move to Allegany."

Brigh smiled, knowing how her friend felt. Cheerleading Captain had always come easily to her because of her leadership skills and her knowledge of football from her dad. Plus, her blonde hair and flexibility were a bonus. She'd been challenged in classes all her life, but never had there been a time when she'd had to seriously fight for something she wanted. *Except*, she thought, *when it came to* her.

Brigh smiled at Felicity's attempt to paint something to make her teacher happy and bit her lip as she started her own. She allowed the pine to invade her nostrils, the cold wind to tease her loose hair. A tune her mother used to sing to her every night when she was a child came to her lips, chapping them after a minute and drying her throat. Green and red met each other on the canvas, quarreling into a russet mess of tree shapes. Faces hid under branches and around trunks, cackling at Brigh's awkward attempt to forget the past.

MORPHEUS

Darius knew very little about humans, having been the one studying with books instead of his owns eyes. On more than one occasion, Morpheus had quelled his friend's many misconceptions about the human race, reminding and somewhat re-schooling himself. Over the years he'd observed that his kind looked upon humans as humans did cattle. Human souls sustained their unfinished existence, one day guiding them to climax as humans themselves. He was sure how he felt. He hadn't been persistent to know who had been murdered or who had died of old age to shape him. Honestly, he hadn't cared. They were figures of the past; forgotten, but put to use.

"I do not understand why you will not come with me," Morpheus said for the second time. Perched on the edge of Darius's cot, Morpheus watched his friend walk around the room, nervously straightening the bookshelves and checking for dust, though he knew in their world dust did not exist.

"I have made my decision," Darius said with a sigh. He turned and leaned against the larger of the two bookshelves, stretching an arm around his stomach. "Why must you keep this up?"

Morpheus smiled. "Because I am thick headed."

A small grin spread out on Darius's face. "True, true. But still. Nothing you say will get me to go with you."

"Will you just trust me," Morpheus begged. "There is nothing wrong with going."

Darius threw him a glare. "You always say that and we *always* wind up in a snag."

"Not always. There have been times where we have escaped with—"

"The skin of our teeth?" Darius interrupted.

Morpheus nodded. "Well, yes. But in all seriousness, I know you will regret not going with me tonight."

A brow rose on Darius's soft boyish face. His shoulders relaxed, slightly. "I do not believe that. But I will go. Just to prove you wrong."

A grin flew to Morpheus's lips. He knew Darius's curiosity rivaled his own in its intensity. He also knew it had been a matter of time before he'd crack and agree. "Then it is settled."

BRIGH

Brigh wasn't a superstitious person. She had no reason to be. Candles were just hardened wax lit to scent the room or ward off darkness in the event of a power outage. Black cats weren't bad luck, neither were crows, or jack-o-lanterns. The fear of all of that was left to Halloween, in her opinion. But her mother had always been...sensitive to all the worlds' superstitions. That night when all the goblins and werewolves emerged from the deep, and the spirits of the long dead tried to slink into our world, was the night when her mother came alive.

Scanning the room as if it were possible those monsters could be lurking in the shadows, Brigh felt the darkness like a blanket. One that soothed instead of suffocated, partly because Felicity was there to help ward off anything malicious, even if she'd use her mouth more than her fists.

Currently, Felicity was on the phone, arguing with Liam. He'd pressured her about sex and she wasn't interested. She *was* interested about sex, just not with him. She'd confided in Brigh that as much as her hormones had flared lately, she couldn't make herself love Liam and hand over her virginity to him.

He apparently was willing to fight for her, but she wasn't.

"What do you want me to say, Liam?" Felicity screeched. "I said no and you didn't listen. I know blue balls are a bitch, but that's what you get for being seventeen. I'm not going to let you fuck me and knock me up like a little tween bitch. If you can't handle that then we're just not meant to be."

Brigh could hear Liam's angry voice through the phone, but she didn't feel the slightest bit of pity for him. Even if Felicity hadn't been her friend, Brigh didn't believe in forced sex just because two people happened to be in a relationship with each other. Sex needed trust. Not marriage or a hot and steamy lip lock. Two people needed time to get to know each other. Sex was a bonus.

"Sorry for your loss," Felicity said before closing her phone and tucking it under her pillow. She wasn't angry any longer and sadness didn't seem to coil in her eyes. She seemed happy, like a weight had been lifted from her shoulders.

"Should we light candles?" Felicity asked. "Say a prayer?"

Brigh eyed the cabinet that held her candles, but shook her head. "It doesn't work that way."

Felicity scooted under Brigh's comforter, concealing her thin, bare legs so only the top, camisole-covered part of her showed. "O-kaaay. But if I get possessed, you're paying for the exorcism."

Brigh smiled. "Deal."

Felicity settled down next to Brigh, their foreheads close. Felicity's breath had a spicy cinnamon smell from her tooth paste, mixing with the scent of her powdery perfume. Taking in a deeper breath of the familiar smell, Brigh rode on the wave of that aroma right into sleep.

MORPHEUS

Like two little angel's, one fair and one dark, they lay together in the peaceful first stages of sleep. Morpheus slunk from the door to Brigh's side of the bed, his gaze traveling over the dark haired Felicity with respect and warmth; he didn't know her particular reason for being with Brigh this night, but he had a feeling it was to watch over the girl. He had witnessed a sleepover only once during his year watching Brigh, and it never fazed him that two women would sleep in the same bed. Had a man been in Felicity's place, he knew his observation of the situation would bend into something morose and acrimonious.

"Oh hell."

Morpheus's attention drifted to his friend. "What?"

"I think I might have fallen in love." Darius grabbed his chest comically and grinned at Morpheus.

Morpheus rolled his eyes, looking back down at Brigh. Even without makeup she was lovely, as though her skin carried its own light, her lashes naturally dark and thick. "I could not imagine one excuse for why you would not find her attractive."

Darius stepped behind Felicity, watching her with the same sudden curiosity Morpheus had been plagued with upon his first sight of Brigh. Felicity lay on her left side, facing away from Darius, with her chin slightly upturned with a rebellious tilt toward the ceiling. He studied the girl like one would a painting, dissecting each piece with the wonderment of what had influenced the creator for certain aspects.

"You did not disappoint," Darius finally whispered. "She is beautiful."

"And?"

Darius sighed, backing away from the bed. "I still do not understand our reason for being here. There is nothing we can do but stare till our empty chests fizzle with an ache that is not there."

"How romantic," Morpheus said. "You are starting to sound like me."

"Perhaps I am." Darius looked at Morpheus, staring at him as though he could see his souls. "There is something you are not telling me."

Morpheus looked away and leaned back from the sleeping girls. "I have not left anything—"

"Liar," Darius accused.

A challenge was sent across the bed between them, accusation and denial flipping each other over like coins. Morpheus saw no way out of not telling Darius about the forest land; neither did he want to share. But then why couldn't he share? Darius knew all of his secrets, not only from being inquisitive and scanning his journal, but from words he'd spilled from his own mouth. So it was only instinctive for Darius to feel betrayed.

He knew he'd been rash in bringing him here, even if only to introduce him to the girl. No one could know of that world, couldn't even suspect that he'd had contact with Brigh. It wasn't natural for their kind to have that power, wasn't foreseeable. He had something no one else could have. He couldn't tell. Not even his best friend.

He stared hard at the bedspread, ignoring Darius's glare. "I am sorry, but I have nothing to tell."

"I do not believe you."

Morpheus looked at his friend, a glare of his own forming without much force. "Believe what you like. A true cohort would not question ones actions, creating lies out of jealousy."

Darius's eyes practically glowed in the dark. "Jealousy? You think by me calling you out as a liar makes me jealous? How dare you accuse me of such a human trait."

"I am starting to wonder," Morpheus began in a voice devoid of friendship, "whether or not you want to become human."

Darius looked shocked for a second, but shook it off. "Your lips are sizzling with lies, but do not spout any about my choices or desires."

Morpheus shrugged, going to move a piece of hair out of Brigh's eyes. His fingers went through her face, her features shimmering and warping so that what lay around his hand looked hideously disfigured. "I only made an observation." He sighed and stood back from the bed. "Go. I can't have you here if you keep ranting about things you do not understand."

Darius was around to Morpheus's side of the bed in a second, glaring slightly down at his friend. "I could understand if only you would quit being so arrogant and tell me the truth."

"I cannot tell you!" Morpheus yelled into Darius's face. This burst of emotion scared him a little. He truly had no reason to yell at his friend other than the fact that he was trying to cover himself and not bring Darius into something he knew would be disastrous if discovered.

Darius seemed to relax a little, but not like he wanted to. He had the strength and the speed but not the intent to use either. Now, standing a little taller than Morpheus, he looked like he could murder. "Why can you not tell me? I am your friend, your comrade through this journey. Why would you not share something with me? Have I done something to steal your trust?"

He'd said the last part like something foul had crawled out onto his tongue. He looked like he wanted to spit, too. Morpheus had no idea how he'd gotten into this mess. Why hadn't he kept this a secret? Why hadn't he been more careful?

When Morpheus spoke, his voice rang with a deep sadness. "Because I do not want to bring you into something that will surely be catastrophic."

"That has not stopped you before."

Morpheus looked at Darius. "I was an idiot. I did not care who I hurt."

"Well, look at me." Darius plucked the fabric of his shirt away from his chest. "I am unharmed. My reputation may have been scathed years ago, but I am still whole. What will this one secret hurt?"

More than you know, he thought.

"I am sorry," Morpheus said again, looking away.

Darius's fists clenched at his sides. "I do not believe you."

Morpheus shrugged. He was at a loss for words. Anything he continued to say would only dig him in deeper. And, as strange as it seemed to strike him, losing his friend to a lie didn't seem as devastating as he'd thought.

As if out of nowhere, a fist connected with Morpheus's jaw, sending him off balance for a fraction of a second. Cupping his jaw, he looked at Darius, his fisted arm raised at his side. His jaw didn't necessarily hurt since pain was a human sensation, but the fact of the action made him pause.

"What in God's name?" Morpheus whispered.

Another punch to his face followed after his words, knocking him back into Brigh's nightstand, the old wood undisturbed. Morpheus barely had a second to think before

Darius was on him, hands at his throat. The two scuffled, throwing each other into inanimate objects, bumping the bed once and then twice. As though they could be harmed, Morpheus tried to move the fight from the bed and the sleeping girls, but that only made Darius push harder. And before either of them knew it, Darius had thrown them onto the bed, sucking them through the sheets, mattress, and flesh into a room neither of them knew existed.

16

MORPHEUS

He opened his eyes to complete darkness and utter silence. Opening them wide and then blinking incessantly only made him wonder if his eyes were still open instead of helping him see. He hoped he had just lost his sight for a moment, but knew his hope a false one. His stomach ached from having fallen on it, weight hoisted on his elbows as he swiveled his head around.

Something gave a muffled grunt, sounding as though coming from his left, but he couldn't be sure.

"Darius?" he called, his voice slightly above a whisper. He wasn't sure where the two of them were and didn't want to find out by something chomping off his leg or the ceiling collapsing from the frequencies in his voice.

"I had sincerely hoped you had died," came a reply from the dark.

Morpheus almost smiled. "Sorry to disappoint. Can you see anything?"

"Dark. Emptiness." Darius sighed. "Perhaps if you tried focusing your eyeballs, objects would appear in front of you."

"Darius," Morpheus growled. "Now is not the time to—"

Something scraped across the floor, the pitch of it high, but somehow muffled, sounding almost like nails on a chalkboard. Morpheus swung his head to the left and then the right, a kaleidoscope of colors dancing before his eyes, but unable to come together and form shadows of anything solid. He waited for Darius to say "boo" or tap him on the shoulder, and when nothing came but another scrape across the floor, Morpheus began to wonder who or what was causing the noise.

"Please tell me that was you," Morpheus said aloud.

He heard Darius gulp. "I was hoping that had been you."

"Well," Morpheus said with a shake to his head, "it was not. We need to find a way out."

"Fat chance of that, mate."

Pushing himself onto his knees, he patted his hand out in front of him. The floor wasn't hard, nor was it soft, but somewhere in-between; a hard foam perhaps. He shuffled forward; knees lifted and set down carefully, quietly. If there was something else there with him, he didn't want it to know where he was.

"Think you can crawl to me?" Morpheus asked.

"It would help if I knew in which direction to crawl."

"Then be quiet and listen to my voice," he said. Slowly, and with great calculation, Morpheus began to crawl in the direction he thought he'd heard Darius. Of course, he took into consideration that they may be in a small four-wall room. His voice could've bounced and echoed from anywhere.

"I do hate being told what to do," Darius lamented. "I am considerably older than you, if you have not forgotten. I should be the one barking orders."

Morpheus grinned. "I am the one who skipped the book lessons and took my studies to the human world instead. I know a considerable amount more about humans than you do."

"Yeah," Darius countered. "But who is more level headed?"

With a tightened jaw, Morpheus changed direction. "Just keep talking. I think I am almost to you."

"Oh, I could go on if you like." Darius cackled unattractively. "Do you recall the time when you left one of our books in the middle of Pennsylvania Avenue to see if the vehicles would drive over it?"

Morpheus sighed, hands skating across the floor. The farther he crawled the clearer things became; outlines of objects slowly appearing in the dark. "You laughed and thought the whole thing unbelievably hilarious, I remember. Your first time in D.C."

Darius's amusement caught his tongue, the pronunciation of his words jumping with laughter. "And what a memory I will have of it. You watched that book all day and night until finally you walked over to it and exclaimed that it was untouched."

"It was an experiment." The room either seemed to be growing as he crawled or it was larger than he'd first thought. Or Darius's babble made the trek seem that much longer. "Say something."

"Anything?" Darius asked. "I do not like your interest in humans."

"Why not?" He only asked to keep him talking and maybe even to humor himself—he wasn't serious. Darius's voice had come from his left, near enough that Morpheus could hear Darius picking at the floor with his fingers.

"It is not healthy."

Morpheus scoffed. "You best get used to spending time around them. You will be one soon."

"We will never be fully like them," Darius said in his scholarly tone, but with a touch of sadness.

"That is half the thrill," Morpheus said, skirting away from the sad truth of Darius's comment. He reached out to where he heard the rhythmic picking at the flooring and clamped down on a hand. Well, he assumed it was a hand. As he felt around, the dips and curves and the texture of the thing didn't match up with any human or almost-human hand he'd ever seen or touched. A sleeve of terror shook its way up Morpheus's spine, pressing in on his ribs and shoulder blades.

"Darius?" he whispered.

The thing underneath his hand twitched and something slithered across his fingers. He had no need of air to live, neither was adrenaline a part of his development, but in that moment he felt what he'd witnessed—and couldn't quite understand—so many times over the years, except *fight* didn't cross his mind.

"What is wrong?" Darius whispered back. He was on the other side of whatever sat between them, his voice untouched by fear.

"Open the stream." Slowly, he pulled his hand away from the thing and pushed back onto his knees. The scratching noise he'd heard earlier started up again, but this time louder and coming toward him. Resisting the urge to crabwalk backward, he instead started walking on hands and knees toward where he knew Darius stood.

For once Darius didn't question the command, a bright white light already slowly forming in front of him. The light helped Morpheus place Darius exactly, but it also shed brilliance on the disgusting abomination directly in his way. Thousands of tiny hairs danced along its body as the thing swayed, clawing its way toward Morpheus faster and faster as it came closer. He saw—and felt as though he might vomit—what had slithered across his hand: a nose-like tube hung from a face of flabby sacks of blubber.

"What——?" Darius started to ask, but Morpheus ran at him so fast, knocking them into the stream, that he never finished the question.

"Think of the hallway outside your room!" Morpheus shouted as they skidded and tumbled through the stream. The lines rushed under Morpheus like concrete—pinching, biting, and unforgiving. Darius sped past him, fighting to right himself on his feet. But the force at which they were traveling there was no way they would be able to.

Morpheus pictured the hallway outside of their rooms, his eyelids attacking each other, lashes tangling as the image replaced the stream and then there was a door. Darius hit the unmoving ground first, and as Morpheus slid to the same ground, Darius had opened the door and was holding it open for Morpheus. They slammed the door shut behind them and ran down the hall and around the corner.

Their kind passed them with odd looks on their faces as the two of them presented themselves in disarray. But nothing surprised any of them more than the screams that followed behind Morpheus and Darius.

Others ran from the hallway, expressions of terror and confusion in their eyes. Morpheus and Darius looked at each other with the same confusion as they were pushed out of the way by the frenzied.

The beast reared on its back stubby legs, drawing out piercing screams from all those around it. Fat, silvery tentacles slithered out from the elbows of the creatures' arms, grasping a fleeing woman around the waist, snapping her in half. Both halves sunk to the floor with a wet slap, erupting into flames and vanishing a moment later.

Morpheus stood in a stunned stupor in the throng of those escaping. Death for a human was inevitable, even he was susceptible to it once he was made. But for him in this present state? He'd never wondered whether they could be extinguished. Never in his studies with Narelle or his classes had they ever discussed death on this plane.

The abomination grabbed a few more of Morpheus's fellows up in its tentacles, ripping them apart all at once as though they were dolls. Pieces fell to the floor in a bloodless heap, igniting and then disappearing right before his eyes.

Darius ran back to Morpheus, tugging on his shirt sleeve for him to run, but still he could not move. He couldn't believe what he was seeing.

"Morpheus!" Darius yelled over the screams, but the name fell on deaf ears. All Morpheus could hear were the thick ripping sounds of flesh, appendages coming off with popping sounds.

Suddenly Morpheus was pushed out of the way, a figure moving in front of him. Alphaeus stood impassive, his long black cloak swirling behind him without air. His arms rose in the air above him, fingers pointed at the creature.

Alphaeus shouted something in Russian.

The creature let out an agonizing cry that made all around it grab their ears. Morpheus had never heard anything like it, neither in his world or the human one. The sound cut into his ears like a box cutter.

And just as suddenly as Alphaeus had come in, the creature disappeared, and those in his clutches dropped to the floor.

Whispers erupted through the growing crowd as those around Morpheus ran to help their friends. Morpheus shook his head, clearing the image of death from his eyes.

"What happened?" Someone asked from his left.

"How did that thing come by us?" Another asked.

Answering questions spun off through the crowd as others continued to question how the beast had entered their home.

"Morpheus."

Morpheus turned to Alphaeus slowly, guiltily. There was nothing that pointed at Morpheus specifically, but he felt as though all eyes were on him, everyone knowing he was at fault.

"Follow me," Alphaeus said as he turned in the direction of his room.

Obediently, Morpheus followed in his leader's tracks, keeping his gaze forward so he wouldn't look into the eyes of everyone staring at him, the word *guilty* metaphorically engraved into his forehead.

17

MORPHEUS

He knew how prisoners felt. Shackled, walking down the row of on-lookers as the door to judgment waited ahead. Alphaeus never said a word, only nodded at those who greeted him, never breaking stride as they continued down the hall of tutor's rooms. All of the doors were the same, all devoid of personality and color. The idea of them being decorated seemed disturbing, even though he sometimes wished they were all different.

At first the walk had seemed too painfully long, but as Alphaeus stopped at a door, Morpheus wished they had kept going.

Like all of their rooms, Alphaeus's was neat and organized, his bookshelves lining every wall, including behind his cot, and bursting with layer upon layer of books. His desk sat positioned facing the wall opposite of the door, as though he did not wish to see those who came knocking.

"Sit," he said, gesturing to his cot. He himself sat at his desk, shuffling papers into neat piles.

Awkwardly, Morpheus sat where he was told. He waited for several minutes before Alphaeus laid down his pen and paper and looked up at him. No emotion rolled back and forth in his eyes, neither compassion nor cruelty. Morpheus didn't know what to think.

"I know what you may think—" Morpheus began.

"I do not care what you assume I think," Alphaeus said in his thick voice. A Russian accent dipped into each word as though he were trying it out. Morpheus suddenly wondered who had given it to him.

"I have the suspicion that you had something to do with the creature, yes, but I do not care about that just now." Alphaeus weaved his fingers, gripping them tightly. "There is the matter of Brianna Elizabeth Breen to discuss."

"What about her?" Morpheus asked warily.

A hint of a smile teased Alphaeus's lips, but it could have been Morpheus's wishful thinking. "I know you have been seeing her."

Morpheus wanted to shrug, but thought the action tacky. "I have visited her world here and there."

Now Alphaeus did smile, but no humor was in it. "*Seeing* implies that you have been with her as you and I are now."

"That is impossible," Morpheus said, scooting back onto the cot. "Our kind and humans cannot intermingle."

Alphaeus stood and went to the closest book shelf, plucking off a brown volume that had seen better days. "What you learn in your studies and what is actually true are two completely different animals." With the book in hand, he turned to Morpheus. "I once was drawn to a woman in the human world."

Caught off guard, Morpheus tried to save the telling expression by rubbing his jaw. He had the suspicion that he was walking into a trap, so instead of asking the how and why questions, he settled with asking about the experience. "What happened?"

"There was a time I thought living to be the absolute freedom."

Suddenly Morpheus wasn't sure he wanted to hear this story. The tone Alphaeus had used to start off signified an unhappy ending. But his curiosity for the story spurred his questions. He wanted to know if this story had anything to do with him and Brigh. He wondered if they were similar in ways Morpheus had never even imagined. "What changed?"

Alphaeus set the book on his desktop, propped himself on the edge of it, and folded his arms across that wide chest. His eyes were glazed over like he wasn't focused on anything in the room. His mouth was curled somberly, but his words were untouched by the emotion.

"Isla," he pronounced the name slowly as ee-sla, as if savoring each sound it gave. "A beauty among her town. She was to be married, an arrangement between her father and a man twice her age. I had watched over her meticulously for months until finally I had the insanity to think I could take her away, make her mine."

"How?" This was becoming oddly a lot like how he felt about Brigh and that feeling didn't bode well inside him.

The look in Alphaeus's eyes changed; back in the present. "Morpheus, are you really so impatient?"

Sheepishly, he looked at his hands. "I do apologize."

Alphaeus nodded in his acknowledgement and then continued. "I appeared to her one night as she lay dreaming. I could not for the life of her understand this infatuation, this need. I wanted so badly—I wanted to know. And then I saw her, looking at me. We were by a stream, a few miles from her home. She looked so beautiful then.

"I told her what I was, told her that I could help her." The small smile biting at his lower lip was sad. "The poor thing thought me an angel of God." He shook his head, adjusting his seat beside the desk as he looked at

Morpheus. In his eyes, Morpheus could see that stream. He could see the two of them in the moonlight gazing at each other as saviors of their misfortunes. Morpheus knew the feeling all too well.

"I told her that I was not ready—that I needed time. She followed me like a child, but damning everything around us, I loved her. Her passion to help others, her radiant beauty, her life. I wanted it."

A sinking feeling unraveled in Morpheus. He stood before Alphaeus, his leader, his idol, and could not believe that such a great being could have made such a grave mistake. He knew the ending to the story already, could see it in the man's eyes and could hear it in his voice.

"What happened?"

Alphaeus looked up at Morpheus as though he'd never seen him before. "We met by that stream every night for weeks when she went to bed. She asked me how this was possible and I told her it was an act of God."

"She believed you?" Morpheus asked just to ask.

Alphaeus closed his eyes and uncrossed his arms. "People then were superstitious. Every plant, animal, and cloud had a God. I watched over her, followed her everywhere she went until we could be together.

"But soon she fell ill." His jaw tightened. "Always tired, always restless. Shadows stained her eyes and cheeks and neither of us knew why, nor could have known. Our meeting, in that world between worlds, was not free. I had conjured it, made it flesh, the energy borrowed by none other than the only thing I loved in either world. This world I loved so much because it brought me to her became a prison. I watched her every night die before my eyes until the morning she was taken and I was the one alive."

If Morpheus had a heart, it would have stopped beating. The similarities were too close. Brigh had grown weaker, her skin pale, her eyes tired. She always seemed so distant and sad. He couldn't have known, he told himself. Before he let his thoughts continue he said, "She was the soul that finished you," like Alphaeus had been waiting for his confirmation of understanding.

"That was why I could not stay away," Alphaeus said. "My love for her is what ended her life."

Morpheus pinched the bridge of his nose, but stopped in mid-motion. Out of all those he knew in his world, none of their nervous gestures included pinching the bridge of their nose.

"But you were human, why are you here?"

Alphaeus hung his head, the hardness in his eyes deepening until their brown depths turned almost black. "The Elders knew of what I had done. They stripped me of that life and chained me to this one. For as long as ours and the human world exist I will remain here, haunted with the memory of her."

"Why don't we know of this?" Morpheus asked. "If it were to happen again, we could stop this."

"It seems a bit late for that," Alphaeus said knowingly. "You love this girl."

"I do," Morpheus confessed, "but I do not mean—"

"You will end it now," Alphaeus said, his voice low but deep with command. "Whether you mean for it or not, she will die. Her time is not yet here, and we do not meddle with the timelines of humans."

"What is the reason for why I cannot see her?" He already discerned the answer, but needed verification. His whole plan had overturned and he felt like a turtle on its shell, fixed to roll and roll and never flip back over.

"She is the last soul that will bring you forth as human."

As it seemed, his shell *had* been overturned in the sun where he lay to bake and rot, for this sudden luck he'd come by had vanished as soon as it had been bestowed.

18

BRIGH

Frustration oozed out of her every orifice as she took in her wooded surroundings. Felicity was nowhere in sight. Every tree looked the same, every moss patch floating in puddles of water in the same exact spots they were always in, and Morpheus, too, seemed absent.

"Just my luck," she muttered, wading a naked foot in a pool of Luke-warm water. Little fish tickled her toes as they swam past, their fins soft and rubbery.

"Fish don't live in puddles," Brigh whispered. "Not in forests, anyway."

"They only come out for humans," said a voice ahead of her.

Brigh's head shot up, but there was nothing in front of her. Rain slid inside the neck of her nightshirt, climbing down her back like a finger. Swinging around to look behind her told her nothing; the woods were a clear and wet thing.

"Hello?" Her voice echoed off the trees. Rain tapped the leaves like tribal drums.

She no longer wanted to be there. Her experiment had failed miserably and she was stuck wondering whether or not she was insane. Now she was hearing voices within the world of delusion. What else would go wrong?

She summoned the words she'd just heard, but could not remember them clearly; neither could she name the voice male or female. Imagining the words aglow in front of her, she tried to pick them apart, place them where they made sense in her mind. But in the end she couldn't recall them, a blunt headache the only reward for her trouble.

A tiredness stemming from her current weak state made her eyes flutter. She wanted to curl up in a nest of blankets and pillows and never wake up. The idea of a never ending dreamland caused a smile, and her weariness made it soft.

"Do not dream just yet," said the voice.

Brigh heard the words this time, but still could not pin down its gender. However, further study of the relevance and meaning of the words caused them to drift apart into useless syllables and letters.

She shook her head. The motion made her dizzy and, falling to her knees, she released that nauseous thought in a patch of neon green grass.

"Why do you come here?" the voice asked.

Brigh hung her head, letting her hair trail in the pool of vomit. "A friend of mine is here."

"I do not see him."

"He will be here." He had to be. The dizzy feeling came over her again, but she swallowed it along with her confusion. She couldn't remember why she'd said that.

"How can you be so certain?" This time the words were pronounced with soft lilting highs, higher so than Brigh's own voice. A figure appeared from behind a short evergreen, its features and figure somehow out of focus.

Brigh rapidly blinked, trying to slow the twitching of her eyes. She opened them for the moment it took to look at the figure until her vision blurred, her eyes stung, and her head felt as though it was going to burst. She felt unsteady and unsure.

"What's going on?" Brigh choked out, holding her head. She had to sit, there was no choice. She sunk to the ground, knocking water out of the puddle as her shirt swam in it.

"Have I frightened you?" The figure's voice sounded closer, but Brigh was afraid to check.

She hugged her arms, pulled up two shaking knees to her chest. "Stay away from me, please."

"Always so proper," it replied. Still, no matter how clear the voice seemed to get, the sex wasn't accessible.

"Why are you here?" Brigh asked, looking out ahead. In her peripheral vision she could make out a foot just beyond her puddle.

"Why are *you* here? Should you not be tucked in your sweet country bed now?"

"I, uh…" What did Brigh have in response? Before she could grasp the words, the question escaped her and she sat there feeling idiotic. "What are you doing to me? Where is Morpheus?"

"He had a prior engagement."

Brigh caught her breath. She hadn't meant to say his name, but how had the figure recognized it and knew where he was? It couldn't be true. Morpheus wouldn't leave her there, not anymore, not since that night. He always came, always read to her and held her within the cover of the weeping willows branches. This thing lied.

"He will be here soon, he will, I know it." Brigh pinched the bridge of her nose to keep from sneezing.

"You honestly believe that he is in love with you?"

Brigh looked up defiantly at the figure and recognized light green eyes the color of moss. The dizziness gripped her again, but she shook it off. She still couldn't make out the shape of the figure, but knew it to be a human shape. "Yes."

"He is not capable of love yet," it said monotonously.

Brigh gripped the moss to her right. "Any being is capable of love if they know what it is."

"Do you know what love is?"

Biting her lip, Brigh sighed, wondering why she was being asked this question.

"If you do not know what love is, how would he?" The thing knelt before her, fingers under her chin, lifting her head so their eyes met. In a swirl of foggy, blurry features Brigh saw nothing except for those bright green eyes, their saturation startling.

"Believe me, my dear, he knows *nothing*. You, on the other hand, I believe know the meaning of love. You are just not positive he is the one for whom you hold that feeling."

Without warning, it dropped Brigh's attention and began walking away. She felt more exhausted than ever, her head drooping as her eyes threatened to close on their own. More than just ill, she felt like she'd had the life sucked out of her.

"One last thing for you to ponder, Brianna Breen."

Her head felt as though it weighed a million pounds as she lifted it to meet the things eyes.

"Not everything is what it seems."

And then she was alone with her thoughts, which, in comparison to her norm, weren't very kind or innocent. Apparently, after this, not everything seemed to be what she'd first thought. And now she was left with even more questions than she'd started out with.

But why was she asking them?

R

Felicity tortured Brigh with all kinds of music whenever she rode in the beetle. Sometimes Brigh wondered if Felicity meant to or if her odd taste in music was just that: odd. But when it came to music in her car, Felicity thought she was Christina Aguilera, talent-wise.

"Do you think I should audition for the spring musical?" Felicity asked as she took the exit for their school.

Brigh grabbed the front of her seat as the turn became sharper and Felicity applied the brake only slightly. Her loose books on the floor of the car slid behind her. "Fee, do you think we could take it a little easy. I'd like to make it to college, if you don't mind."

Felicity leaned forward to check for cars as she proceeded to merge onto the road leading to the high school. Her hair was partly pulled back into a ponytail, the rest of it floating in the air as she rolled down her window. "Seriously, do you think I could make it in? My voice is pretty good. Maybe not amazing, but decent, right?"

"You sure you can do all that singing for that long?"

Felicity grinned at her. "I've sung a whole Abba record."

"Then yeah, I think you can make it."

Felicity turned up her music and started singing along. Brigh wasn't sure whether the lyrics were in another language or not, but she wasn't too fond of what she was hearing. What she really wanted was to talk about the experiment and to maybe find out why it hadn't worked. She remembered being in the forest, cold and confused and with soaked pajama pants, but nothing spectacular had happened. Like a comically horrifying clown crouched between them in the tight little beetle, they refused to acknowledge its face of failure and disappointment. But sometime, and she didn't know when, her and Felicity were going to get to the bottom of this dream world, whether they wanted to or not.

The schoolyard loomed ahead of them as they followed a line of cars into the parking lot. Several groups of people were clustered outside of the building, staving off the suddenly chilly air. Amelia and Chandra were already parked and waiting in Amelia's red Honda Civic with the engine running a few rows down from Felicity's spot. They headed over to the beetle as soon as it was parked, leaning into Felicity and Brigh's open windows.

"Got the heat on high enough in there?" Chandra remarked. Her afro was tied back with a paisley scarf. She looked like a singer form the seventies.

Felicity stuck her thumb in Brigh's direction. "Cold ass over here was complaining."

"I was not complaining," Brigh retorted. "A side effect of my medication is the chills. Give me a break."

"The Gateway beat me to it," Felicity said, and then opened her mouth like she was shocked she'd said such a thing when Brigh really knew Felicity was just being a smart ass.

Brigh smacked Felicity's shoulder lightly. "Help this cold ass out of your tiny car."

Felicity cut the engine and popped the emergency brake, joining Chandra and Amelia on Brigh's side as she opened the door. All three stood back, waiting for something to do, something to hold, or to help Brigh out of the car.

"I'm not dying," Brigh said, and then she pushed herself out of the low car. Felicity put a hand on her shoulder and she felt calmer from her doing it. There was something about seeing weak in front of her friends. Felicity had seen it before, and Chandra and Amelia to an extent. But she didn't want to seem or feel weak at all.

"Has anyone gotten the memo about after-school activities?" Amelia asked as their group moved slowly toward the school.

Felicity held her hand lightly against Brigh's back. "You know I don't read the newspaper."

"No," Chandra interrupted, "it wasn't in the paper. They passed out something from the county in first period. I didn't read it, so I don't know."

"Chan'," Amelia groaned. "You're supposed to bring the paper home for your parents. You didn't read it?"

"I was supposed to bring it home?" Chandra smiled at Brigh conspiratorially.

As Amelia gave Chandra the third degree, Felicity kept pace with Brigh's slow crutch-walk. "Those two are crazy."

"Crazy in love," Brigh said, looking over her shoulder at the pair holding hands. She smiled and then frowned. Would she and Morpheus ever be able to hold hands in public?

"I don't know why they need all the rest of us to know, though," Felicity remarked, looking uncomfortable.

Brigh smirked. "It's the same as a girl and guy going out."

"No, it's not."

Brigh sighed. Some people just didn't get it, and she knew it was futile to try to change Felicity's mind on the subject. "When will Kyle be back to school—have you talked to him?"

"He should be back in two weeks," Felicity answered with a shrug. "His mom is still holding onto him like a freaking stuffed animal."

"I hope he's okay," Brigh whispered. She didn't feel quite the same way about him as she had before. Suddenly it dawned on her that she hadn't thought of him much, and for that she felt guilty. They had both fallen through the floor. Their current predicament was the same, but she was the one able to move around, even though she used crutches.

"Me too," Felicity whispered back.

They headed through the wide doors and made their way through the throng of waiting teenagers. The hallway was full of laughter and cell phones ringing. Teachers stood outside the crowd trying to maneuver them further into the school, but none of their tactics seemed to work.

Until they walked in.

The noise level lowered, but didn't completely cease as Brigh and Felicity climbed through the large group. Whispers exploded around them, questions about Brigh's crutches and talk of that night at the Gateway. Felicity pushed people out of the way, being the older sister she always played, even though Brigh was older than her by five months.

The whispers drew her back into the past, back to the day after the accident. People had gawked at her then, whispered and sneered at her. She hadn't felt comfortable or completely safe then and now she felt its symmetry.

Once they'd broken through the gossipers, Felicity placed Brigh in front of their lockers while she ran to the bathroom for some paper towels. Brigh hadn't even noticed she'd been crying. Her cheeks were dry, but her lashes stuck together with her tears. She was tired, tired of everything and everyone. She wished people would give it up and stop talking about her. She was a different person from last year. What happened to her now had nothing to do with her a year ago.

Or did it?

"Was someone dumped over the phone?"

Brigh blinked the blurry image of Marissa into focus. She wore her hair in her face, whether to hide or to appear shy and sexy, Brigh wasn't sure. Skinny jeans hugged her thin legs without appeal and her shirt was bright pink and short sleeved. Her Coach purse hung heavy over one shoulder.

"I don't have time for your bullshit," Brigh said in a sigh.

Marissa was taken aback for a second, the shock clear on her face. Recovered with a sneer she said, "You think you're so hot, don't you."

"You have that covered for both of us." Brigh gave a little smile.

"Bitch," Marissa snarled in Brigh's face. "Just because you killed your mother, doesn't mean you're exempt from life."

Brigh sucked in a breath. She couldn't believe it. "You have no heart, do you?"

"At least mine isn't black like yours." Marissa pushed her hands onto her shapeless hips.

"Take that back!" Brigh said. She leaned into the wall for strength. She wanted to hide.

"Everyone knows you did it. Everyone knows you murdered your own mother."

Brigh bit her lip, trying to hold in the tears that threatened to escape.

"Just admit it," Marissa continued. "You didn't care about her. You never did. That's why you pushed her over the cliff."

A fist came out of nowhere and Marissa was suddenly on the ground. With wide eyes and a shocked mouth, Brigh looked over at Felicity. Her fist was still raised and her mouth in a thin line. Brigh had never seen her best friend so angry, and she'd definitely never seen her violent.

"Fee," Brigh whispered.

Felicity looked at her, her expression softening, and then followed Brigh's eyes to Marissa as she tried to stand. Felicity didn't move, didn't say a word. Her expression seemed peaceful almost, as though she'd accepted her actions. Brigh's heart raced as a teacher emerged from the curious group standing around them. He didn't look happy, especially when he saw who was involved.

"LeBlanc, McAllister," he said with a cigarette roughened voice. "Follow me to the principal's office."

Without a word or a backward glance, Felicity followed the teacher out of the hall toward the main office. The group dispersed after them, whispering and laughing, leaving Brigh alone and crying.

The chairs in the main office were unusually hard and uncomfortable, as though the administration wanted visitors to feel unnerved in the tiny waiting room. The walls were a sickly off-white color and the floor a dusty black carpet that showed every hair and bit of dirt. Brigh's guidance counselor had greeted her and so had the lady at the main desk, but she wasn't in a chatty mood, so they'd left her to her silence.

A shadow appeared at her feet.

"Ready?" Felicity asked.

She didn't have the happy-go-lucky smirk she always seemed to have. "Principal give you the third degree?"

Felicity shrugged, looking out the office windows, and picked up Brigh's backpack without comment.

Pushing herself up from the hard pleather chair, Brigh grabbed her crutches and hobbled behind. "What's wrong? What'd she say?"

Brigh's backpack dangled without security from Felicity's left shoulder. She didn't look back. "She suspended me."

"*What?*" Brigh gasped.

"Three weeks," Felicity said with a sigh. "I had the choice of in-school, but that's—it's bullshit, all bullshit."

Brigh hadn't felt so guilty in her entire life. It felt as though her heart had sunk past her ribs. "You should've let me handle it."

Felicity stopped in the middle of the hallway, her shoulders slumping slightly. Turning to face her, Felicity's long chestnut hair hid part of her face. "What would you have done? You used to be able to stand up to people like that."

Brigh looked at her feet. Her one leg was still wrapped in a cast while the other foot had on a bubblegum pink Chuck Taylor. Last year she'd almost broken that same leg. Funny how she'd managed to actually break it this time just from falling through a floor.

"There are a lot of things I used to do," Brigh said sadly. The truly sad part was that she still had the ability to do such things; she just didn't have the drive. Cheerleading used to be the only thing she ever thought about. She had originally planned to find a team to try out for and then see if they had a decent college in which she showed interest. But the drive for life after high school had somewhat died that night with her mom.

"I miss her, too," said Felicity. "She was there for me when my own mom couldn't be."

Brigh nodded, unable to speak. Her throat began to burn as the first few tears fell. Biting her lip and holding her breath usually staved off the rest of the tears, but as people started to stop and stare at her, she felt like a circus freak and the tears of sadness turned into tears of frustration and anger.

"Show's over!" Brigh screamed. "*Get out of here.*"

Felicity grabbed Brigh's arm and guided her through the hallway toward the auditorium exit. Few knew of this exit, and those in theatre production weren't quick to give it away. A lonely granite bench was pushed up against the side of the building, cigarette butts littering the dirt patch beside it.

"Let's sit for a little while and calm down," Felicity whispered soothingly. She sat Brigh down on the bench and knelt in front of her, holding her hands tightly. "Everything will be okay."

Brigh shook her head; her lips pulled back, eyes unloading a storm cloud of salt water. "Nothing's been okay. Everything's been screwed up ever since she died. How could I be so stupid?"

"Honey," Felicity said, shaking her hands, "it wasn't your fault."

Brigh's eyes bore into Felicity's, seeking refuge. "It was my fault. I let her go. *I let her go.*"

"No one would've been able to do what you did. *No one.* You hear me?" Felicity dropped Brigh's hands and grabbed her shoulders. "Listen to me. Your mom was going to fall. No matter what you did. If you had gone any further you would've fallen too."

"I don't care," Brigh yelled, her words coarse from crying. "I need her—I want her back!"

19

BRIGH

She'd never thought being home could be more depressing than being in school. Sitting in her bed reminded her of all the sleepless nights and wet pillowcases. The four walls surrounding her were filled with images and shadows of her past. Her father had always scolded her from the doorway when she'd misbehaved or when her and Rich had gotten into a little brawl. Rich always invaded her privacy, no matter how many times she'd yelled at him. Having her room locked made no difference. Locks were only good for honest people. Not that Rich wasn't trustworthy, he just wasn't when it came to terrorizing his older sister.

Brigh found herself looking at her mother's painting as she sometimes did when she was a slave to her own thoughts. The thick, harsh strokes of the Easter-egg-color acrylics instantly brought a smile to her face. At a quick glance, the canvas looked like someone had just splattered paint and drug a brush through it, haphazardly rubbing it in. But a second look would show the observer that a house lay hidden in those swirls and waves of paint, a house and animals of several species and people whose emotions could not be fully interpreted.

Just after her mother had finished the painting, she asked Brigh what she thought the people were thinking. Brigh told her mother that the people were happy, though not always pleasant to be around. But together they seemed at ease with their existence and whether others found their company appealing didn't matter to them.

Brigh's interpretation of those people changed over the years since her mother framed it and hung it by her door, but her feelings about them had stayed positive. Now, as she glared at the dust blowing away from where it clung, she saw nothing positive about their bent and protruding statures. The various shades of green from her own paintings crowded her bed like a protective circle. Looking at them after critiquing her mother's work, she saw nothing original or fantastic within their small glimpses of the world.

The door swung open and a crop of brown hair was the first thing Brigh saw.

"What do you want, Rich?" she asked, suddenly finding a small tear in her comforter fascinating.

He pushed his way into her room, knocking over a painting. Bending to right it, he looked up and around her room. "Want anything from the kitchen?"

"No thanks."

"Want any movies?" he asked, standing straight. "I bought *Scrubs* on DVD yesterday."

"No thanks."

Rich sighed and made his way through the din to sit on the edge of her bed. "Billy asked about you the other night."

"Billy?"

He gave his sister an awkward smile. "Yeah. 'Poker Bill.' He and dad kick each other's asses every Sunday night."

Brigh nodded. "The guy with the long gray hair and Jack Sparrow mustache?"

Rich laughed. "Dad says the next time he wins he's making Billy shave that thing off."

Brigh shook her head. "Never going to happen."

"Nah, I guess not."

Brigh caught her brother's eye. They were a lighter green than her mother's, but slightly darker than her own. His cheekbones weren't as sharp and defined as their fathers, but they hinted at the possibility. Once upon a time, Brigh had felt near murderous about wanting her brother's hair, but now she accepted and appreciated their differences. He was more like their mother, and her like their father.

"Its mom, isn't it?" Rich asked suddenly, his voice somber as he adjusted his seat on the bed nervously.

Brigh opened her mouth to breathe through it. "Isn't it always?"

Richard looked away, rubbing his face and then his hair. "I thought it would go away. The questions—how people could be so horrible."

"People will always be that way; today, tomorrow, forever. A single event in history wouldn't change a thing."

Richard stood from the bed so fast he knocked off a blanket. With a sigh he bent and picked up the blanket, constricting it between his fingers. "I wish last year didn't happen."

"Mom wouldn't want that."

He turned on her, the blanket dropping back to the floor. "What the hell do you know about what mom would've wanted?"

"I mean that she wouldn't want you to have missed the state championship. You guys won."

"I don't care about that," Richard said. His cheeks grew red, a reaction to a twist of anger and embarrassment their mother had always exhibited. "I wasn't the one who won the game, so what do I care?"

"Rich," Brigh said in shock and exasperation. "Don't say that. It was a phenomenal game and you know mom would be happy for you."

"I can't talk about this," he said quickly. Without picking her blanket up like he would on a normal occasion as the sweet younger brother, he pushed aside the many canvases—both finished and near completion—and practically ran out of her room.

He wasn't her brother.

She wasn't herself.

They, along with their father, had died the night their mother had. Richard had seemed to be the only one who'd walked away unscathed. But apparently Brigh's assumption wasn't correct. What had once made him her brother was gone, and the only thing that would change it would be the life whose end had ruined them all.

She nestled uncomfortably further under the blankets and between her pillows, hoping to hide from reality and the image of her mother's painting. The figures stashed away in a sea of colors no longer mattered. They no longer had feelings. No longer bore hearts. No longer breathed.

"Please," she pleaded as the first tears fled her eyes.

She needed to see him, needed his arms cradling her like a newborn, speaking words of hope that he would never truly understand. She needed his false hope to continue.

Closing her eyes, she waited for sleep to come. For many minutes her thoughts lay far back in her mind. Her fingers relaxed, toes twitching from the silence of commands. The ache in her shoulders seemed to dissipate. But after those minutes of relaxation were over, when she opened her eyes, her room was still wrapped around her.

Fear invaded, and suddenly her heart rate piqued like she'd been running a marathon. Snapping her eyes shut, she pictured the forest, imagined liquid mud making disgusting noises between her toes. The scent of pine and holly and earth met her nose, and when she opened her eyes this time, she was in her forest.

He was there. His broad shoulders and thick torso were so still he didn't look alive. With his back to her, she thought he didn't know she was present. Her heart flipped, her air intake dwindling as she spurred forward, calling his name. He turned just in time for her to jump into his arms. She hugged him tight, his solidity comforting her more than anything she thought could.

Kissing his cheek, she spoke his name. He felt more real than any living thing in her world. But as she hugged him tighter, she noticed that his arms weren't holding her back and that his spine was tall and straight and stiff.

Pulling back, she looked at his face. His eyes were unmoving, looking at something away from her. There were frown lines around his mouth that she'd never noticed before and his eyes looked haunted.

"What's wrong?" she asked, the sinking feeling in her chest growing.

He didn't say anything, looking as though he couldn't manage to force his mouth to open. His eyes found hers, though, after a moment, and in them her thoughts of insecurity, misunderstanding, and fear were mirrored.

"Morpheus?" she asked again. "Say something, please, you're scaring me."

The ground earned his attention as he looked away from her. "I cannot do this."

Several times she blinked. The rain started to pick up, soaking her clothes, pasting her hair to her neck. "Can't do what?"

As though it pained him, he looked at her again. His jaw was clenched, lips thinner as he opened his mouth. "I cannot see you anymore."

Never before had it felt as though she were falling and couldn't find an end to it. An ache started in her chest, a pinch that made her eyes fill with tears and grab her chest. She shook her head like it would make his words go away or make sense.

"This, between us, it is wrong," he said.

She opened her mouth. Sucked in a sob. "Did I do something? Something w-wrong?"

His eyes widened slightly, his features screwing up in a beautiful mess. "No—not you. It—I—" Hanging his head, he wouldn't look at her. "This just cannot be. You and I—it is vile and disgusting."

Anger reared its ugly head within her. She wanted to run, scream, and hit something. Hitting him seemed preferable to a tree, but she couldn't make herself do it. She couldn't hurt him even though he was slowly tearing her heart apart.

"How can you say that?" she spat.

He jerked like she'd hit him, but other than that he didn't seem affected. His eyes were pleading with her to understand. "Because it is. Can you not see it? The both of us, this place—it is all terribly wrong."

Fat, hot tears snaked their way free. Her cheeks burned with humiliation and an anger that made her whole body catch a fever. "*If you felt that way, then why didn't you bring it up before?*"

He stepped toward her, which made her step away. "Because I did not feel it before."

"Feel?" she screamed. Her throat felt clogged and gross. "You can *feel* now?"

"Brigh, I—"

"No!" she shouted, getting up in his face. She punched his chest, and punched him again when the first didn't seem to faze him. She wanted him to feel, to hurt like she did. How could he come to her like this in the world he'd drawn her to so many nights, make her believe there was something between them when everything was a lie. "How dare you tell me you *did not feel it before*. What do you think I am—an idiot?"

Anger blazed in his eyes as she hit him again with his words. He grabbed her forearms, the strength in them biting her skin, scaring her. "You do not understand. You are young and still have much to learn."

She pulled out of his arms, tugging with all she was worth. "You're an expert on humans now? You're not even alive! As far as anyone's concerned, you're a figment of my imagination!"

His eyes hardened. "Then treat me in such a way."

A sob wracked her angry stride and all she wanted to do was touch him and for his arms to comfort her. "I love you, Morpheus."

His jaw tightened once more, but this time there was finality to the look in his eyes. "I do not love you."

"We have something special and you know it," she yelled, trying to find a reasonable argument that would change his mind. She'd been top of her debate class. "Why are you going to throw it all away and be an asshole?"

He grabbed her shoulders, shaking her like a doll. Any hint at the possibility of the kindness she'd wanted from him was no longer there. "*Listen* to me damnit. Nothing you do or say will change my mind. What we have is not real—this world is not real. I cannot pick you up from school or meet your father. I cannot take you to the theatre or cheer in the stands with your friends at a football game."

"I don't care about that." So this is what this was all about? He felt impotent when it came to her? How could that be? She'd given him power over her, even though the action was unintentional. She'd given him her heart long before she had the word for what was flowing through her.

"In time you will," he said. "You are still young—it will take time for you to understand."

She hadn't liked her mom and dad telling her what to do and Morpheus definitely did not receive a pass when it came to her free will and choice. "Who are you to say I'm young? You haven't even lived."

"I have been here for one hundred years."

"It doesn't matter—it's not the same thing." She choked on the words, the tears coming, the nauseous feeling in her stomach rising. She couldn't catch her breath, but she pushed through to finish her thought. "You haven't had to make hard choices or do things you didn't want to. You don't need to breathe or sleep. How can you stand there and tell me I'm young and that I don't understand?" She shook her head. She couldn't continue. She couldn't find the words to express the way she felt. There were none. "I never should've come here. This was all a fucking waste."

Turning, she walked away from Morpheus's still form, never chancing to look into his eyes. If she saw any remorse or sadness she would break and give him another chance. If he felt anything for her, she'd go to him. She knew it was hopeless to think that she no longer loved him, that she hated him. It wasn't possible to go from loving someone so unconditionally one moment and then hate them the next. The hope that maybe he did love her made her turn around. But there was only empty space between the pine trees. She sat heavily into a mud puddle, the water sluicing around her, clinging to her pajamas.

The rain began to pour.

20

MORPHEUS

Her sadness and hatred for him had been palpable, and it took every ounce of energy he had not to go back to her and try to explain and apologize. Not that she would listen to him. She was too smart to make such an idiotic mistake.

He knew the subject of idiocy very well. He'd compromised his whole existence to be with her and had in turn done the same to her. She just didn't understand, couldn't know. He'd thought explaining the whole situation to her would help her deal with what he was asking of her. But when he'd seen the joy and relief on her face when she'd come to him, it had crushed the kindness he'd hoped to use. For if he'd shown her any, she wouldn't hate him. Hating him would help her move on; help her understand in the end that he could be nothing more than a figment in the past of her imagination. She would move on and find someone. Perhaps Kyle or someone of equal intellectuality to her own. He couldn't help hating the idea of her being with another, but after what he'd just put her through, he had no right to complain.

Pushing open the door to his room, he stopped mid-step in the doorway as the image of his occupied cot filled his vision.

"Get out," he growled.

Narelle rolled her eyes. "I missed you as well."

He strode across the room and grabbed her arms, yanking her to her feet. "How could you?"

She stumbled away from him, rubbing her arms. "It is rather simple. You see, I—"

"You told him," he yelled in her face. "You...told him about Brigh. How could you betray my trust? I thought you cared."

Pushing him back, she glared as he stumbled. "You truly are bent if you think it was I who gave you and your foolish obsession away."

He shook his head. "You expect me to believe that? You have never approved or particularly liked the idea of her."

"I did not approve of your infatuation with her. This had nothing to do with her, Morpheus. You sought her out, *you* created this obsession. *You* not *her*. She is the innocent. You are the one at fault."

Morpheus wanted to rip his hair out. The woman was insane. "Your jealousy is suffocating."

"At least now you notice," she said in a small voice.

"I have known," he admitted. Allowing her knowledge of this fact made him feel uneasy.

She marched across the room to where he now stood, her hips persuading his masculinity. "Then why not confront it? Why not abandon this love affair that is never going to last and accept my adoration, for we truly can be together."

"It is because our union can be so easy that I do not want it."

And before Narelle could respond, he left her standing by his cot and shut his door on any retorts she may have created through her shock and embarrassment.

R

He was talking with another when Morpheus punched him in the face. Bloodying it gave him satisfaction, for the hideous mess he'd created would no longer attract those of his kind, even if only briefly. The thought of his destruction only being brief didn't squander his inner celebration.

"What in the name of—"

"Good," Morpheus said. "You are bleeding. Seems your humanity will soon be rewarded."

Morpheus didn't offer a hand to help Darius stand and neither of them made comment of the lack of friendly interaction.

With a sigh and looking sullen, Darius blotted his nostrils that were no longer spouting blood with his shirt. "My apologies."

"No apology will ever right what you have done."

Darius shook his head. "It was not right to keep something like this from Alphaeus. He needed to know."

"I should have been the one to tell him," said Morpheus. "Not you."

Darius shrugged and then turned from Morpheus and sauntered down the hall. Morpheus took a step forward with the intention to follow Darius, but thought better of it, and headed in the direction opposite from his traitorous friend and jealous mentor.

21

BRIGH

As fall descended upon the quiet town of Cumberland, the days became cool and the nights a deadly freeze. The trees had already begun to lose their leaves, piles of yellow, maroon, and pink littering the ground. A dull sky hung over the empty streets, abandoned factories, and train track that'd once been the town's main source of income.

Felicity and Brigh rode in silence on the way out of town, the radio a small noise in the corner of their tensely knit suppression of words. Mountains chased them as though wanting to follow their escape, brightly colored leaves dancing in their wake. As Brigh stared out the window, her mouth dry and her throat scratchy, she watched the last of the houses disappear behind them as they hit the highway.

"What exit?" Felicity asked monotonously.

"Twenty-two," Brigh replied without looking at her.

Felicity's reflection in the window nodded. The music grew louder, some seventies band vibrating through the car.

Brigh clutched the leather parcel tightly in her lap, her fingers pinching the thin suede ties holding it closed. The leather was brown and aged from years of use, years she hadn't seen. Stains colored the hide darker in spots from spilled paint and charcoal smears that'd never been cleaned. Her mother hadn't been particularly careful with her possessions, which was why everything she'd owned had had paint stains on them: clothes, hats, shoes, dishes. Nothing in their house had been saved from her creative monster.

One specific instance Brigh treasured above all others was the first time her mother had brought her to Tinker's Hill. The giant mound wasn't really a hill, but a little manmade mountain. No one knew for sure who'd built it, but many had come out in the past to paint and take photographs.

"Which way?" Felicity asked.

Brigh took in a breath and let it out. "Left at the fork. Ignore the stop sign. No one comes down here anymore."

Felicity nodded in acknowledgement and took the left. So much had changed since Brigh was a child. So many trees had burned or been cut down for firewood. The brush no longer crowded the base of each tree, vines that were big enough for Tarzan to swing from were also absent. Ten years since the last time she'd set foot near the mound, and she regretted every second.

"Sure you don't want me to wait?" Felicity asked, as they came to a crawl through a narrow path between the two walls of trees.

Brigh couldn't take her eyes off of the tall dogwoods surrounding them. Their smooth bark was interrupted by the carvings of sweethearts and dates and quotes. Somewhere, her father had carved his and her mother's initials, but she couldn't remember which tree he'd branded.

"You can if you want," Brigh mumbled. "But I'll be a while. You'll get bored."

"I could stand to practice my lines."

Brigh wanted to draw the warmth from Felicity's words, but inside she felt so bitter. She forced a smile to brighten her face even though the energy taken to do it made her tired. "If you can help me with my supplies up the thing I'd appreciate it. But after that I'll be fine."

"I know," Felicity said. She didn't look at Brigh, as though knowing a glance would crumble her confident façade. She hadn't spoken much about her suspension, neither had she mentioned Brigh's quiet and miserable mood. "You just have a tendency to fall down a ways. Someone needs to be there to catch you."

"If I fall, there's something wrong with me," Brigh said, "Not what I'm falling off of. The mound isn't steep or even that tall."

Felicity sighed and turned off the radio. The breaking of sticks under tires snapped Brigh's attention quickly away from Felicity's inner turmoil. Several more trees and they'd be near the clearing. Soon the natural and the modern world would switch, and the sounds of birds and squirrels knocking twigs and evergreen needles from their posts would replace the blaring car horns and obnoxiously loud radio music she had to deal with every day.

"I'm worried." Felicity stopped just inside the clearing under the shade of some trees. The mound was still there, the almost neon green grass unruly and tall.

She'd have to stamp down a patch of the grass to set up her stool and canvas, but other than the time that would take, nothing about what stood in front of them worried her.

"I'm not," Brigh said with a smile. She unbuckled her seatbelt and slowly pushed herself out of the passenger seat. The air was cold and crisp, the smell of a burning woodstove in the air. The sun hid behind passing clouds in the shapes of disfigured animals, but the light was just right for her to paint.

"Help me?" Brigh asked as she rounded the rear of the beetle.

Felicity nodded, looking over her shoulder.

Brigh grabbed her canvas and sketch pad and left her stool and paints for Felicity. Curling up and around the mound was a smooth, dirt walkway outlined by boulders of a gray color. The first step brought a memory to mind, one she had thought lost to her.

That day had been cold and snowing instead of the start of fall. Her mother's blonde hair had been splotched with melted snow, cheeks pink. She'd carried all the supplies without a word of instruction, and led Brigh up the mound.

"Why are we here?" Brigh had asked, her gaze to the sky as dark clouds rolled in.

"We," her mother grunted, setting down her equipment in the middle of the mound, "are here because this is the best view in town."

Brigh had wrinkled her nose in complete confusion. "All I see are trees."

"That's because you're not looking hard enough." Setting up her stool and canvas, she untied the leather parcel and pulled out a fat charcoal pencil. Before Brigh knew it, lines were beginning to curve on the canvas, creating shapes she'd never dreamed of.

"I still can't see anything, momma."

The disbelieving look on her mother's face made her laugh, and in turn a giggle burst from the older woman's throat. "Don't look with your eyes. You have to feel it."

"That makes no sense," Brigh said defensively.

Her mother put down her drawing pencil, wiping her blackened fingers across her jeans, and patted her knee for Brigh to sit. With one arm wrapped around Brigh's stomach, her mother pointed at the trees, flicking her fingers to grab attention.

"See there? The bird in the tree?"

Brigh saw the black bird, which her mother explained to her was a raven, and couldn't understand why she pointed him out. It was doing nothing spectacular, except maybe twitching its head back and forth constantly. She had never seen a bird dressed all in black, especially since it seemed like it was ready for a funeral. Its eyes, body, and legs were as dark as coal.

"What do you see?" her mother asked.

Brigh bit her bottom lip, sucking it in until her flesh ached. "I see black."

"Excellent!" she exclaimed with a gorgeous smile on her face. "Where do you think he'll be off to?"

"A nest?"

Brigh's mother nodded, hugging her daughter so tight she thought breath would never come back to her. "Can you imagine all of the places he'll see? They're very smart, but they're always alone. Why do you think that is?"

Brigh shrugged. "He's big. Maybe the other birds are scared of him."

Her mother sighed. "It's possible. I think it's because they're so smart. They want more out of existence than nature gives them."

"Do they like people?" Suddenly Brigh wanted to pet the creature, especially after it looked in their direction with a knowing gaze. Did it know who they were discussing?

Brigh's mother shook her head. "Well, maybe. Mostly if you have food. But I wouldn't let it get too close. It might peck."

Felicity walked in front of Brigh, destroying the image of her and her mother so long ago. The branches that the raven had been clutching to were bare, shaking in the rushing wind. Brigh's loose tangled hair fluttered around her like the ghost of so many lost or forgotten memories she did not wish to remember.

"You okay?" Felicity asked.

Brigh sucked in an icy breath and winced as her throat burned with it. "I wish people would stop asking me that."

Felicity shrugged. "It's better to be asked than to be ignored. Have everything you need?"

With a nod, Brigh sat on the stool, ignoring the tall grass around her. "Yeah. Pick me up in an hour?"

Felicity tucked her red fists inside her jacket pockets. "I'll call you before then. Just to check in."

"Thanks," Brigh said with a smile. "See you soon."

"Yeah," was all Felicity said before she turned and disappeared down the hill.

Silence settled lightly on Brigh's shoulders. The wind swirled around her, creating little tornados of hair in her face. Birds chirped and sang in the distance, the loud feathery sound of the grass filling her ears with music. Unwrapping the parcel in her lap, she pulled out her mother's charcoal pencil. She studied it for a minute, at how short it was, how dull and rounded the tip. Of course her mother had many pencils like this one, but the one in which she held was the only one she remembered.

Picking up her empty canvas, she set it up on her easel and began drawing. She didn't allow herself any thoughts, didn't allow anything to travel through her brain except the music around her. The tips of grass tickled the back of her neck, catching in her hair. It felt as though someone else was there with her. Her muse, maybe, but maybe even some essence of her mother. She'd loved this hill, had traveled the half hour to it every day and would stay for hours. Her father had had to call her home for dinner most nights because she'd lost track of time.

Brigh wanted that. To lose track of time, to escape into this wilderness her mother had founded and cultivated as her own. She needed the wind to help her breathe, needed the songs of the animals in the woods, and needed the grass to sway. Only then did she fully exist, and only then did she feel complete.

"Go away," she whispered.

The feeling of being watched hovered over her like the thing she knew to be watching. But he'd turned her away. He couldn't be watching her—she was imagining things. The hope was too much.

But she whispered again, as though repetition would push him out of her mind, "*Go. Away. Morpheus.*"

MORPHEUS

Her words hit him like a fist, unrelenting and unforgiving. But he took them and bottled them so they would last and he would fully understand the pain they meant to inflict.

But he couldn't leave her. Not yet. She seemed so sad on the outside, but a calmness he didn't understand floated around her pupils. He knew he'd destroyed a part of her, but he wanted deeply to patch the hole he'd created. If only he hadn't been chained against seeing her. If only he hadn't been found out. Deceived. Betrayed.

"I will see you again," he muttered. And by *see* he meant touch and kiss and hold. She would be his again. He just did not know how.

Yet.

22

BRIGH

"Where have you been?" Jairus asked Brigh right as she opened the front door.

She hadn't expected anyone to be home. Richard was most likely off with a football buddy and Jairus was supposed to still be at work. Felicity had helped Brigh put her art supplies in the garage and then she'd left with just a wave.

"I've been out," Brigh said. The front door stood half open behind her. The vulnerability she felt by standing with her back to an open door made her shoulders tense and want to lock it. But any movement would spur her father on and she wanted to get away from this awkwardness and head to bed.

Jairus uncrossed his arms. He was still in his work clothes, mud spackled and caked to his blue jeans like a lost lover clawing its way to serenity. "Where were you?"

"It's none of your business."

Jairus bounded through the hall to Brigh, towering over her with his unshaven face and dirty hair. "It is my business when you're skipping school."

Brigh held her ground. She didn't much care for intimidation, but he was her father and she respected him. But at that moment she just wanted to climb into bed and sleep to the point of death. "So what if I skip one day? I've had perfect attendance until this accident."

"You're graduating in a couple of months," Jairus fumed, "do you really want to throw thirteen years down the drain just because you don't feel like going anymore?"

"It's my life," Brigh yelled back. "I can do whatever I want."

"I am your father!" Jairus screamed, grabbing hold of her forearms. "You do as you are told, by me, until you are eighteen and out of my house. Got it?"

"Mom wouldn't have cared," Brigh muttered.

Jairus let go of Brigh like she was a scalding hot stove. "Your mother would've beaten your ass for back talking. She definitely would have cared."

"How do you know?" Brigh shouted. "The last couple weeks of her life you two never talked. You were never home. She was always out painting. Why are you taking it out on me that she died?"

"Because you let her go!" In his exclamation, Brigh saw so many things. She'd felt that he'd blamed her. But she'd never received confirmation of the fact.

"You think I meant to let her go? Do you think I wanted her to die?" Tears stung Brigh's eyes and burned along her burning cheeks. "You are a fucking asshole if you for one second think I wanted mom to die. I never...I never wanted...she was my...you worthless, unfeeling son of a *bitch*."

Feeling cold all over, Brigh turned and ran upstairs as fast as her cast would allow her. Her door slammed so hard behind her, her arms prickled with the vibration. As she faced her room, the first object in her line of vision was a painting leaning against the side of the bed. It was the largest canvas she'd ever used, the size of which being so large she could curl up on top of it and leave edges untouched by her body.

Her eyes narrowed. Something about the painting just didn't click. The different shades of green didn't blend well—she could see the lines. Her circles and squares were misshapen and ultimately disfigured the artwork. She couldn't even see the purpose or the subject of the piece. What had she been thinking?

With the growl of a dissatisfied artist, she strode to the painting and tore at the edges of the canvas, ripping it free from the wood. Once in two pieces, she continued the havoc of ripping and shredded the painting in frayed sections. But her fury didn't end there. Every painting in her gaze received the same annihilation as the last until her floor stood as the battleground of an enraged teenager. She cried out in frustration once there was nothing left for her to tear apart.

Wait...

Slowly, she turned to her wall, to the painting that had collected dust and scrutiny and aversion. What had made this painting special? Out of all her mother's pieces of art, why had her eye been drawn to only this one? Their garage was full of them. Canvases, sketch books, furniture that had been attacked by pencil and brush and fingertips.

She grabbed it from the wall, thrusting her fingertips underneath the edge of the fabric, breaking it free. Slashed and split and gashed, she decimated the piece before any form of rationality met her. Soon the multihued painting was nothing but dusty rags in her hands, shaking with dwindling adrenaline.

Thorburn whined from under her bed, his nose peaking out underneath the edge of the comforter. His perpetually drooping eyes seemed even sadder as he gazed up at her.

"Thorburn," she called, patting her knee. She dropped the remnants of the painting, hearing the material smack thickly against the splintered wood at her feet. A sob wracked her and the dog came immediately, rubbing against her thighs.

She clung to his coarse hair for a moment, savoring his warmth and solidity, then locked her door, led the animal to her bed, and helped boost him onto the mattress. He waited until she'd changed into her pajamas and situated herself under the covers before relaxing and curling up alongside her, his head resting heavily on her stomach.

Absentmindedly, Brigh patted and petted her dog's head for a while before her throat tightened and a replay of her father's face and angry words resurfaced. Once again she was lost in a rocking sea of sorrow and pain, her mind torturing her with different plays of his words. Images of the paintings lost under her hands.

She wanted to curl up on her side and die, like the world was going to crash on top of her. But when Thorburn whined again, nudging her hand with his frigid nose, she abandoned all hopeless thoughts and curled around the animal instead. His body anchored her, made her feel again. She tore at his hair, pulled on his ears, clinging as though she were falling into a bottomless abyss. She whispered apologies and promises to him, and as much as she feared she'd hurt him, Thorburn didn't whine again, the animal already beginning a quiet rumbling snore.

MORPHEUS

Without a word to anyone, he pushed himself into their domain, awakening them from an immortal sleep that made them see their future. Some shuddered, some exhaled discontent, and some just stared at him as though, through him, they saw nothing.

Their attempts to give him any excuse possible were faltered as he shouted, "Elders! Do not play me any longer. I beseech you in the most humble of ways. Tell me when I will be made."

Whispers erupted, and though Morpheus could not understand their language, he did understand anger as they glared at him.

You have no say of what we do.

You are no more than a fledgling.

Your time has not yet come to us.

"How do you know?" he asked. "Tell me. How is it you determine us? Did you make us? Do you create our timelines?"

He heard a sigh go through them as they all settled in their chairs around him, but one leaned forward, its shadowed face seemingly empty and abandoned. As it spoke, long arms extended forward from its cloak, large hands flicking back and forth with its words. *You ask too many questions that we cannot, by any order, answer truthfully. Every being's energy is different and most times difficult to analyze.*

"Can you change it?" he asked. "Is there any way you can speed up the process or change a certain soul we are meant to consume?"

The Elder's hood swayed side to side. *Meddling in the affairs of your ascension is not in our interest, and not at all in your best interest. Altering something can intersect lines of the future that are not meant to cross. Who knows what could go amiss.*

"But if you knew of what lay in the future," Morpheus went on, forcing his words out without thinking of the consequences, "could follow the lines and know of what is to occur, you could rearrange them to fit without great sacrifice?"

There was a collective pause throughout the Elders, all back to whispering in that awful language that wormed through Morpheus's brain like needles. He didn't feel pain, just an uneasy sort of invasion of privacy.

Since your last visit we have determined your time, said an Elder from his right, directly across from the first Elder who spoke.

He felt sudden annoyance at this news, as though he wanted to jump in their face. "And why wait to reveal this intelligence?"

The Elder cocked its hooded head to the side. *Your questions would not have led you to this knowledge.*

Morpheus shook his head, blinking several times as though nothing would come in focus. "Do you know of the name of the soul?"

All of the Elders nodded in slow, synchronized movements.

Most precious, it is.

A piece to the puzzle.

Very glorious, we are sure.

"Who is it?" Morpheus demanded, his patience escaping him.

Brianna Elizabeth Breen.

He hung his head, fists growing tight at his sides. He'd known. But knowing and being told were two completely different animals. Knowing, without interference from another source, there is a biased opinion and hope. Whereas, with the subject of being told, one allows another's morals and opinions to either mix with their own or destroy what they once believed. Being told always hit deeper and harder than one expected.

"It cannot be her," he whispered.

The Elders leaned forward, with what looked to be resemblances of nostrils peaking out of their hoods. *You question our ability?*

Morpheus shook his head. "Can this be changed? Can she be saved?"

There is nothing we can do; her essence has started becoming a part of you. Can you not feel it?

He shuddered at the thought of his recently changed eye color and nervous tendencies and knowledge of things he'd rather not know. "I do not want this for her. She needs to live. Her family and friends need her."

She has no choice, the Elder nearest him growled in his brain. *Her soul is not her own, and it will be split without need of her consent.*

Morpheus felt like he'd been slapped. The Elders were not commonly gentle creatures, and their voices no louder than a whisper, but the intensity of their words could easily anger or sadden any being. Right then he felt hopeless. How could he stop the inevitable? He thought it possible to be reassigned another soul as though every human were like stocks in a version of their own stock market. But any hope that vibrated with certain negativity was bound to end badly.

"What is the date of her death?"

The thirty-first of October of this human year.

Morpheus's head snapped up, running an image of the human calendar through his mind's eye. "No. That cannot be right. You have given me tomorrows date—"

And we have not failed or misrepresented ourselves.

Morpheus searched the darkness of their domain, the complete lack of anything material or light. Could these creatures be wrong? He did not think so. So many of his friends and teachers had been made flesh on the exact specified dates the Elders had given them. They'd predicted many human tragedies, as well as inhuman, that had been made true. Whether they held sway over events throughout the dimensions, Morpheus wasn't sure. But he did know the Elders could not be wrong.

They knew far too much.

23

BRIGH

The forest dream world came upon her without her knowing her eyes had closed. This world around her seemed frozen. No longer did rain pelt the leaves above her or the puddles at her feet. Bird calls were silenced, and the common sounds of the wind in the trees were also gone.

She clutched at her forearms, rubbing the chill she felt from this silent world. The ground was still muddy, pools of fish all over the ground and water dripping from the leaves above. Why this world had seemed to stop, she didn't know. The answer wouldn't have calmed or satisfied her. There were many things she didn't know about this world, and she was positive the answer to her question would not be one she would like.

A rustle in the brush to her left caught her attention, her body turning and walking toward the noise almost on reflex. Curiosity pushed back any uncertainties she may have had about investigation.

"Morpheus?" she called softly.

What if the noise hadn't been created by him? What if she wasn't truly alone in this forest? Again, questions she'd rather not have the answers to.

Instead of calling out his name a second time, she decided to head toward the noise. Images of idiotic blondes in horror movies walking to their deaths came instantly to mind, but she didn't care. That was fiction, this was reality. Well, even this world wasn't her reality, but a manipulation—a play—on what she'd known for seventeen years.

She picked through the brush, carefully escaping hideous rose bushes whose petals had all but wilted and rotted on their stems. Rotten logs tried tripping her, but after the first two that were hidden beneath leaves under her feet, she made sure to test the ground ahead of her before putting all her weight on her foot.

An outline came into view through the thin trees, and she noticed it only because it kept moving. Her skin felt too tight, the intensity of identifying this thing almost driving her mad. She wanted to run to it, wanted to touch it and know the creature's chemical makeup.

Pushing two full tree limbs out of the way gave her a clear view. From the rear, it looked like a dog, the tail curled up as though it'd been clipped off. But on further inspection, she noticed the legs were covered in scales of colors that changed when she blinked. Without view of the head, she wasn't sure if this creature was a dog.

A dark red caught her eyes, dragging her gaze to the ground at the creature's feet. Another animal lay still beneath it, one Brigh couldn't identify. Several gashes crawled up the injured creature's legs, the source of the blood pool coming from a slash in its throat. Clouded eyes stared at her from beneath its predatory victor.

She stifled the intake of breath she knew was going to be loud. Backing up, she lifted her feet high enough so she wouldn't trip, all her movements slow and calculated. *Like in gym*, she thought. But in gym they hadn't had an obstacle course filled in with wet and dry leaves, mud puddles, and fallen trees. She reached behind her and grasped tightly to a thorny vine, gasping as the pain from the puncture marks leapt up her arm.

She bit her lip, continuing her backtrack when the creature's head shot up unexpectedly fast, startling her so much that she slammed her foot down and tripped backward. She didn't fall, and for that she was grateful when she saw that the creature's eyes were looking into hers, crimson blood dripping from its lips, bits of flesh crammed in between giant incisors as it snarled. When its lips pulled back, she noticed that half of the left side of its face was missing. Bone and muscle shone slick and red around giant teeth.

Brigh had no choice in the matter—she screamed. She felt her cheeks grow red and her throat lock up as she turned and ran. A loud snapping noise followed her and she swung to the left, but was cut off as the creature leapt in front of her.

Like a giant black Australian Bandog infected with rabies, led by long snakelike wisps emerging from all over its body, the creature bared its teeth with what looked to be a grin. It seemed artificial somehow, the coat thick and glossy—but the shine came from a dark liquid suffocating its grimy hair. Intelligent citrine eyes measured her every move, and when she stood stock still, she imagined it watching her every intake of breath.

Never before in her nightmares had such a creature appeared. Her mind kept trying to shut off the questions concerning the purpose of each extra tentacle or row of teeth, but the answers seemed to file in long before the question marks were vanquished.

"Good doggie," she found herself whispering. She took a slow step back, moving at the speed of a timid box turtle. But the thing matched her step, only its stride overpowered hers by at least a foot. Now it was closer to touching her than it had been before she'd moved.

She weighed her options, corresponded the probabilities with the growing speed of her heartbeat. The time it would take to turn and run in the direction behind her would give the beast the advantage and it'd be on her in seconds. Right or left would buy her some time with the close-knit forest, but she didn't know for how long. The odds weren't in her favor, and that fact glued her feet in place. No matter what angle of this she dissected, there was the possibility that she was wrong.

"Wake up, Breen," she urged in a whisper to herself, her fingers twitching with the need to pinch her arm. In the back of her mind she knew such things wouldn't work, for this was not a normal nightmare. The air, though saturated with a sulfuric odor, had the same distinct scent and feel to it as her forest dreams. And by realizing this, and the fact that she was as close to being real in this world as she was her own, she was struck by the terrible truth that she could die here.

Without further thought, she bolted left, throwing herself through the tiny gaps between the trees in a frenzied run. The creature howled behind her, and the loud *snap* and *crash* of trees breaking and falling followed her path. Air was becoming an issue with each hurried gallop; she couldn't get enough of it, and when she did take a huge gulp, the back of her tongue turned to sandpaper against the roof of her mouth. But she couldn't stop running. An instinct so ancient and basic had kicked in, the adrenaline burning the veins of her legs and arms. All she knew in that moment was to run as fast as she could, dodging brush, pits of mud and leaves, and trees that seemed to grow in diameter as she approached them.

The bass of the creature's howls intensified, the echo from the crashing trees slashing at her eardrums. She wanted to scream, herself, but couldn't find the air when she opened her mouth. The trees seemed like they would never end; nothing but wood and leaves surrounded her. She wished for a miracle—didn't care what form it came in.

Ahead of her the forest began to clear, and beyond that sat the Gateway. Never had the enormous, lonely, and dilapidated piece of property looked so good. No light illuminated the boarded up windows, and the poor excuse for a driveway was vacant. But the place sent her the promise of shelter from the beast behind her.

Without thinking, she stole a look over her shoulder. The beast was closer than she'd thought, now accompanied by a shadow larger and darker than itself trailing behind. Two against one was never good; especially two gigantic creatures that her world had never seen against an average size human being.

Death was inevitable.

MORPHEUS

Morpheus had stared at his ceiling in loneliness on more than one occasion. But before, the loneliness had only been a feeling he'd conjured for himself during those moments of silence and privacy. Something to feel. Something to try out. He'd experimented with so many things, hoping to know how each and every emotion felt before he had to go through with them in life.

Now the hole he felt in his chest was because of her absence, one that needed to be eternal. No one had said anything about him not stepping in and watching her, but there were reasons and suggestions for why he shouldn't. He'd found out such reasons on that hill. She hadn't seen him, but somehow she'd known of his presence. Being near hurt her and nearly destroyed him. To be so close and not be able to touch...he'd have been better off never seeing her than having her and losing her.

Pushing himself up from his cot, he walked around to his desk and pulled out his chair. His journal would've been covered in dust had such a thing existed. The front cover flipped over in his hands like it always had, the edges sharp and the pages crisp as though brand new. The pages were not numbered or dated—time for them moved at the same pace as the human world, but time had no meaning among them for they had it in abundance. There was the occasional fear or excitement of becoming human, but other than that no one paid too much attention to time.

Time was all Morpheus had. Each day was another he didn't exist. Each moment he spent in his room or in a classroom was another moment lost within the world of humanity. Becoming something had been his dream for a century. He hadn't much cared for what he'd become; anything would work.

Settled in his desk chair, he thumbed through empty pages to the first one he'd chosen fit to write on. Not necessarily anal, but he hadn't cared for how the first several pages curled up over the rest instead of lying flat.

I do hope no one will find out. We kept perfectly still and hidden until they had left. Narelle will not be pleased, but I do not particularly care. Darius has run back to his room to hide. Coward. I would have stayed to see Alcorn sit in his chair and not be able to rise, but they would have known the culprits for such a prank. Most likely they knew even without my attendance. Even still, the consequences will not be harsh.

They never are.

Morpheus smiled at the memory. His history teacher had been a crabby old being with whom he and Darius greatly disliked. So, on the way back from a trip to the human world, he'd stopped in on the twelfth dimension and stolen saliva from a Larjmack demon. Darius hadn't been sure whether the plan would work, but Morpheus convinced him that the saliva was the stickiest substance in all dimensions. A Larjmack demon could capture prey by simply spitting on them. They would stick to whatever they came into contact with, making them easy to detain.

He flipped through half the book, feeling the near perfect pages beneath his fingertips. His handwriting hadn't even indented the paper. Though this didn't stop him from being drawn into the page. Her name stood out from every word around it, the B soft and curled around itself. He remembered the first day he saw her, the memory forever ingrained in his mind.

It has been two human days since last I wrote, and it is because of her. Brianna. I passed through Maryland to see the Baltimore Harbor as well as the Annapolis one and decided to head west to the mountains. In comparison to the congested cities with their ambling, wide-eyed tourists, the country was peaceful and quiet. But uneventful. Edwina had once mentioned that every being should see the old little cities of the world and that Cumberland was the sweetest.

Morpheus had found it interesting that every person in the streets knew everyone who passed them. They even recognized people's vehicles, leaving them little notes under windshield wipers. He'd walked the old streets, unable to resist the pull he felt toward the privately owned shops. The bookstore had their door open invitingly, but no one entered. The store opposing it had signs plastered all around the windows, showcasing handmade gifts from around the world. Again, there was no one, he could see, inside the store.

And then, as he'd thought to turn around and head back into the heart of town, he'd seen her. She'd stepped out of the art gallery, dressed in mostly black, her head and hands protected by a dark green fleece. Once in the street, the smile that'd been on her face was no longer present. At that moment, he'd wanted to make that sadness disappear. The day had seemed to dim with her somber expression and he wanted it to brighten.

So he'd followed her home, met Jairus and Richard, and hadn't wanted to leave her since. At first he hadn't questioned his immediate attraction that he couldn't pin on lust. He coveted many things, even her, but the feelings within him did not seem like lust, at least by the definition with which he was familiar. As puzzling as she was, he didn't care for any answers. He'd known she was meant to be his. He just hadn't figured out her role in his life.

He grimaced, pushing himself back from the desk and journal. Almost as though he couldn't get away from his words fast enough, he tripped over his feet as he hurried over to his bookshelf. An assortment of handbooks and human novels were shrouded in shadows on his shelves. *An Introduction to Humanity. Biological and Cosmetology of the Human Race. A Million Diseases of Humanity.* The list went on. Of course, his collection was incredibly smaller than that of, say, Narelle. Being around longer definitely showed through her collection of tomes, but she also enjoyed reading more than Morpheus. He enjoyed action, the art of doing. Reading was so isolating. Being around humans was more intimate than any book he could've read on them.

He was meant to be an expert on what it was to be human by his Time. Of course, the only drawback of this, and it had been observed throughout the centuries, their kind often didn't do well emotionally and mentally once thrown into the human world. Often it was because they knew too much and could make sense of the insensible that humans usually ignored. Statistically speaking, their kind committed suicide more often than humans who hadn't been remade.

He couldn't escape death. It was everywhere. Death was inevitable. She was going to die, and there was nothing he could do.

A growl reverberated through his chest, escaping into a howl that shook the books on their shelves. He turned, hauling the bookcase into the air, and hurled it across the room. Feeling unstoppable, he picked up his desk and tossed it onto the cot, smashing the tiny bed into pieces. He went to wrench the door from its hinges, but was interrupted in his stream of consciousness when a whisper slipped inside his mind.

He took another step toward his door, shaking his head. Insanity wasn't entirely implausible for his kind, but it wasn't common. He'd never heard of them hearing things either, so his plan to obliterate the door set back into motion.

Until he heard her scream.

He swung around to see his room, but she was nowhere behind him. With fast feet, he looked into the hall. He didn't see her.

He shook his head again, pinching the bridge of his nose. He was sure she'd sounded near him. Her scream had been so piercingly loud that he'd been almost certain she'd found some way into his world.

"Impossible," he muttered.

Then he heard his name again, only this time a multitude of colors, sounds, and smells knocked him back into the doorway of his room. He was running before he knew why, knew where she was without knowing how, and how he'd get there was already forming between his hands.

In the hall he passed Darius conversing with a female whom Morpheus had never met. Past them he saw Narelle and Alphaeus locked in conversation, their bodies close to conceal anything of importance. They all looked up at the sound of his running and sent questioning glances his way. Narelle even tried stepping out in his path, but Morpheus already had the stream open and was diving in head first.

24

BRIGH

She darted through the thick and lush greenery toward the Gateway, avoiding anything on the ground she couldn't identify ahead of her. She'd already tripped twice and each time had cost her several seconds of which the monsters had taken advantage. Several more monstrosities followed behind and in front of the larger two she'd started with. These smaller creatures, from what she'd gathered while peaking over her shoulder, were either more human shaped than the larger beasts, or were drastically far from their neighboring hunter's appearances. Squeals and shouts collected throughout the sea of beings behind her, each inhuman sound piquing her heartbeat higher.

The front steps bowed under her clamoring footsteps as she raced to the front door and slammed it shut behind her. She flipped the old lock before running up the staircase. Looking to her left and then her right, she hauled herself into the room furthest from the stairs and slammed the door shut. Her hands shook around the door knob—there wasn't a lock. Shadows closed in around her hand, but she couldn't see anything around her—the room was pitch black.

"Shit," she spit in a whisper. She'd only been on the second floor of the mansion once and that'd also been in the dark. She had no idea how any of the rooms looked or if they were even still furnished.

Backing up with careful steps, she avoided any creaking floorboards as soon as her weight triggered a tiny creak. She held out her hands behind her, fingers lightly clutching at the air to steady herself once she came into contact with something. She hoped she would touch something with her hands before she fell through a hole in the floor, if there were any.

Downstairs, a pounding at the door sounded, the sudden noise scaring a shriek from her throat. With one hand she covered her lips, the other still searching for somewhere to sit and hide. Another *boom* hit the door and then a *crash* and *slam* followed shortly after. Echoes of scampering feet and haughty squeals rang in her ears. She tried to stop her heart from climbing out of her chest, even held her breath to keep from hyperventilating.

Her knuckles grazed something behind her and she grabbed a hold of it, and then let go as soon as the pain registered. She felt it slice into her palm, cutting into layer upon layer of skin, muscle, and nerve, deeply severing the smooth skin between her thumb and forefinger. The hand covering her mouth tightened, her teeth biting the flesh of her thumb in hopes that that pain would make her forget the other.

Cradling her hand in the crook of her elbow, she felt with her feet for a clear space to sit. When she found one, in what felt like a corner, she lowered herself carefully. Her hand ached almost as much as her broken leg had, but that wasn't really much of a comparison. She had no pain meds readily available to chase away this excruciating pain. She also had no reason to believe that she was getting out of this world alive. No matter how many times she pinched herself or closed her eyes, she didn't feel the transition between this world and hers. And it was only a matter of time before those creatures slithered up those stairs.

There was a scratch at the door, a long teasing noise that made Brigh's body jerk in resistance to its otherworldly sound. She pulled her good leg up to her chest, the other bent at the knee as much as the cast would allow. The creatures hadn't even made it upstairs until she'd thought about the possibility. She was slowly coming to the conclusion that somehow her thoughts controlled what happened around her. Or perhaps her fear and hope were answered in the form of objects. She wasn't sure, didn't even want to think of the possibility. How could something like that exist? This was the stuff of science fiction.

She needed to run, she had to run. But she had no choice. Something stood between her and freedom. The only other option was to find a hole somewhere and sneak through it. But she doubted there were any.

The sudden splintering of wood and the crash of the door giving way made Brigh hide her face behind her knee. The movement forced her injured hand beneath her elbow. She bit her tongue, letting the pain out in a shallow breath.

Something was in the room with her. The room was so dark she didn't even know in which direction laid the doorway. No floorboards creaked, nothing rustled in the air. All was quiet, even downstairs.

I just want them to go away! She screeched inside. *Please go away! Leave me alone!*

Then she heard the first one scream.

MORPHEUS

He heard the first awful scream before quickening his pace. He had never truly known, until that moment, through the scream that would perpetuate the following events and change both their worlds, who and what he was. Finding the direction to take through the woods wasn't very difficult. He'd been planted just outside their clearing, the weeping willow at his back. Ahead of him were broken trees, limbless trunks and gigantic footprints in the mud. A feeling he'd never experienced before gripped him, making his strides longer and his run into a gallop.

Fear.

What had he once thought of such a sensation? He didn't know. He'd felt joy and grief, sadness and hatred. But never fear. Never true terror.

"Brigh!" he shouted, leaping over decapitated trees and uprooted plants. "*Brianna!*"

There was no answer and, like a fool, he'd expected and hoped for one.

Ahead of him the tracks stopped and with them, so did he. The footprints ended at a clearing, the grass a dark brown in contrast to the intense green surrounding him. Death of the vegetation suggested something once stood in front of him, but he couldn't see any rubble or any piece of true evidence for a previously existing structure.

Bending down, he ran his fingers through the dark grass, hand coming back red with blood. A nice slice to his thumb sluggishly ejaculated crimson down to his wrist. The wound didn't hurt, but the fact that his body, his shell, produced any liquid shocked him. Blue lines pushed for freedom beneath the paleness of his skin where red had yet to touch. They weren't distinguishable enough to name them veins, but the promise of them was there.

"No," he whispered.

Before any spec of sense reached his mind, something bolted into him and knocked him to the ground. Snickers erupted as something hit him in the stomach, flipping him onto his back. Frantically, he searched for the assailant, but there was no one to be seen.

Quickly, he gathered himself and was on his feet before the next attack. He felt the air against his face before his jaw took a hefty blow, but couldn't keep himself on his feet. He watched the grass bow under an invisible weight and rolled to the side before something connected with the ground where his head had been. He looked up, but still saw nothing. A gurgling noise brought his attention to his left, and he put out a hand above his head just as something came down, slicing his already injured hand.

"*Gish maneyuk*," gurgled something from his right.

"Bryshlocke?" Morpheus said incredulously. How had a Bryshlocke demon happened upon this forest? Bryshlocke's never ventured out of their dimension, for they bred their prey and enjoyed the disgusting slime of their own world.

He didn't spend any more time musing the oddity of the invisible creature charging at him. Morpheus turned and ran for the dead grass, tripping, banging his head, and sliding on things he could not see. He knew many beings could make themselves transparent to those around them, but he'd never heard of Brishlocke demons having the ability. Was there something else here with them? Was Brigh here, just invisible to his eyes?

"Brianna!" he yelled, running around the clearing to keep away from the persistent being. He heard the twigs snap behind him as he ran, felt the weight of each bounding step getting closer and closer. He could run forever if he had to, he knew nothing of exhaustion. But the beast would catch him sooner or later. Morpheus would falter in his step, trip, or lose the battle of acceleration.

"*Brianna, where are you?*" Morpheus yelled again, putting every ounce of energy he could into his voice. Something rattled to his left, the sound of hinges coming loose.

Running straight for the center of the circle, he caught a glimpse of something that he couldn't make sense of. A door that hadn't been there during his previous lap now hovered slightly above the ground, dilapidated and solitary. In his haste to reach the door, he tripped over something invisible and then another. Finally he realized that he was falling on steps. He hopped until he stood in the doorway.

As he turned to shut the door behind him, the demon that'd been chasing him appeared in front of him so suddenly, that the shock nearly made Morpheus forget the open door. The large wooden door slammed, shaking the house, and a considerable amount of dust, in the demon's face. The lock snapped tight into place, and then Morpheus was off running up the crumbling staircase. Blindly, he ran to the end of the hallway, to a door on his right, knocking it off its hinges.

"Alesch zuknei," a voice growled from the shadows.

He took two steps into the room and then, as though growing out of the shadows, a figure lunged at him. Morpheus caught the small multicolored demon in his fists and then hurled it at the wall to his left. The demon's teasing snickers ended abruptly on impact, its body sinking to the floor in a foul smelling heap. It wasn't dead, but thankfully unconscious.

"Brianna?" Urgency, fear, and worry vibrated in his voice, growing stronger as the seconds ticked on that he did not see her.

A muffled grunt came from several shadows ahead of him. The thought of the noise coming from another demon toyed with his mind, but he confronted the source, marching up to the pile of cloth covered objects. She lay curled in on herself in the fetal position, head protected beneath her folded hands. The fact that both of them still resided in the house meant that she wasn't dead.

Kneeling beside her, his hand hovered over the left arm thrown across her face. "Brianna."

She let out a pitiful moan, but didn't show any sign of moving. Her clothing was dirtied and torn in places; hair tangled in knots spread around her head. Her left hand was stained a dark color, and when Morpheus opened her palm, he saw the dots of bloodied holes and the deep slice across her flesh.

He slid his hands underneath her and lifted her without difficulty—to him, she barely weighed anything at all. Clutching her to his chest, he left the room, the house, and the clearing. The Brishlocke demon had sometime left, most likely becoming bored and hungry and wanting to hunt. The forest around them was silent.

Morpheus traced his steps back to their clearing and snuck beneath the willow tree, flinging raindrops behind him as the needles caught his shirt. Brigh stirred as he sat her in front of the tree, leaning against its trunk. Her eyelashes fluttered open, and then closed repeatedly as though she couldn't keep them open.

Cupping her cheek, he held her face up to him. "Brianna."

The commanding tone in his voice made her open her eyes. Though they stayed open, her eyes wouldn't focus on him or anything else. Thinking she might rouse, he shook her by her shoulders. Her head snapped up, eyes gone wild. She struggled within his grasp, pushing at him like a frightened animal. This change in her took him off guard, but he stole back control over the situation and shook her again.

"Brianna, calm down."

"Away!" she shrieked, pushing and prodding him. "Stop! Alone! Away!"

"*Brianna*," Morpheus bellowed. "It is me." Pulling her into his arms, he held her tightly, rocking them back and forth. Her screaming became sobs and her pushing into clutching. He smoothed her ragged hair, patted her back.

When she'd calmed to the point where she was only sniffling, Morpheus pulled her back from him to look into her face. "How are you feeling?"

"Horrible," she whispered. Her words were sharp from a scratch in her voice.

He pushed unruly clumps of hair out of her eyes. "You are hurt. What happened to your hand?"

Brigh looked down at her hand completely smeared with blood. Her eyes watered again. She opened her mouth to speak but stopped when something caught her eye. Morpheus followed her gaze, but didn't see anything of great interest.

Taking his left hand in hers, she uncurled his fingers to reveal several clean uneven holes in his skin and a clean slash between his pointer finger and thumb. They gasped in unison as she brought her hand next to his to compare the holes and gash. They matched perfectly. Size, shape, and placement.

"You need to wake," Morpheus said abruptly, tearing his hand out of hers.

"No," Brigh hurriedly said. "I can't lose you again."

"You will not lose me." It hurt him to lie to her. The only other person he'd outwardly lied to was Alphaeus, and neither of them deserved such a treatment. But revealing the truth to Brigh would only further complicate things, and he wasn't completely sure about what happened next.

"You must leave," he continued. "You are not safe here."

"I am safe with you," she said so innocently it nearly killed him.

Part of him regretted having wanted her in the first place, but the larger more dominant piece of him needed her more than life itself. No harm would come to her. He'd follow her everywhere if he had to just to make sure of her safety.

He sighed. The future didn't seem very bright or easy. "The only place you will be safe is in your world."

She smiled. A simple expression, but it lit up her face. "Come with me?"

Sadly, he grit his teeth. "You know I cannot."

There was a pause between them as he tried to think of something to say. He couldn't be harsh with her again, couldn't lie to turn her away. Kindness would only prolong their presence in this world and he wanted her as far away from it as possible.

But she surprised him by being submissive. "I will wait for you," she whispered, a soft smile curving her lips. She caressed his cheek before closing her eyes and fading out of sight in front of him.

25

BRIGH

As she was plucked from the dream like a dying newborn from its crying mother, Brigh sucked in a breath as though she couldn't quite catch it. Feeling lightheaded, she twitched her fingers to rub her temples. And opened her eyes when her hand caught on something.

A groggy, half unconscious Richard clutched her fingers just below an IV drip pulsing in the back of her right hand. His usually artistically messy hair lay flat and frizzy over his eyes. His trademark classy brand name clothing had been replaced by black sweatpants and a red varsity football hoodie. She wanted to ask where her brother was and who could have possibly wanted to take his place. But when his eyes opened, and that first flash of green lit up in the low florescent lights of the hospital room, she knew the unshaven young man couldn't be anyone but her brother.

"What happened?" Brigh asked, trying to sit up. "Why are we at the hospital?"

Richard licked his lips, quickly let go of Brigh's hand, and sat back in the uncomfortable looking wooden chair beside the bed. "Keep it down. Dad's snoring."

Brigh saw him on her left, sitting upright in a matching wooden chair. His head had lolled to the side and the lines in his face had softened, but his mouth was tensely closed. How long had he sat there watching her like a hawk? Brigh and her father hadn't gotten along for a while, but his protective nature had increased since her mother's death, and when she was hurt or in danger, he was a force to be reckoned with.

"You wouldn't wake up," Richard said in a small voice. He was looking down at his hands as though searching for something. "Doctor's couldn't figure it out. You were breathing on your own. Seemed to just be sleeping. It's not right when the doctor's can't find a cause."

"I'm sorry," Brigh said. She wanted to hold her brother, to reinforce the fact that she was there and wouldn't leave.

Richard looked at her, balling his hands into tight fists. "You can't apologize for not waking up. No apology for that."

Brigh shook her head. "No, I meant sorry about our little thing. I shouldn't have said those things. I wasn't thinking."

"No, you're right," he said. "Mom may have been a little weird and insane about her art, but she always wanted me to win."

"We should wake him up."

Richard shook his head. "Let him sleep. He wouldn't until I pretty much threatened him."

Brigh let out a long, throat drying yawn. "And how'd you do that?"

"I tried to use my height for intimidation," Richard said looking sheepish. "Didn't exactly work."

Looking at her father, Brigh bit her lip. She couldn't stay in the hospital any longer. Any place surrounded by life and death made her uncomfortable, as it would for any person. Being in a hospital bed, alive and well, while others who needed the room more than she did had to wait, made her uneasy. She wished she could wake her father, but he'd want her to stay for tests, nurses, and doctors to prove that she was healthy.

"Rich," Brigh huffed as she pushed herself into a sitting position, "get my clothes."

His right brow rose in question, lips pursed and ready to deny any request. He didn't need her to explain to understand her reasoning's. Most times they thought alike, almost as twins or kindred spirits would. Once the brow had dropped back into its low, uninterested droop, Richard pushed himself up from the chair and went to the table across from the bed to retrieve her clothes.

"I need you to put the things that monitor my heart on dad," Brigh instructed after Richard handed her the clothes.

Both brows shot up into his hairline. "Are you nuts? You just want to waltz right outta here?"

Brigh nodded. "If you follow my lead, we'll be fine."

"You sure *you're* fine?"

Brigh grinned. She was tired and ached all over, but besides physical discomfort she felt better than fine. "Right as rain. Now, take these and stick them to his chest."

Shaking his head, Richard quickly took the wires and did as he was asked as Brigh tiptoed into the bathroom.

"I'm so going to hell for this," he said with a sigh. "And I'm saving you a seat."

 R

"You're nuts," Richard whispered as they walked around hospital staff and patients toward the elevator. He kept enough distance between them to where one couldn't discern whether or not they were together, but close enough so he could protect her if they were questioned.

"You already mentioned that," Brigh panted. She found quickly that her body was more exhausted than she'd thought. Two corridors down from her room and she could barely catch her breath.

"Seriously though," Richard continued, motioning dramatically with his hands. "If we're caught, we're dead. And not just dad. Billy's a cop. He'll cuff us. Definitely."

Brigh gave him a disbelieving look. "If you shut up, we won't get caught. Act natural. We're on a stroll. And quit giving me The Brow. It's conspicuous."

"What does that even mean? Sis, I think the drugs messed up your mind or something. We're not getting out of here alive."

"Overly dramatic much?" Now *she* felt conspicuous. Richard kept talking and she kept quiet. All eyes that saw something seemingly suspicious were trained on her. She rolled her eyes at the psychology. Here Richard was the one making noise and drawing attention, but it was her silence that made her interesting to others. How quaint.

Richard led them into the elevator after two doctors emerged from the bright box. Once he'd pushed the button for the lobby, he put his arm around Brigh's shoulder and leaned his head on hers.

"The door's closed," Brigh said with a smile. "You can drop the act that you like me."

With a laugh, Richard hugged Brigh to his side before pulling away from her. "You're just jealous because the hot guy hugging you just now is your brother and there's nothing you can do about it."

"I wouldn't date you even if our last names were different."

The door opened and Brigh walked out, leaving her brother and his puzzled expression inside the elevator. She looked over her shoulder to see if he'd moved, but the only thing that'd changed was his face.

"Really?" he asked in confusion, his brows and lips dipping with it. "You don't even think I'm cute?"

Brigh laughed. She couldn't help but razz her brother. Besides, if she didn't, he would get her first. "Ask me that again when we get home."

"Tired?" Richard pulled the keys to Brigh's BMW from his left back pocket.

"Exhausted," she said with a sigh.

The two of them rounded the corner of the hospital that led to the parking garage. Stars peppered the sky in different shapes, all slightly dimmed due to rolling clouds from the north. Brisk air rushed through Brigh's gnarled strands, pleasantly tickling the nape of her neck. A gasp of undiluted pleasure tore from her throat. She'd missed nights like this. When the cold air smelled of burning cinders and the world lay quiet and calm. The change in seasons left her wanting more instead of wishing for warmth and greenery. She craved snow like some craved whiskey. Skiing, ice skating, winter coats, boots, hiking...all the things there were to do around Cumberland and she'd rushed past it all.

Richard grabbed Brigh's hand, pulling her to a stop and out of her distant dreams. Her head jerked up in the direction of a shadow leaning against a pillar off to the right. A sudden glow in the dark signaled a long drag on a cigarette before it fell to the ground and disappeared. The stench of Marlboro Lights floated over to Brigh and Richard, drawing a short cough from them both.

From within the shadows dispersed Jake MacRae in a plain navy tee and faded boot cut blue jeans that'd seen better days. His cheeks shimmered with sweat from the small light above them, but the rest of his features were doused with darkness.

"Hey, Jake," Richard said in a voice full of masculine challenge.

Brigh elbowed her brother. She didn't understand the hostility; neither did she want to experience the finale. Jake wasn't bothered by the less than welcoming start of the conversation; at least he didn't show it.

"Rich," Jake announced as though he hadn't seen him standing there. The grin plastered between his cheeks screamed sarcasm, but Richard didn't seem to notice. "What are you doing here?"

"I'm taking my sister home," he replied. "What are *you* doing here?"

Jake shook his head as he laughed. He ran an unsteady hand through his messy crop of russet hair before looking Brigh in the eye. Something swirling in those hazel depths unnerved her—she couldn't dissect the parts of his eye because they were hidden beneath a sleeve of darkness. But by the upward quirk of his mouth, she identified the possibility of something ominous coiling around in that head of his.

Breaking eye contact with her, Jake settled his gaze on her brother. "I need to talk to her for a sec."

"Do you know what she's been through?" Richard spat. "She just got out of the hospital for Christ sakes."

Jake's hard stare did not falter, neither did his insistent and determined stance. He looked like a frazzled cat whose back hair stood on end. She couldn't remember a time where Jake had appeared so antagonistic or harsh. His father was always absent in his life, never attending his games or any school events, although everything Jake did had plenty of funding behind it. His mother had long ago divorced his father, leaving Jake without nurturing care that he desperately deserved. Most times she felt sorry for Jake. She didn't know what was worse: having a mother leave of her own free will or one being taken without choice.

"Rich." Jake spoke in an eerily calm voice that did not match his personality or the expression on his face. He looked about to grab someone's throat if he did not get his way.

"*Jacob*," Richard responded in a much more heavy tone laced with challenge.

Brigh stepped in Richard's line of vision. "Rich, listen to me. You don't want to start anything."

"He's the one starting things," he said without looking away from Jake.

Brigh rolled her eyes. "Look, I'm tired and not in the mood for testosterone battles. Please, let's just go home."

Richard clenched his teeth. "Someone needs to teach them a lesson."

"Teach who a lesson?" Brigh asked in confusion.

"Money needs to learn that it's not above others."

Brigh shook her head. "Rich, can we not do this now?"

Richard's squinted eyes relaxed, as did the tightness of his shoulders. He shook his head with an embarrassed smile and blush creeping over his face. "Sorry, sis."

Brigh nodded in acknowledgment and turned around to face Jake.

And that was the last thing she remembered before everything went black.

26

MORPHEUS

The anticipation of owning or having something disappears as soon as it is within reach. Once the coveted has been possessed, the excitement leaves, and not long after, another thing is coveted and then another and so on. Such a pattern falls into conflict where the person is either out of money or out of options of something new to covet.

Life had been something Morpheus craved for nearly a century. He was a pup compared to his peers and mentors, but that had never been an issue. To most, he was an unrealistic dreamer and sometimes he thought that himself. But his dreams never ceased to build, repair, and renew. Every day brought something else he wanted to the point that he thought the need he felt within from the wanting would surely make everything happen. Or madness would engulf him whole.

The only flaw in his dreaming of being human was that he'd never thought of what, who, and where he would be. Who would he surround himself with? Would they be music lovers, poets, or a combination of every art? What would his parents look like? Would they have the slightly crooked nose of his or the attractively long lashes Narelle commented on every so often? Did he want to be a doctor? Could he handle the solitary isolation of a desk job? Or would he enjoy being outdoors more so than something that kept him inside for hours on end? Did he want to be the older brother type who watched over everyone close to him? Would he have a sister or a brother? Would there be twins?

So many questions without answers, and with life being so close to him, sheer terror flooded. How could he not know these things? He'd thought of the places he'd go and the people he wanted to meet, but he had never stopped to think of what his life would be like. He would have no choice. His parents would be chosen for him; the life that he was supposed to follow already carved and laid out ahead of him. His human age, position in life—everything was decided for him ahead of his ascension by monstrous beings who did not know him.

Suddenly he found it all unfair. How could someone else decide what he was going to do in his life—who he was going to be? Once he'd thought the whole thing a free thrill ride and all he had to do was sit back and relax. Now he felt what freedom he'd had scurry away from his outstretched hands. Standing in the middle of his ravaged room, he felt vulnerable and unsteady.

A doorway for the stream appeared before him without much thought. Minutes later he was deposited before Brigh's door, the unforgettable R carved into its wood glowing a bright green. Her room was dark, the faint light from a nearby street lamp illuminating her blinds. One step forward and he saw the shreds of canvas and splintered wood strewn all over her floor. A path had been made to the bed, but there was no room to walk anywhere else. The blankets had been stripped off the bed and bundled haphazardly on the floor.

What had happened?

The same shot of fear surged through him that had in the forest until he heard the front door open and voices break the silence in the house. Laughter and jokes floated up to him as he ran down the hall and down the steps.

Instead of Brigh and Richard, Alice and Owen stood in the doorway smiling and laughing at something one of them said. Alice wore a beautiful light blue knee-length dress and heels, and Owen stood handsome in a dress shirt and jeans. Neither of them could keep their eyes or their hands off of the other. They smelled of alcohol and cigarettes and cheap food.

"Jairus?" Alice called as she shook off her coat and hung it on the hook by the door. After no reply, Alice's features wrinkled in confusion. "Where do you think he could be?"

Owen shrugged, keeping his leather jacket in place. "He's *your* brother-in-law. He may be at work. Call him."

"Nah," Alice said as she walked down the hall to the kitchen. Several lights flickered on in her wake. "I don't want to bother him just in case he's out on a date or something."

"I doubt he's on a date." Owen glanced at Morpheus, raising his brows in question before following Alice into the kitchen.

Morpheus's eyes grew wide. Had Owen just looked at him? Or looked *through* him? He headed into the kitchen and watched as Owen leaned against the counter and Alice check the answering machine messages. Owen didn't look at Morpheus again, and for a second he thought that he'd imagined the recognition he saw on the man's face. But he was certain their eyes had met. He'd seen the old look in his eyes and felt Owen's ancient soul reach out to him like an old friend.

The answering machine ran through a message Alice had left earlier in the day and then one from a co-worker of Jairus's. Alice headed to the refrigerator and had pulled out a bottle of water when Richard's rushed and worried voice, punctuated by a distant siren, came over the speaker.

"Alice, I don't know if you'll come by our house, but if you're there, we're going to the hospital. Brigh...something's wrong. I don't know what. I'll call back later. Bye."

Alice turned to Owen, the water bottle dropped onto the counter. The force from which Alice had let go of the bottle propelled it over the side of the counter, hitting the linoleum with a plastic *smack*.

"Do you think she's okay?" Alice was past Owen before he could answer the question. She shook her arms in the air in panic, grabbing at her coat and trying to tug it on. "I mean, she has to be alright, right? She's strong. She's fine."

Owen grabbed Alice into his arms before she could go out the door. Holding her tight, he looked over her shoulder at Morpheus. In them Morpheus saw command. He saw anger and disgust, as though Owen thought this his fault.

"She's fine, Al," Owen whispered, rubbing her back.

Alice pulled back, shaking her head, tiny tear streaks running along the curve of her nose. "She's been through so much. She doesn't need anything else."

"I know," he said. "But we don't know what's wrong yet. Maybe it had something to do with her leg. We don't know."

She sucked in a breath. "I'm going to the hospital."

"I'll drive. I'll meet you out there in a sec."

Alice nodded and went outside, wrapping her wool coat tighter around her.

Owen sighed and turned to Morpheus. His calm and soothing expression had disappeared and was replaced by eyes infused with hatred and fury. Morpheus could count the number of times he'd seen Owen on one hand and have fingers left over. He had nothing to compare this man in front of him to the man he'd only briefly observed, for he knew nothing about him.

"The girl better be alive," he spat.

Morpheus was affronted. "I do not know what you are talking about."

Owen stepped up to Morpheus as a challenge. The man's head came up to Morpheus's eyes and he was built much smaller. But it was obvious by his serious expression that the knowledge he carried surpassed Morpheus's by centuries. Although he felt wrongly accused, and although Owen could not physically touch him, he did not wish for a confrontation.

"You know exactly what it is I speak of. You are meddling with forces that you have no right to touch. She could die."

"You think I do not know this?" Morpheus shook his head. "I have stayed away, put away my feelings to keep her safe. Do not accuse me of something I do not even have knowledge of."

Owen pulled car keys off of the key ring by the door, but before he opened the door he turned back to Morpheus. His expression had softened to one of worry and grief. "I hope you love her enough to keep her safe. Let her go. It's best for everyone."

Owen shut the door behind him, running off to the car, leaving Morpheus in the empty, deathly quiet house. The car roared out of the driveway and disappeared down the street.

A humorless laugh escaped his throat. He rubbed the back of his neck, pulling at the neckline of his shirt with discomfort. To any onlooker, he'd done nothing wrong.

He had never sought her out with malice or ungentlemanly thoughts or devices.

"No. I have done something far worse." Shoulders slumped, he let out a sigh and made his way to the hospital, hoping that his girl would be safe.

The fiasco that surrounded him as he stepped foot into the hospital made him pause. The staff were not strangers to madness and mayhem, life and death, but they normally weren't surrounded by security guards and police, unless such madness escalated to something even they could not control.

"What is wrong? What is going on?" he shouted to a frantic nurse and an angry doctor he passed in the hall. No one answered. He heard yelling further down the hall, and when he rounded the corner he found the source of anger.

"How the *fuck* did you miss two teenagers walking through the hospital by themselves?" Jairus yelled. A group of police officers and nurses circled around him as he shouted. Everyone looked shocked or angry, all eyes trained on the man pointing and cursing at those around him.

"Sir," a nurse feebly stepped closer to him, "I assure you we did not know—"

Pushing his fist at the ground, his pointed finger at attention, he said, "I want my children found. *Right now.*"

The officer closest to Jairus nervously put his hand on the butt of his holstered gun but made no move to draw it. "Jairus, calm down. Our officers are looking for your children as we speak."

Jairus took in a deep breath to keep from tearing up. "You—"

"Dad?"

As if synchronized, everyone, even Morpheus, turned to face Richard, whose bloody nose and slightly swollen left eye caused several nurses to rush to his aid. Jairus stood behind the throng of busy nurses, his cheeks reddened from yelling and hands tightly fisted at his sides. Morpheus himself could not move. The sight of Richard shocked everyone around him, but Morpheus still found himself confused. What had happened to Brigh and where was she?

"Ask where she is," Morpheus pleaded with Jairus. The man did not answer, but stared straight ahead at his son. The nurses started leading Richard away, but the boy was shaking his head and pushing against their insistent hands.

"You have to find her," Richard said. "He took her."

"Who?" both Morpheus and Jairus shouted at once.

"I can't remember." Blinking as though trying to recover the memory, Richard stopped struggling against the nurses and looked around him for answers. The nurses, too, stopped and waited for the boy to finish.

"There may be brain trauma," one nurse said, followed by several agreeing nods from the other nurses.

Every second that Richard said nothing, Morpheus felt at the brink of imploding. Brigh had been taken and no one knew who or where.

With a gasp of knowledge, Morpheus drew in close to Jairus' ear. "The cameras. They must have shown up on the cameras."

Jairus walked over to his son and placed his hand around Richard's shoulder. "We'll find her. Let the ladies clean you up."

Richard, looking defeated, gave a short nod and turned to leave. Jairus was turning away when Richard blurted, "Jake!"

Everyone stared at Richard as he said again, "Jake. He's the one who knocked me out."

"Peter's son?" a young, pretty, and petite nurse asked.

The officer closest to hearing range of the situation pulled out his radio. "We have a patient missing from the fourth floor. May have been kidnapped by Jacob MacRae. Patient's name is Brianna Breen." To Richard he said, "Son, I need you to tell me everything you remember."

Everything else the officer said was unimportant. Jake MacRae had taken Brigh—Morpheus was sure of it. The reason for the abduction did not cross his mind, but he didn't really care. Where he'd taken her was something else of which he was certain.

Again he tried talking to Jairus. At the Gateway he'd reached Brigh. He knew not how he'd completed such a task, but he was willing to try anything. Time was surely running out and he was the only one who knew where to look.

Morpheus stood close enough to Jairus that the man's form flickered as though he didn't quite exist. The man's facial hair had reached past the point of calling it stubble, but short enough to where one wouldn't consider it a full beard and mustache. Being up this close made Morpheus notice the short graying hair and lines making the man look older than he was.

Old or not, Morpheus leaned into Jairus so that his lips were close enough to touch his ear. Each second of uncertainty made Morpheus frenetic. Seconds ticked by, seconds that Brigh kept losing because he wasn't capable of putting fear of incompetence away. But he had to find her. He knew it wasn't her time. It couldn't be. She was merely a babe in this ancient world of theirs and he knew he'd trade places with her if it were possible.

Morpheus whispered anything and everything into Jairus's ear, hoping something he said would spark acknowledgement in his deadened hazel eyes. He described the man's daughter to him, how Brigh looked through Morpheus's eyes. How beautiful and courageous she was; how intelligent, intellectual, and talented. How never in his hundred years had he met anyone worth remembering until her. She was perfection incarnate.

Images of the Gateway poured out of his mouth like vipers striving for the gates of heaven and their promise of absolution. He left nothing out of his words to Jairus. Every detail of the dilapidated building was conveyed, and only once Morpheus had nothing left to share did he step back to watch the man's reaction.

Jairus showed no sign of acknowledgement. He kept staring straight ahead where Richard had been ushered away, his eyes seemingly lifeless, his body just the shell of a man.

Morpheus's speech had been for nothing. When it came to the parts of life and death for humans, Morpheus had nothing to play. He was merely the final vessel for lives that had moved on and vanished from the human world. He could do nothing for her.

Then an idea struck him. So swift was it that he'd almost missed the clue to this riddle. At the Gateway Morpheus hadn't attached himself to Brigh. He'd merely stood behind another and unknowingly skewed the boy's words that were close in meaning to his own so that what Brigh heard was his voice.

Oppression. The key to opening a human mind and riding in their body wherever an Unfinished liked. Domination. Force. Subjugation. Putting away the human as though in a box until what the Unfinished sought was completed and they released the unknowing human. Simple in theory, but in action it stole energy from the host they used.

But it was myth. He'd read mention of it somewhere in the library texts that weren't meant for students. He vaguely remembered having asked about its origin, but no one had any answers. Whatever the Unfinished knew about oppression was securely locked in the minds of those who had come before them and ascended before anyone knew to ask.

But he'd been able to carry the oppression through with no issue. Now all he needed was someone who knew Brigh and was thinking about her. Jairus apparently wasn't thinking of his daughter since the oppression hadn't affected him at all. Richard was somewhere in the hospital most likely under the influence of pain medications. He was of no use to him.

Looked like he had run out of options.

Until the elevators opened behind him and Alice and Owen emerged. Alice ran to Jairus, embracing her brother-in-law. Owen stayed close behind Alice lest he was needed. The officer and band of nurses had departed awhile ago so the sudden interruption to the quiet hallway made several women at the nurse's station lean out.

"Is Brigh okay?" Alice asked Jairus once she'd pulled away from him.

Jairus briefly closed his eyes and looked away. The man had shut down.

"What happened?" she asked again. Grabbing hold of his forearms, she shook Jairus. "Jairus! What the hell? Where is she?"

Owen stole a glance at Morpheus, an annoyed roll to his eyes as he looked away. He was as uninterested in Morpheus as he was with Jairus.

"Owen, listen to me," Morpheus pleaded. He didn't move, didn't walk to Owen and get in his face like he wanted. Intimidation would just make Owen shut him out and he was the only one who could help him. "I know where Brigh is. Someone took her."

Owen gave Morpheus a questioning glare. He couldn't respond, otherwise the others would ask questions. He couldn't leave Alice's side because he'd be seen as a selfish and inconsiderate man.

Morpheus would do all of the talking, which was just fine. "Brigh was here, I do not know for what. But a boy her age by the name of Jake bloodied Richard's face and abducted her. No one knows where he took her, but I have an idea."

Walking over to the corner where Morpheus had placed himself, Owen turned around to face the others. But before he turned, he whispered the question Morpheus had been hoping someone would ask him.

"Where?"

27

BRIGH

Her mother had always told Brigh that her heart was too big. She couldn't stay mad at anyone for long, nor could she stand it when people fought. Violence irritated her. Ignorance confused her. Neither of them made any sense.

She'd seen the color of blood only once and swore she'd never see it again. Her mother's dead body had been the first. Thankfully she couldn't remember much of that night or the way her mother had looked torn up on the rocks at the base of Lovers Leap. And then there had been her and Morpheus's bloodied hands covered with more than enough blood for one to see in a lifetime.

Blood?

The pain in her head was more intense than anything she'd ever experienced. The world filled in around her so fast that at first she couldn't form clear thoughts. A gasp tore from her throat, smoldering her flesh as though flame had touched her vocal chords. She was cold. Curling in on herself—the slight movement making a tremor travel up her spine, through her head, and around her eyes.

"Finally awake?" a voice asked.

Brigh fought hard against the groan forming in her throat. She didn't want to talk, didn't understand why her whole body felt like someone had smashed it into pieces. She hurt so much she wished death would fall swiftly across her shoulders. She nearly welcomed it, succumbed to such a sweet escape that sounded so easy.

Something slapped her face, and when her eyes drifted slowly open a figure came into view. Her cheek stung, lip burning and dripping something warm she couldn't see. Her body felt suspended, but she knew she was leaning on something for her side ached with the pressure.

Blinking rapidly, she tried to focus on the figure. Doing so only called another slap to her cheek. She fell backward, unable to bring up her hand to massage the pain away. She gasped, spitting what tasted like blood and smelled like vomit.

She knew she was going to die. She felt a coldness seep into her limbs as she tried to push herself upright. Her brain felt as though it would explode, such throbbing in her temples made her want to vomit. She pushed herself to sit up straight, arms wobbling uncontrollably as she tried to apply weight to them to help her stand.

Hauled up by her elbows, the rest of her hung limply in the hands of someone strong. She still couldn't focus enough to make out a face, but she knew whoever it was had to be male. She smelled cologne on the expensive side and the rough handling of her arms only signified a man who did not know his strength or one who acknowledged such strength for intimidation.

"Bitch," he spat in her face, little drops of saliva clinging to her skin. "I never thought you'd wake up."

She tried to say, "Who are you?" but the question sounded like a drunken slur, even to her, when it slunk out of her mouth.

He shook her hard, her head bobbing back and forth. She was going to vomit. She didn't care where or on whom. She let out a cough and expelled the nauseous sea roiling in her stomach. She felt herself fall, but did not have the mind enough to catch herself. Her elbows stung, the quick vibrations snaking up and around to her shoulders. She wished to be numb; she wanted it more than anything.

Quiet sobs wracked her, made her choke on blood and saliva. Who would want to do such a thing? Could someone hate her this much? What had she ever done?

She made the decision to remember her killer's face. She needed to know what he looked like, who he was, and why he'd chosen her to be at his mercy. She had to draw enough energy to open her eyes and focus on the figure for as long as it took to memorize his face before she closed them for the last time.

Rolling on her back, she let out a painful growl, hugging her arms to herself. She didn't know how much her body could take, so she quickly opened her eyes. She looked above her, seeing nothing but blurry brown and black blobs. Blinking several times, she tilted her eyebrows up and the movement was rewarded with something thick and wet and warm crawling its way down her forehead. It seeped onto her left eyelid. Distantly she thought it might be blood, but she wasn't sure.

Something pressed on her stomach, hard enough to make her gasp. A slow crack made it hard to breathe, and she realized that the pressure wasn't on her stomach, but her ribs.

She wanted to cry or scream, but taking in oxygen to complete such a task would cause her more pain.

"Trying to get away?" he asked.

She tried to focus on the figure while still seeming docile and out of it, neither of which being difficult to create. The blurry pieces began merging into something recognizable until she could make out a nose, lips, and eyes.

Jake? She screamed inside.

How could he? What had she done? They didn't necessarily get along, but she had never done him wrong!

He leaned down, moving his foot to the floor by her side. Kneeling, he leaned close to her face. He looked so angry, but in a way, also pleased. Pleased that he had her where he wanted her was the only thing she could think of.

"You always were so beautiful." He ran two fingers along her jaw, tracing the curves of her lips until her skin tingled with his touch. She'd never seen such detachment on his face before. He didn't look real. He didn't look like Jacob MacRae. Disappointment marred his dreamy expression and then he abruptly stood.

Between his legs Brigh saw an old rusted hammer lying useless on the wooden floor. Looking around at the old empty picture frames and sheet-covered objects that she'd never had the interest to inspect, she knew where she was. They were on the second floor of the Gateway—the same room in her dream.

Suddenly she didn't want to die. She wanted to fight. Jake walked away from her, his stride unhurried and calm. She needed another boost of energy to propel her forward for the hammer. She had to wait until he came back and was close enough to strike, or she had to grab it without a sound and hit him over the head while he faced away.

Could she do it? Could she actually be brave and face death and get away? Even if she made it outside of the house, she still had miles of dirt road until she saw cars and asphalt. She felt the fear of failure and then the hope of success swirl together in a building mixture of adrenaline. She could do this. She had to.

Jake was still facing away, his gaze attached to a window facing the front of the house. He wasn't moving, seemingly a statue. She knew to take no chances. She had to keep silent. First she made sure all limbs were on board for movement. Legs were stiff, but moveable. Her arms sore, and at first ignored her commands, but then twitched back to life.

Putting weight on her heels, she dug them into the floorboards and moved slightly sideways. Pain erupted from her ribs, but she sucked in her lip and bit down hard, breathing carefully through her nose. Thankfully no creak came from the floor, but she wasn't sure that luck would be found again. Another small section of floor was covered the same way, her arms shaking as they helped carry her to the next spot, the pain from her ribs threatening to tear a groan from her mouth. She was in reaching distance of the hammer. A surge of happiness ran through her. She grasped the old thing and laid her arm close to her side, so that if he turned around he wouldn't immediately see it.

Jake's silhouetted figure still hadn't budged from his place at the window. This was her window of opportunity.

She was about to sit up when Jake turned from the window, a small smile playing on his face when he saw her. Her window had closed just as suddenly as it had opened. He came toward her, still with that slow, easy walk. It was dark enough that he didn't see the hammer, and she was hoping it would stay that way.

"The moon's high tonight," he said with that smile. "I wish you could see it."

She swallowed. He just had to lean down enough for her to get a good shot at his head.

With a sigh, he looked away from her. "You never did like being with me, even as friends. You know, I could've been a lot for you. Most popular guy, star quarterback, dad owns most of the town. I could've helped smooth out those rumors about you killing your mom."

Brigh grit her teeth. The bastard had only to bend down a little and this speech of his would come to a close. She didn't need to hear about the mistakes she'd made. She just needed to get out of this one, the biggest mistake of trusting him.

Jake shook his head, looking grieved. Setting his eyes on her, a small devilish smile pulled his hazel eyes into a dark brown. His white teeth glinted in the darkness. "I guess it won't be too bad without you. I still have Marissa to fuck me."

At the same time Jake leaned down, Brigh shot up and slammed the hammer into his head. She didn't wait to see if he fell. She threw herself out of the room, stumbling in the dark, wincing at every sharp turn or step. She nearly fell down the staircase and almost dropped the hammer when she hit the floor.

Which way?

Would she make it by hiding in the house or was she better off in the woods? Hiding in the house tugged at her inner child, but there were no beds or even furniture to secure her safety. She didn't know the woods that well or even in which direction to take. If she kept close to the road, he'd find her, and her attempt to escape would have been for nothing. Slipping out of the door, she ran as fast as she could toward the woods. The leg on her cast ruined the ease with which she ran, but the pain from her chest threatened to double her over. Rain pelted her through the trees and soaked her clothes before she'd gone a hundred feet. Keeping low, she ran as far away from the road as she could and then turned in the direction she thought the long dirt road headed.

"Bitch!" Jake yelled from behind her, his voice off in the distance. "I'm going to cut your throat!"

Brigh's heart rate skyrocketed as she turned again to change her path. If Jake was smart enough, he'd follow the mud spatters along the tree and the shoe prints left in the thicker mounds of mud. She tried to avoid the puddles so as to keep the noise down, but sometimes she had no choice.

With one giant adrenaline rushed step came another that was slower, shorter. Panic set in, which she thought would help her move faster, but it didn't seem to change anything. She was slowing down. The adrenaline rush was ending, and the damage that'd been done to her body was telling her brain to shut down. Little black spots flew around her vision every time she blinked. But she was determined to make it out. She had to.

MORPHEUS

Morpheus had always ridden in the backseat of Brigh's car whenever the thought of spending the day with her made him exultant. He was forced to the back because either Felicity or Richard would be in the front seat and he needed them to open the rear side door for him to get in. He couldn't simply materialize; there had to be a metaphysical door.

Right then he was in Jairus's car, but instead of the older man driving it was Owen and Alice upfront and Jairus in the backseat with Morpheus. Owen sped through the streets, passing illegally and without signaling. Alice scolded him several times, but after the first thirty times he broke a traffic law, she kept quiet and sunk down a little lower in her seat.

"Are we almost to the road?" Owen asked.

Alice sat up a little straighter and squinted through the rain. Owen had the windshield wipers on high and still visibility was low. The headlights made the shapes of signs acknowledgeable, but the actual words and symbols weren't seen until they came right up to them.

Alice bounced in her seat as she pointed. "There!"

"Where?" Owen shouted.

"Right, turn right! Here, here, here, here, here!"

Owen swerved to the right, barely making the turnoff for Lovers Leap and the Gateway. They were nearly there. Morpheus could've traveled ahead, but there was nothing he could have done had he found anything. And if he was wrong and they were not there, he would have to wait for the three of them and then try to figure out a next possibility.

The dirt road had become a sloshing mud stream that flowed against the car. They had about a mile until they hit the trees lining the road. Ten minutes at the very least.

"I want to know why he would take her," Owen suddenly said. Alice's shoulders rose in confusion, but the question had been aimed at Morpheus. Owen looked up at Morpheus's figure in the backseat every so often as they continued up the road.

"I do not know," Morpheus replied. "They have never seemed anything but classmates at school. No quarrels of any kind apparent."

Owen nodded and turned back to the road. "Al, do you know about anything?"

Alice shook her head, massaging her temples. "Jair works for his father. They've never been particularly fond of each other, but the kids have never had any problems as far as I know."

"As far as you know," Owen said. He looked back into the mirror at Morpheus.

"You think I brought this," Morpheus said without question.

Owen's eyebrows rose. How could he not think that? Brigh was in trouble and it was because of something Morpheus had a hand in. But then again, Morpheus wasn't sure of his involvement. He didn't even know why Brigh had been at the hospital.

"Why was Brigh in the hospital?" Morpheus asked.

Owen couldn't answer him. "What was Brigh in the hospital for? Did you find out?"

Alice nodded. "She was in a coma and the doctors had no idea why. She has no history of seizures, diabetes, and she didn't take any medications other than the prescribed amount for her leg. It's almost like she fell asleep and couldn't wake up."

"A coma," Owen repeated with another glance at Morpheus. "And now she's up and walking, and Jake, the bastard, took her."

"We'll find her," Alice said obstinately. "She'll be fine."

"And why are no police involved?" Jairus spoke unexpectedly from his slouched seat in the back.

They entered the long line of trees that ominously lined the driveway. The rain created what seemed a solid curtain around the car, but that didn't stop the fact that at any minute an animal could run between the trees and in their way.

Owen shook his head. "They would further complicate things. Jake is a boy. We can handle him."

What Owen meant was that *he* could handle him. Morpheus could attempt oppression if he had to, which he thought he might, but he wasn't sure his lack of experience was going to do them any good.

"Alice," Owen began, "you're going to stay with the car by the house. If you hear anything or you hear me yell your name you call the police right away. Got it?"

"Yes," was all she said.

Morpheus was surprised at how quickly Alice gave in. But when he thought about it, Owen's plan seemed logical. If everyone went in together, there might be safety issues, depending on whether or not Jake was armed. Also, there was the possibility that Brigh was hurt and would need medical attention. Keeping someone in the running car would be ideal because they could quickly put the girl in the backseat and drive off.

Would Jake hurt her?

He'd abducted her—he certainly had the capacity to inflict pain, although he'd never shown any reason to do so before. If he hadn't done anything to her yet he definitely would once he saw them coming, he knew it.

"Turn off the headlights," Morpheus said to Owen. The man gave him raised eyebrows, but Morpheus nodded. "I have a feeling."

Owen rolled his eyes but reached over and turned off the headlights on the old car. They were near enough to the Gateway that missing the lights weren't a total loss, but their absence made the trek much harder.

"What was that?" Alice screeched.

Morpheus leaned forward trying to see out of the windshield. Without the lights and the rain falling like it was, he couldn't make out anything. Owen pulled the car to a stop and sat for a minute studying their surroundings.

"What did she see?" Morpheus asked.

"What was it, Al?" Owen asked her.

Alice shook her head and took a deep breath. "I'm sure it was nothing. I thought I saw something run in front of the car."

Owen looked up into the rearview, and in his eyes Morpheus saw fear; raw and inescapable fear. With that look Morpheus was suddenly filled with the same emotion. Alice saw some*one* run in front of the car not some*thing*.

Owen turned to Alice with the face that a general wears before he sends his troops into battle. He'd erased the expression of fear and replaced it with control and demand. "Al, stay here with the car. Lock the doors. Stay in the driver's seat, and if you see anyone coming toward the car and it's not us, floor it. Call the police. You got it? Don't go out for anything. Call the police first."

Alice nodded as Owen opened his door and stepped out into the rain. He was soaked during the two seconds it took to open the rear door for Morpheus to slide out and Jairus to do the same. Morpheus led the two men into the woods in the direction the figure had gone. Rain pounded into the ground around him but not a drop touched his hair or soiled his shirt. The drops shimmered when they came close to him but changed direction and slid around his figure before hitting the ground.

He could see through the wall of rain and darkness better than Jairus or Owen, so he led them at a fast walk. His feet never got caught in the mud; neither did he trip over mossy logs.

They were moving too slow. Morpheus wanted to turn and yell for the men to move more quickly, but he knew they were trying their hardest. Owen was keeping a hand on Jairus to help him over the tough spots they encountered. The older man still didn't seem alive, almost as though he'd crawled into a shell and didn't feel it was safe to crawl out.

Morpheus was about to look over his shoulder at Owen and Jairus when a scream rocked the forest. Morpheus ran, forgetting the men behind him. Another scream ricocheted through the trees making Morpheus change his direction to follow the sound. He shouted Brigh's name uselessly, but he hoped somewhere in the world that some being would grant his voice access to this world so she could hear him coming.

The trees began to clear as his thoughts turned to Brigh. He stumbled, grabbing at the tree branches around him, and frowned when they bowed under his weight. The rain still didn't hit him, but the tree reacted to him in a way nothing ever had. Shaking his head, he continued forward until he hit the edge of a clearing and caught sight of two figures on the ground. Morpheus ran to the pair, and then suddenly halted as he registered what was happening.

Jake's back was to him, leaning over Brigh's still body on the ground, her eyes staring out ahead of her before they slowly closed. After several more seconds, Jake released his grip around her neck and backed up with a sadistic grin on his face.

A painful snarl erupted through Morpheus as he felt Brigh's essence enter him. The person he felt the most disgusted with was himself because he'd wanted this. He'd wanted for so long to be alive.

Now he wished he had never existed.

28

MORPHEUS

"No!" he screamed.

An earsplitting ringing started in his ears and he brought his hands up to cover them, but the pain in his chest stopped him. The first beat took him from his feet and the second stole a scream from his mouth as he fell on his side. His airways burned as the lungs expanded and air whooshed through his chest. Every hair in his nose tickled as he breathed. He felt the blood circulate in his hands, his feet, his calves, his shoulders, tingling. A numb and burning sensation came over his lower extremities and then a bitter cold he'd never experienced before.

What's—

The memories hit him all at once, the sounds loud and vibrating, the colors vivid and blinding, and the smells sickly intoxicating. He tried to spit out the flavors of cheap meat, expensive wines; the taste of blood and virginity between his teeth, her teeth. Different lives, different times, they all flowed through him quickly, birth marks forming on his shoulder blade and ankle, tiny scars curving around his knuckles. His favorite color blue, her favorite scent of lavender, their prejudice against the Africans; none of them matched what he had made himself to be, but in the end they were all a part of him. He witnessed every birth and every death as though they were his own. And in a way, they were.

Once the pain numbed every inch of body and mind, Morpheus lifted his head from the ground and looked around with what he felt were new eyes. The night no longer seemed so dark, but the temperature was definitely a shocking chilly surprise. The hairs on his arm stood at attention to such a chill, but were smoothed out by the rain's cold embrace.

"The fuck?" Jake gasped.

Morpheus's brows drew so close together his head began to swirl in pain. He stood, turning to look the murderer in the eyes. Four thin streaks of blood flowed across his cheek; blood drawn by Brigh's nails. There was a cut on his lip, a red crusty mess billowing around the openings of his nostrils. But that wasn't all he saw; old bruises, old, brittle blood. Not by his hands, but surely by his doing.

She hung from the edge of the cliff, dangling by fingers chilled by the October air. She'd gone to find her daughter, knowing where the girl's favorite spot had always been. She'd been in love with the old house since she was little and had seen the magic of its beauty in her mother's paintings. She'd come thinking she'd find her daughter aimlessly drawing in front of the old fireplace, but the girl had not been inside.

No, she'd found her daughter out back behind the house, nearly unconscious and naked and at the mercy of a boy. He'd glared at her as she'd drawn near, cursing her for ruining what he'd been wanting for so long. He'd hit her, tried pushing her over the edge. One fatal push and she'd tripped on loose soil. Her husband was right around the corner, but the man had missed seeing the boy, and his wife was already sliding down the mountain and into the rocks below.

Jake had murdered Brigh's mother.

When he clenched his fists, and his arms grew hot with tension, Morpheus realized for the first time what it felt like to be angry. Every time Narelle had gotten to him, the few times Brigh had pushed him the wrong way, and the times Darius had said the wrong thing to him, he hadn't been angry. Anger was just a word then, not a feeling. Now anger was more, it was a fever, searing his insides. Coursing through his veins with anticipation.

The scream that ripped from his throat vibrated in his chest as his heart tried to climb out. He charged at Jake faster than he thought his legs could carry him, and before the boy could put up his hands, Morpheus picked him up and threw him to the ground.

"*Why?*" Morpheus yelled in Jake's face. He picked the boy up again, his arms straining slightly from the weight, and slammed his body down on the ground.

"Man…" Jake mumbled. Mud dripped inside his ears as he coughed.

Morpheus had to admit the boy looked pitiful. His face was a bloody mess and the rain wasn't making him look any better. Morpheus wanted to add to the cuts and bruises already on Jake's face, but something stopped him. He relaxed his fist and let his arm come to his side. Jake was cowering, hands held out in front of him, pleading incoherently. No, he wasn't pitiful. Jake was something Morpheus had no words for.

"You—" Morpheus shook his head. *You are not worth it*, he'd wanted to say.

Closing his eyes, Morpheus stood and turned to find Brigh.

A roar was heard from behind him, and before Morpheus could turn, he was attacked and forced to the ground. Mud gathered in his nose and between his teeth before he was pulled back and turned around. Jake's fist connected with Morpheus's nose and a crack sounded.

The pain was almost too much, but the fury jetting through his body reminded him what Jake had done, what Morpheus had let him do. The guilt melded with the fury and the combination tore another scream from his throat. Grabbing Jake's shirt collar, Morpheus pushed him back enough to punch him. His knuckles burned with contact, possibly broken, but it didn't compare to the sound coming out of Jake's mouth.

"Fuck you, man," his words slithered out on a stream of blood and saliva.

Morpheus pulled his arm back again.

"Let the boy go, Morpheus," Narelle chided.

With a growl vibrating between his cheeks, Morpheus shot a look at Narelle behind him. "Who the fuck is she?" Jake squealed, looking back and forth between the two.

The new breath stilled halfway out of Morpheus's mouth, causing a short vaporous tendril. He looked down at the terrified expression shadowing Jake's face, and then searched Narelle's new rosy red complexion. He dropped the boy in the mud and stood to face his jovial, and human, mentor.

"Simply *smashing*," she said as he approached her. She took the wet folds of his shirt fabric between her spindly fingers and stroked and tugged, her nails dancing around his chest hairs.

His breath came back to him fast, and he didn't understand the warmth spreading through his veins. And then she looked up at him, a coy smirk soiled with fat drops of rain. Water beaded along her hairline like a delicate crown and then slipped down her nose and into her eyes. Eyes that were as green and beautiful as Brigh's.

"Get away from me," Morpheus snarled.

The smile dropped from her face, taking a few bits of rain with it. "How dare you speak to me in such a way."

"I may speak to you however I like, *murderer*."

"The girl's existence no longer mattered. Our right to life has been fulfilled."

"What right is it of ours to steal?" Morpheus yelled. "She was innocent; she had barely even begun to live. You took over that boy's body clearly knowing what the consequences would be. You took his memory of that night and amplified it. You are no better than the memory of what he did."

Narelle slapped Morpheus hard. His cheek vibrated. "Do not forget your place, *child*. You wanted humanity more than anything. Do not tell me you are not happy to be alive."

Morpheus tightened his jaw. Shook off the pain. "Touch me again and worse will come to you than it did the boy."

Narelle's eyes widened slightly, but anger still clouded them. "The way you see this will change."

Morpheus backed away from Narelle and turned his back on her. "Never will I forget what you are."

This time Morpheus didn't allow himself to be surprised. He measured the noise of splashing from puddles and crunching of leaves and turned in time to catch Narelle before she jumped his back. Her thin neck fit into his fist perfectly, his fingers meeting at the nape. A look of surprise took over her face, quickly replaced by pain and lack of oxygen.

"Do you not realize what you have done?" he yelled into her face. "You took a life. Your heart will not be spared, neither will your soul. You are filth in my hands, and this world would do well without you."

Tears welled in her stolen eyes and Morpheus realized they were more from sadness and anger because his fist had already loosened. He took a step back from his mentor and looked away. So many things pushed at his lips to be spoken, but he couldn't bring himself to let any of them free.

"Just go," he found himself saying.

She gasped. "Morpheus."

He didn't look until he heard her scream. On both sides of her, grasping a long pale arm in their gray and bony hands stood two Elders. Their faces were in shadow underneath their black hoods, but Morpheus knew what lay underneath and the image made him shiver.

Before him came another Elder, this one taller and wider than the two holding Narelle. He nodded at Morpheus and then turned to face his mentor.

Narelle, the Elder facing her said in a rough voice that tickled the lobes of Morpheus's brain. *Newly Finished, do you agree to the charge of stealing a life?*

"No," she responded quietly.

Do you plead guilty to this charge?

She looked at Morpheus. Her eyes pleaded with him for help, tears streaming down her face with the rain. Morpheus broke eye contact and turned sideways with his arms crossed. A few seconds passed and then Morpheus heard Narelle utter the word he'd wished she'd say, but hoped she wouldn't. "Never."

Then you are banished to the Hall of Damnation for all eternity. So be it!

Lightening shot across the sky once, twice. And then, in a strand of electric brilliance, a bolt swirled down from the clouds and struck Narelle square in the chest. Morpheus had to cover his ears and shield his eyes from the blinding light and Narelle's horrific cries. And then all was quiet.

All was calm. The only sound was that of rain hitting the ground and zipping past leaves. When Morpheus looked up, both the Elders and Narelle were gone.

A light shone on the ground across from him, shadow figures dancing crosswise in the muddied leaves. Jairus knelt on the ground, his back facing Morpheus, his shoulders shaking. The flashlight was at his feet, the light facing away. It was a small manmade contraption laying across from Owen whose haunted eyes stared at the ground. He must have brought the flashlight from the car. Owen met Morpheus's eyes. The other man nodded and then turned and left them alone.

With more energy than he thought he had, he pushed himself up from the ground, stumbling at first as if he didn't know how to stand on his own two feet. The walk to Jairus felt too long, and when he walked around the man he wished the walk had never ended.

In his lap was Brigh, still and silent as Morpheus had never seen her. And when he looked to Jairus questioningly, the old man meeting his gaze, Morpheus saw the tears in his eyes and the way the muscles stood out in his forehead.

He wasn't sure how he got to his knees, he really didn't care. He couldn't blink, couldn't speak, and couldn't take in oxygen for a long time. His beautiful enchanting Brigh looked…so wrong.

As if giving up a dead bird for burial, Jairus motioned for Morpheus to take his place without questioning who, why, and how, and when Morpheus caught the weight of her body, he knew.

He held her in his arms, fingers clutched tightly around her elbows, shaking and white. Her skin was warm, soft, and slick under the water and his tears. But no beating force came from her veins, no heated breath from mouth or nostrils. Her lips parted without a smile, rain dipping through the creases of her skin.

"She's gone," he heard someone whisper.

"No," he growled. She couldn't be gone; he'd just gotten her.

In his anger and panic, he shook her hard, her head lolling to the side. An arm fell heavily to the ground, the rain splattering mud along her hand. He watched the mascara leave trails of black around her nose as if she were crying, and waited for the lashes to twitch and her eyes to flutter open. But nothing happened.

"*God damn it,*" he yelled. He didn't know what to do. He was cursing a God he'd never known, never worshipped, never thought to exist. But as he knelt in the pouring rain, his knees cutting into the muddy ground, he began to wonder if there was a god. And if there was such a being, he'd begun this life hating it.

Breath was lost to him as a deep searing pain curled through his chest. His jaw shuddered after his throat tightened, and he felt something hot and wet meld together with the rain on his face. He could feel the heart trying to break out of his chest, the lungs unable to expand as he choked out a sob. He wasn't sure if the drops on her cheek were the rain or his tears.

"You cannot be gone," he whispered. "I just found you."

"Son," Jairus choked out. "There's nothing you can do."

"There has to be," Morpheus cried. "Something. Anything. She has to come back."

Jairus closed his eyes and pinched the bridge of his nose, something Morpheus had seen Brigh master over the past several months. For as long as he'd followed Brigh, he knew Jairus was never one to crack many jokes, or smile too often. The man was always quiet, somewhat reserved, with a broken slope to his face.

Now he looked lost, a line of forfeit creasing his lips. He'd given up his daughter like he'd given up his wife, and that made a patch of hate slip across the place Morpheus had made for the older man in his heart.

"You are just going to stand there and do nothing?" Morpheus growled.

"There's *nothing* we can do," Jairus barked.

"Most likely not," a deep voice rumbled behind him.

Morpheus watched the others out of the corner of his eye. The bloodied Jake and the grieved Jairus reacted just as he suspected; Alphaeus was an enormous presence, with his alarming rugged and slanted looks, a face forever lost in shadows of guilt and sorrow. Jairus took two steps back, held out his arm as if to protect his daughter from a monster. Jairus hadn't yet realized that the real monster was the one holding his daughter.

"Peace, my friend," Alphaeus went on, his Russian accent sharp and emotionless. "I have not come to wish any harm."

Not that he could, thought Morpheus. His confusion on what his kind could and could not do was still there, but he knew one thing was true: they could not touch.

"Who are you?" asked Jairus.

"I am known as Alphaeus. You might be Jairus?"

Morpheus watched Jairus try to force out his reply, but in the end he nodded and took a deep breath. Tears still shined in the man's eyes, a few escaping to hang in his lashes. His jaw was set tightly, his lips quivering slightly, and Morpheus counted the seconds before the older man would crack and break open.

"The boy?" Alphaeus inquired.

"Alive," Morpheus whispered.

Alphaeus threw him a look. "Do *not* regret letting him live. You are human now. Killing him would have crushed everything you have dreamed of, everything you have worked for."

Barely an audible whisper, Morpheus said, "He took everything of which I have ever dreamed."

Alphaeus didn't blink as he bowed his head. "I am sorry. Truly."

Morpheus caught his gaze and the sadness and want of revenge shown in his eyes like fire so hot tears welled. Alphaeus nodded, understanding, but set his jaw. Morpheus knew Alphaeus wouldn't allow the murder, even though a part of him agreed. He also knew that if he did commit the sin, he would pay for it in his next life, if such a thing were given to him.

"What's going on?" Jairus asked, his tears and pain set aside for the moment.

"I will allow Morpheus to explain everything to you later." Alphaeus addressed Jairus politely, though Morpheus noticed that a little annoyance edged his voice. "Morpheus, please stand."

Morpheus hung his head. "I cannot."

"I told you to stand." This time his voice trembled with caged anger.

"And I told you I cannot." Morpheus met his eyes and felt his own fill with tears. "I know what I have done. I know the consequences. Would you rob me of a few seconds more to grieve?"

"What did you do?" Jairus asked, looking back and forth between the two men.

"Grieving is for the weak," Alphaeus continued, his Russian accent deepening with anger. "For the last time, you will stand or I will make it so that never again will you have the ability."

"Did you not mourn for your Isla when she passed?" Morpheus shouted. Two tears rolled across his angry cheeks. He was surprised at how warm they were against his cool skin as they dripped one at a time from his shaking chin. "If not for me, then for the memory of her, leave me to grieve the death of my own love. I only ask a minute."

Alphaeus's eyes darkened. "You *selfish, inconsiderate—*"

"Take it back!" Morpheus shouted.

"What?" Alphaeus asked incredulously.

Morpheus wanted to yell, but couldn't ready his throat for the pressure. He took a painful deep breath and closed his eyes. "Take it back. I no longer want it."

"*What?*" Alphaeus snapped.

"Life." Morpheus looked Alphaeus in the eyes. "It is not what I thought it was. Take it back."

Alphaeus gritted his teeth. "You cannot just give back a life."

"Find a way. There has to be something. Anything. Bring her back."

"There is nothing I can do."

"Then the Elders, they have to—"

"*Nothing can be done*," Alphaeus growled.

Frantically, Morpheus searched around him for anything that might aid him in bringing Brigh back. But all that lay around him was a grieving father, a murderous boy, and a being so old and powerful who denied giving help because of a few technicalities. As Rich would've said, he was screwed.

He hung his head and let the tears fall. "I would rather experience a thousand different deaths than live one life without her."

"Boy, I—"

Morpheus's next words caught in his throat as Alphaeus paused and stared fixedly at Morpheus's chest. He eyed his elder with curiosity on the verge of being concern when the man didn't meet his gaze.

"Alphaeus, what—"

Morpheus heard someone suck in a breath and choke. Only once he heard, "'When these sunny days are vanished'..." slowly, the words harsh from a bruised throat, did he look down at his lap to see from whom the noise was coming.

His face slackened of any emotion. Her eyes were closed, her lips slightly parted as they had been when Jairus set Brigh into his arms. Was it possible...?

Morpheus cleared his throat. "'When the charm of youth is fled'..."

He held his breath. Waited.

One minute.

He tried again. "'When the rosy bloom is banished'..."

Two minutes.

Her lips barely twitched. "'...age's frostiness, instead'..."

His breath rushed out as a sob. How was it possible? He didn't give it another thought. "'When the eye has lost its brilliance, and the voice is weak and old, will I lose this heart-surveillance'—"

Her eyes fluttered open. "'Will this love of thine grow cold?'"

"Never," whispered Morpheus, the force from the sudden change in elevated emotions and holding of breath robbing him of sight and consciousness before he could get out another word.

29

MORPHEUS

Six months had passed between them. She'd been busy with healing and him with his new life. His parents were very kind and very young for their generation, both filling him with love and attention. He found he enjoyed football the most because his friends all made the game cunning, ruthless, and exciting. If they weren't all graduating from high school in a couple of weeks he would have joined the varsity football team.

Never had he thought life would feel quite like this. Like the air outside had become soft as silk and the ground so solid and still. Sometimes he felt like he could fly, felt like his shoes barely touched the ground as he walked. He let his hair grow longer so the wind had more with which to play and his clothes tapered to fit him perfectly. He found himself liking the clothes those of his generation coveted, even though some outfits once seemed so ridiculous. He was popular at school and in line for valedictorian. His only match was Brigh, but she hadn't been in school for several months and had been denominated by the class advisors.

Jake was in jail, facing manslaughter and attempted murder. The police had no proof that Brigh had died, except for Morpheus, Jairus, and Owen's testimonies. The case against him for Brigh's mother's death was still being put together. Peter was beside himself. Morpheus had caught sight of him yelling at the principal in the main office several times, but he didn't know what was being done.

He'd had no problems about his sudden appearance to everyone. They all thought him and Brigh had been friends for the year since he moved to town. He worked with Jairus as a carpenter's apprentice at a job in Berkley Springs, West Virginia. Morpheus drove to work every day with the man. Somehow Jairus talked more with him than anyone else. Morpheus thought it might be because of how close his wife was within him that drew a smile out of Jairus, but he wasn't sure. Either way, he was close with the man. Even Richard liked him. The only person he hadn't seen much of was Brigh. Jairus didn't say it, but Morpheus knew it was because she wasn't ready to see him. To her, he'd just been a figment. Seeing him for the first time in the hospital interacting with her family had shaken her.

His eyes were no longer brown, but a bright peridot green that rivaled Brigh's in beauty. Looking in the mirror did nothing to change his mind about his appearance. Though he didn't look like anyone in town, and though many girls sought his company, he did not find himself incredibly attractive. He knew his knowledge of the world surpassed even that of his teachers, and for that he felt above them, but he didn't feel above people when it came to appearance. He was comfortable with what he'd become, but not so much that he wanted people to see him and only him.

R

Like so many times over the past months, he found himself at her door. Jairus was at a contractors meeting and Richard at school. Alice was home taking care of her niece like she had been every day since she got out of the hospital. Morpheus would stand there, silent, his hand twitching toward the doorbell, but he'd never press it.

This part of life was harder. He couldn't just go to her room and watch her, or follow her around everyday anymore. He had to patiently wait and be asked to come in. He was always afraid she would turn him away. She hadn't shown any desire of seeking him out and she hadn't personally asked for him. He'd taken it upon himself to do the seeking. What a coward he'd turned out to be.

Before he could get enough nerve up to knock on the door, or enough cowardice to head to his car, the door opened. He stared up at a breathtaking Alice who'd let down her curly hair and worn something a little more feminine than a t-shirt and jeans. Perhaps Owen was coming to pick her up. They'd been publicly dating for several months now; the whole town, knowing it was inevitable.

"Morpheus?" she asked.

At least she was smiling at him.

"Alice," he said with a nod. "I was just seeing if Jairus was around."

Her smile grew into a grin and she ducked her head in amusement. "I don't think you come here every other day and stand on the porch for an hour just to see my brother-in-law. Face it, he's not that interesting."

Morpheus felt his cheeks grow a little hot, no doubt red as a cherry. "I do apologize. I just…"

"I know why you're here." Backing away from the door, she held it open for him to enter. He followed her through the house to the kitchen he'd seen a million times and waited for her to bring out the pitcher of homemade lemonade from the fridge. She poured two glasses and set them both on the island in front of the sink and dishwasher. He stood as immobile as always, waiting to see what he was to do or say next.

Alice leaned against the cabinet where the coffee pot sat, still brewing even one in the afternoon. She looked tired. "I know things aren't how they seem." She gave him a motherly look, one his own mother gave him when she knew he wasn't being completely honest. "She asks for you. Not when she's awake. She talks in her sleep and says your name. She wakes up and it's like nothing happened. She doesn't want to go to school; she doesn't want to see anyone. I don't know how much longer I can hold off Felicity. She's getting creative."

Morpheus smiled and then couldn't help but laugh. Then he drew himself up to his full six-foot-three-inch height and looked Alice in the eye. "I need to see her."

"I know," she said. "But you have to follow what she wants. I like you, Morpheus, I do. I wish you two happiness. But what I want doesn't matter. It's up to her."

Morpheus nodded in understanding. He didn't like it. He knew she'd say no. He knew it like he knew he wasn't entirely human. There was something about him that made him different that made everyone notice. He wore their clothes, he'd started adapting to their way of speaking, and he drove their cars, but he wasn't one of them. He knew he wasn't.

"May I?"

Alice nodded. "She's out back. Take these." She handed Morpheus the two glasses she'd poured. He took them with a nod and headed for the backyard with his head held high and his heart fluttering in his stomach.

ᚱ

He found her sitting on the rocks of the small manmade pond by the tall, wooden property fence. Her face was hidden by a wave of long blonde hair as she leaned over a hardback book in her lap. The arm and leg casts were gone, the bruising very slight and faint shades of brown and green. He knew the brace around her ribs was still there even six months later.

He set the two glasses of lemonade on a piece of flagstone and shoved his hands in his jeans pockets. Instead of dawdling like he wanted so badly to do, he loudly cleared his throat, kicking the grass sprouting between two large pieces of Allegany Rose flagstone. He knew Jairus would be annoyed about the grass, if he wasn't already, because he'd gone against the professional opinion of Arnold at the nursery about using polymeric sand instead of a thin layer of regular sand. The polymeric would harden after being moistened, and it would keep weeds from coming up between the stones as well as create an even walking ground.

Morpheus had spent two days helping Jairus lay everything out, and now that half of the hard work had been for nothing he felt cheated. But those two days had spread through him an enormous feeling of achievement. He'd spent a total of twenty four hours laying everything down in hope that Brigh would watch him and feel obligated to come down and see him. Well, she hadn't come down, but he'd had the feeling of being watched on more than one occasion from her window.

Brigh didn't jump from the suddenness of his presence, but turned slowly, languidly, with a dreamy expression still on her face. He wished she would smile, but once the reality of his presence sunk in he could see her start to retract. She closed her book, finger holding her place, and stood to face him. He watched her wince at the pain in her ribs that the movement had cost her. He wanted to erase such pain, wished he could go back to that night and change everything.

But what he needed now were some cue cards to get the conversation started, or at least completed. He hoped she would say something, but worried that if he didn't start talking she'd lose patience and leave him standing in the yard by himself.

"I've missed you," he said. He wasn't too thrilled with the choice of words, but they'd have to do for the moment.

Warily, she eyed him like someone she'd never met. At some instances he wondered if she recognized him at all. "Why are you here?"

He cocked his jaw painfully to the left. He hadn't been expecting that reaction. "I don't know if you've noticed, but it's been six months since last we saw each other."

"Yeah. So."

He shook his head and laughed. He pulled his sorry carcass out of the nervous wreck he'd created and walked toward her. "This is all so obscene. You ignoring me. Your absence from school; absence of any room in your house that inhabits life of any kind when I come over. Anything to do with me and you shirk away."

Now he was right in front of her, so close that he could smell the mint scented sunscreen she'd recently applied. Her eyes had lost a little of their emerald brilliance, but everything that made her Brigh was still intact.

"I want to know why," he whispered.

Her eyes hardened in challenge for a minute, but then lost their frigidity when he softened his gaze. She shook her head and sunk down into the nearest lawn chair, stretching out until there was no pressure put on her ribs. Morpheus took the seat on the side of the pond where she'd previously perched. He leaned in close, ignoring the fear of pushing her away because he wanted to be close. He needed the solidity of her to know she was real. He needed some comfort in life.

She didn't speak right away. Her attention was reserved for the book in her hands. An old brown book falling apart at the spine. Some of the pages were sticking up outside of the covers, unbound and aged. He couldn't make out the title; it'd been worn away over the years, but it looked familiar. He hated that he couldn't place it.

"I don't know how to…be…with you," she whispered, her eyes focused and still on the book.

Resting his elbows on his knees, he threaded his fingers and rested his chin on the formed steeple. "I wouldn't know how to be with me either. Kind of a frightening thought, actually."

She smiled. A little. "You're not helping your case any."

"Didn't intend to."

She looked up at him finally, the smile no longer there. "You're insufferable."

His brows knotted in confusion. "How do you figure?"

"Sorry, insufferable was the wrong word."

"Oh, good."

Again she shook her head. "You're insane."

"Undoubtedly the best adjective to summarize me."

She narrowed her eyes. "How can you make a joke about this? You waltz right into my house and think you can carry me away with your good looks?"

"Whoa, whoa," he said as he stood. He ran four trembling fingers through his hair as he turned in a small circle before meeting eyes with the siren whose song unnerved him at the moment. "For one thing, the hostility is unwarranted. And for another, I do not, have not, and will not ever plan to 'carry' you away with my 'good looks.' Once I had hoped my selfless and unconditional feelings toward you would suffice."

"You stole me, Morpheus," she yelled, holding her stomach as though her ribs wanted to charge right out of her skin. "I felt you take my soul. You raped it and then spit it back out. How else am I supposed to feel? Do you want me to say congratulations about becoming human? Because you won't get it. You didn't even tell me my soul was the one that would finish you. You didn't say a word, and for *that* I hate you."

He walked over and grabbed her shoulders, carefully hauling her to her feet. She struggled in his hold, but he only tightened his grip. He wanted her to see his eyes, how they reflected her own. "See this? Do you see what I have to look at every day when I stand before a mirror? Do you understand how the very sight of them makes me want to gauge them out of their sockets, to take everything back? Every hour of every day for the last six months has been nothing but a sickening reminder that I stole from you.

"But I stole from myself, too." His grip loosened as the first tears rounded her flushed cheeks. But he continued on. He had to unload because he knew he'd never get another chance. "If I couldn't have you I didn't want to exist. You made me feel alive when I was with you. And now that I have breath, it doesn't matter. Because the one reason I wanted to be alive doesn't want me."

Her lips pursed against the shower of tears cascading down her skin. But her eyes never wavered from his. "I was so afraid. When I died. I thought I was never coming back. I was all alone. I'm all alone."

Morpheus wrapped his arms around her as she sobbed. She clung to his t-shirt and he clung to her. This wasn't about him taking her soul. It was about her dying painfully, slowly, and alone. She resented him for not saving her, for not being there when she needed him the most. But most of all, she thought he'd taken her soul so that he could live.

This realization made him pull back from her, his eyes growing warm and full from his own tears. "You think I wanted you dead—that I wanted your soul?" He shook his head, his face lost in an expression of horror at the thought. Grabbing her face between his hands, he kissed her forehead fiercely. He wanted to eradicate such a thought, wanted to suck it right out of her mind.

"I would do anything to secure your happiness and safety. Do you understand?" He felt on the edge of hysterics.

She nodded, choking out her next words. "I've missed you so much. I wanted you here...I wanted to know you were real. I didn't want to just imagine you."

"I'm as real as you are." Being able to say it felt odd to him. But it felt right. He'd wanted to exist in the human world for so long he'd known nothing but the want, the need. He kissed the top of her head, pausing at her brow, then pulled back and looked her in the eyes. Tears still glittered there, but a smile brightened her face.

"May I kiss you?" he asked, afraid that if he didn't she would reject him.

"You did so well with the rest of my face," she said with a laugh.

With his arms wrapped around her, he leaned down and touched her nose with his. She exhaled, leaving her lips partly open. He wanted to claim them with his own so badly but wanted to savor her soft features first. Trailing kisses across her brow, he spaced them apart slowly, wiping away the tears in his wake.

He pulled her closer as he came to her lips. Her eyes were already closed, her head slightly tilted back in waiting. She looked so innocent and sweet. He hated to kiss her knowing that he was slowly stealing that innocence away.

But she's mine, he thought.

A smile broke out on his face. She was his and no one else's. "I will love you until the end of days, until our bodies no longer bear breath and life. I have and always will cherish you, Brianna."

A laugh escaped her tiny mouth as a few tears escaped her lashes. "I love you, too."

Until the end. Who knew when that would be? The thought of death frightened Morpheus, made him pull her so close that no space came between them from head to toe. He pressed his lips against hers and kissed her as though they'd never have another day together. Maybe they wouldn't. Neither of them knew. Death came so very easy among them, even Morpheus was no exception. When he'd lost her he'd lost everything. There was the possibility of losing her again, and the fear of that poured into the ferocity of his kiss. He sucked on her lips and her tongue as though they were her life source. He needed to keep her safe, if not for her then his own sanity. He couldn't live without her. He couldn't see a world without her.

Until the end.

He prayed there wouldn't be one.

30

MORPHEUS

Joshua and him had gone to the local dress shop and rented tuxes for prom. Morpheus was glad that his friend hadn't known about formal wear anymore than he did. The women there had been very helpful and had laughed at some of Morpheus's choices for a tux. He'd gone for frills and pastels. Jodi had explained to him that those two things hadn't been in vogue since 1986. He'd laughed with the girls and looked confused with Joshua. Neither of them had a clue about color schemes or fit.

Standing at the head-to-mid-thigh mirror hung slightly crooked on the back of his door, he adjusted his tie for the thousandth time. He wouldn't match her dress, but he wasn't going to prom with her either. He had begged her to tell him the color of her dress, but she'd resisted, saying that a girl's prom dress was second in line to her wedding dress. It was a surprise. No one could know. Felicity didn't even know anything about it. So she claimed. But the surprise made him antsy. He wanted to see her. He had to see her.

A knock at the door made it bounce back and forth in the frame. "Morpheus? Are you decent?"

He smiled at his mother's soft voice and backed away from the door. "You can come in."

She peaked around the door first before coming in. Her dark hair was pulled back in a loose bun, her cleaning bandana securely wrapped around her head. Her brown eyes winked at him as the smile lines grew prominent. Her eyes went wide at the sight of him. He hoped he didn't look a fool; he'd never put on a tie or a cummerbund before. "You look amazing, dear."

Letting out the breath he'd been holding, he tugged at his black tie. It felt too tight all of a sudden. "You think so? I still can't get the tie right."

"Oh, no worries." She started undoing the tie and fixing it. "You're just nervous. Had you gotten up the nerve to ask anyone to go with you?"

He gave her a sardonic look. "The person I wanted to ask already has a date."

"What a shame," she said. "I'm sure Jairus had a fit."

Morpheus looked away from his mother. "I didn't ask him."

"Well why not?" She smacked his shoulder lightly and then stepped back to take him in. "I'm sure if you'd talked to him about taking his daughter he would've said yes in a heartbeat. You look wonderful, stop fidgeting."

"I feel like an idiot in this."

She sighed. "They all do, dear. Even your father hated the prom. Until his friends spiked the punch, that is. I still have a Bacardi stain on my dress."

Morpheus closed his eyes. "I don't want to know."

"I know, I know," she said, going to stand by the door. "But let me just say this: prom marks the end of an era in your life. You're supposed to enjoy this night, not sulk. Have fun, and you better ask her to dance. And if you don't, do not even think about coming home."

Morpheus rolled his eyes. "I will, don't worry."

"I know," she said. "You wouldn't last a day out on your own without someone to fix you a hot meal."

He grinned. "Exactly."

"Hmm. Give me a kiss."

Morpheus gave her a hug and planted a kiss at her brow. She teased him and gave idle threats and he loved her for all of it. She entertained him more than anything when she tried to enforce the fact that she'd given birth to him and he had to follow her rules. She was fair and loving. His father was the same way.

"I'll be down in a minute," he told her when she went for the door.

She smiled. "Don't forget your ticket. I had to stuff your fathers in my bra so he wouldn't lose it."

He closed his eyes away from that image. "Sometimes information is just too much."

He heard her laugh as she went down the stairs.

With a sigh, he picked up his ticket and stuffed it inside his jacket. When he looked up into the mirror, Alphaeus stood behind him. The man hadn't changed at all during the six months he hadn't seen him. The empty expression on his face gave away nothing. Whether he was angry or happy was lost on him.

"Alphaeus." He bowed his head.

Alphaeus responded with a nod of his own, but didn't move. "I hope all has been well."

"It has been better."

One smooth brow rose in question. "The girl has not been satisfying?"

He tried keeping the blush at bay but wasn't sure if he'd been successful. "Things have been...stressed. I do not know if we will become anything."

"Pity."

"Why the interest?"

Alphaeus walked across Morpheus's immaculately clean room to sit in his large leather computer chair. He sat in it more gracefully than Morpheus. But where

Morpheus made the chair rotate and rock as he sat, the chair didn't react to Alphaeus at all.

"I just think the girl's reaction to your sacrifice is very selfish and unbecoming of her."

His brows drew together in confusion. "Sacrifice?"

"Do you not remember my story?" he didn't look pleased about Morpheus's lack of remembrance. "I was not spared from the fact that I had stolen her soul." His eyes narrowed. "You, on the other hand, were granted clemency where Narelle was not. Do you wonder why?"

He didn't like where this was going. Was Alphaeus here to tell him that his short period of time alive was just a joke? That everything he'd made would be taken from him? Was he threatening Brigh's life?

"I have not given it any thought," he admitted.

"This is obvious," Alphaeus said. Standing from the chair, he now towered over Morpheus by a good two feet. His face was now corrupted by the down strokes of anger and boredom. "I am also sure you do not remember what you said that night."

"Do remind me," Morpheus taunted.

Alphaeus's eyes glazed over, and for a second Morpheus thought the man might strike him. But his hand never rose toward him. "'I would rather experience a thousand different deaths than live one life without her.' Do you remember saying these exact words?"

He really didn't like where this was heading. "Yes."

"At least you retain something." Alphaeus sighed and suddenly looked sad. "By expressing this aloud you made a bargain. In exchange for the girl's life you offered your soul infinitely, for as long as the world exists. You will not age, neither can you die. For her life, you will live a thousand or more. One's energy for another."

"Excuse me?" He hoped his hearing had been off. Immortality didn't exist. It was the essence of fairy tales and romance. Nothing lasted forever. Someday he would grow old and rot in the ground just like every other human. He was no different.

"You gave this girl a second chance," Alphaeus said. "I was too selfish to save my Isla. I wanted life more than I wanted her."

"I thought you were exiled from the human world because you took her essence."

The taller man shook his head, a solemn expression sliding fluidly over his face. "Because I felt there was no penance or reparation to give for my actions, intended or not, I was punished. You chose differently, and, therefore, were presented a different outcome. But nothing comes without a price. Yours was just easier, for you gave it willingly."

Morpheus shook his head. "I didn't know."

"What's done is done," Alphaeus said with a half shrug. "We cannot change the past. All we can do is move on."

"Easier said than done," Morpheus muttered.

Alphaeus nodded. "Now, I see you are going to prom."

"My first. Sort of."

Alphaeus smiled for what could have been the first time in one hundred years. "This one will be different, yes? Enjoy today, for tomorrow may bring sorrow."

"Thank you for the optimism."

Alphaeus bent at the waist in a formal bow with a wide smile. "Most welcome."

Then he was no longer there.

ᚱ

As Morpheus stepped into his recently paid for panther black Pontiac G8 GXP, he wondered whether or not going to the prom was worth it. Brigh would be there, but so would Kyle. Her date. He'd asked her to homecoming, and since neither of them had made it because of their fall in the Gateway, he'd tried again with prom and she'd agreed.

She'd agreed. The thought left a disgusting taste in his mouth. He turned the key in the ignition and smiled at the roar of the V8 engine. 415 horses galloped beneath the hood, the rumble of their arousal vibrating through the dual hood scoops. He ran his fingers around the steering wheel and patted the dash lovingly. The car was the first thing he'd bought with his paychecks and he couldn't have been happier.

He glanced at the empty passenger seat, trying to imagine her sitting there with the back of the seat slightly reclined and her arm hanging out of the window. Her hair waving in front of her face as they listened to some song with a fun bass beat.

With his lips set in a firm line, he pulled out of his driveway and headed toward the school. The wind curled his hair into knots and the loud music slowly deafened him to anything other than the road ahead. Not many people were out at this time. Parents were already at the school putting the finishing touches on the gymnasium for prom, and the students were either out to pre-prom dinners or pre-prom alcohol binges. Neither of which had sounded interesting to him, so he'd politely avoided both invitations. Joshua wasn't into the drinking part, but him and his girlfriend were going out to dinner beforehand and would meet with Morpheus at the school.

He didn't mind so much about the isolation the car offered him. He loved being with others, but he loved being by himself more. His parents had already been giving him ample amounts of space as though they knew he was an introvert at heart. But to his friends, he allowed them to drag him to parties, games, and other activities. He was a part of the honor society at school and made sure to make all of the meetings. He'd signed up hoping to see more of Brigh. But with her recovery, and then little spurts of agoraphobia, he'd hardly seen her.

The school parking lot was full of cars, vans, and SUV's with Mary Kay, Pampered Chef, and Creative Memories stickers in the rear windows. The town mothers were hard at work inside, and even though Morpheus felt inclined to go in and help them set up, he stayed inside his car and relaxed into the instruments of his favorite music.

Before long, other vehicles joined him in the small lot, their cars rumbling and vibrating with loud music. Only when he spotted Joshua and his date did he leave his car. People crowded around in little clusters outside of the gymnasium. Amy, Joshua's girlfriend, gave Morpheus a hug when he came up to them. Even with heels, she was a foot shorter than Joshua, and a foot and a half shorter than Morpheus. The trio pushed themselves through the throng of waiting students and took up space by the gymnasium entrance. Both Joshua and Morpheus stood with their backs to the door, arms crossed over their chests as though they were the ones hired to keep order among everyone.

As more people showed up, girls giggling and screaming over each other's dresses, and guys grasping hands and half-hugging, the doors behind Morpheus opened. A small lady walked out and waved her hands to get everyone's attention. When no one even moved toward her, Morpheus and Joshua simultaneously yelled out for everyone to be quiet. Even people just coming out of their cars or limousines by the curb quieted.

Morpheus grinned at Joshua and the other guy did the same. The small lady turned and smiled thankfully at them before facing the growing crowd. A little thing, her salt and peppered hair was teased into short, tight curls. The blue in her eyes flashed out at everyone as they regarded her with respect and a little fear. As the principal, she held sway over who did and did not graduate. But everyone knew her to be the sweet little old lady she appeared, unless otherwise provoked.

"I want to welcome you all to prom," she yelled in her soft voice.

Everyone cheered before she could go on. Morpheus found himself cheering as anticipation and excitement settled over everyone. He wasn't the least bit embarrassed to be without a date, but the loneliness slowly set into his shoulders. He shook it off and clapped his hands.

The lady turned to share her own excitement with everyone. Her cherry colored cheeks rose in a smile. "There are just a few ground rules." Everyone groaned in unison, which made the lady laugh. "No drinking, no drugs, no sex." Everyone groaned again, but this time theatrically and followed by snickers of amusement.

Shaking her head, she stepped back for people to enter the gym. "Have fun! Don't party too hard!"

Joshua turned to go in and stopped when Morpheus didn't move. "You coming?"

Without looking at him, Morpheus said, "In a minute."

Joshua looked out at the crowd, trying to pinpoint whoever he was looking for. Amy tugged on his arm and he was suddenly lost in the sea of milling prom goers.

People passed Morpheus with smiles on their faces and a variety of greetings. But within those going into the gym he didn't see her. Since she was a little shorter than Kyle, Morpheus began looking for him. But even after the last couple skipped into the gym, he still searched the front walk. They weren't there.

With a feeling of defeat, he walked inside and forfeited his ticket. He wouldn't be able to come back into the gym if he left, but if he left he didn't intend on coming back. The ladies inside were very sweet and offered him drinks and food, but he shook his head. He wasn't hungry. He wasn't ready to dance. He didn't feel much of anything. Suddenly he wanted to be anywhere but there in the middle of couples happily dancing to a fast paced techno song.

He spotted Joshua up by the DJ stage caught in a dance move that would make even Michael Jackson laugh. He couldn't help the smile creasing his face, even though he wanted to yell in frustration. Again he surveyed the room, but didn't see them. The strobe lights and techno colored floor paintings blinded him. Squinting, he ran for the bathroom and ducked inside. The small room smelled strongly of Clorox and Lysol, but he was grateful that the place was immaculate.

Leaning on the sink counter, he closed his eyes and took in a deep breath. As he exhaled, a shudder ran up his spine. Whenever he breathed deep he felt like he was floating, like he couldn't get enough air. Certain songs gave him that free fall feeling where oxygen wasn't readily available. Brigh made him feel this way often. Looking at her would incite such strong emotions within him he'd have to sit from the impact.

Even though he had no idea what her dress would look like, he knew whatever color, style, or shape, that she would look stunning and heartbreaking in it.

"If she ever comes," he told himself in the mirror.

BRIGH

Kyle, even with his small limp to his left leg, held the door open for her after he parked his Mazda. The parking lot was full of cars, but mostly empty of people. A few girls were running back to the school, their high heels held in one hand and the bottoms of their dresses in the other. Brigh didn't see Felicity's car yet, but she'd said she was going to be late.

Kyle took in a deep breath and held out his arm. He'd already complimented her dress and how she looked, but still he couldn't keep his eyes off her. "Ready?"

"Yeah," she said, and then took his arm.

Her dress reminded her of royalty on the way to a ball. It was a rich gold color with a sweetheart bust and corset fit, cascading in gold glittery tulle that met her toeless heels from her hips. She felt like a princess, with her hair freshly curled in angelic waves around her face. She'd expertly applied her makeup and allowed a little bit of black eyeliner beneath her lashes for an added dramatic effect. Her father had been speechless when he saw her, but her aunt had saved the silence from becoming awkward with her screams of surprise and excitement.

"Nervous?" Kyle asked her as they stepped up onto the curb.

They could hear the bass of the music pounding through the school and she knew that every girl inside had let their hair down. The boys looking exceptionally handsome in fitted tuxes, holding onto their sweethearts like this night would end all others. But for some couples it would. She'd heard rumors of several girls planning to lose their virginity to their boyfriends, while the guys were busy making the arrangements. She hoped the guys who were planning without their girlfriends understood what they were getting themselves into before they made a big mistake.

She looked up at Kyle, watched his relaxed jaw, his soft pink tinted cheeks nicely rounded from a gentle smile. She knew Kyle enough to know that he wouldn't force her into anything or suggest something she wasn't comfortable with. He played tough with the guys and teased Felicity more than the girl could stand sometimes, but when it came to her everything changed. He was gentle, caring, and attentive. He knew when to say no and how to ask for what he wanted from her, which wasn't much.

"You okay?" he asked, once catching her gazing at him.

A blush rose to her hairline. "I'm good."

Smiling, he took their tickets from his pocket and presented them to the woman at the door. They ignored the drinks and the food and headed into the mass of seniors. "Good, 'cause we have some dancing to do!"

"Where the hell have you two been?"

Brigh and Kyle's heads shot up at the unmistakable annoyance in Felicity's voice as they turned to face her. But the smile on the girl's face didn't match her tone. With one look at each other's dresses, both Brigh and Felicity screamed and hugged each other.

Brigh was the first to pull away, taking in her breathtaking best friend. Felicity's dress was the most daring outfit she'd worn yet. A black satin halter, embellished along the plunging neckline with silver sequins and beads, the dress revealed enough of her curvy figure to be sexy and mysterious. The sides were cut out, held together by small black circles of fabric. A mid-thigh slit completed the dress, revealing her pale legs and four inch heels.

"Felicity, you look amazing!" Brigh couldn't help but squeal.

Felicity's eyes grew wide as she beamed. "I look nothing like you though. You won't be able to get this one off you."

Kyle shook his head at Felicity's finger pointed in his direction. "Do you realize that almost half your body is showing in that thing?"

Felicity shrugged. "I haven't heard any complaints."

"That's not what I meant," Kyle said under his breath.

"Don't listen to him," Brigh said, tears coming to her eyes. "You look great. Fabulous. Gorgeous."

"I get it," Felicity said. "Now let's move on." Felicity's eyes glittered a little with her own tears as she looped her arms through Brigh's. "I can't believe prom's here already."

"Believe it," Kyle said. "You're wearing a come-fuck-me dress with come-fuck-me heels."

Felicity gave Kyle the death glare. "Brigh, can I talk to you alone for a minute?"

Brigh wanted to talk about whatever it was in front of Kyle, because she was almost positive that it was about him. But she kept her mouth shut and followed Felicity to the punch table, leaving Kyle behind to joke with his jock buddies.

Brigh went for the blood red punch, smiling at the older woman watching over the table. With a quick sip, she turned away from the table and faced Felicity.

"Look, I know Kyle can be forward and sometimes obnoxious—"

"I already know all this," Felicity said in exasperation. "I brought you over here to tell you that your hot sweetie-not is here."

Brigh's heart fluttered in her chest and for a second it was hard to breathe. "I had a feeling he'd be here."

"He doesn't have a date," Felicity said pointedly.

Brigh didn't want her punch anymore. "Why should I care? I have a date."

Felicity rolled her eyes. She took Brigh's cup and tossed it in the nearby trash can and then pulled her by the arm, dragging her around a large group by the stage. After she'd positioned Brigh in the right spot, Felicity pointed through the crowd. Morpheus leaned against the DJ stage with his arms folded tightly across his chest. The DJ leaned down and whispered something into his ear and Morpheus's impeccably sexy frown turned up at the corners as he laughed.

Brigh swallowed. His black tux fit him perfectly, accentuating his broad shoulders, long torso, and warrior height. Hair left loose and curling into layers around his shoulders, he was the prime candidate to be the cover model for any historical romance novel.

When he turned, she caught sight of his gray undershirt. She was disappointed that they didn't match and wished that they coincidentally had. She shook her head and closed her eyes, feeling Felicity's questioning gaze upon her. Once she'd taken a deep breath, she opened her eyes and looked at her friend. Felicity didn't look angry or frustrated. Her face painted a picture of unconditional love and concern.

"I'm here with Kyle," she said.

Felicity smiled coyly. "Some rules are meant to be broken."

"Wait, where's your date?"

Felicity's smile widened and she laughed. "I'm single tonight."

Brigh noted the devious glint in Felicity's eyes and shook her head in amusement. "You planned this."

"Yep," Felicity said, beaming. "No date means I can dance with whoever I want. But just because you have a date doesn't mean you have to stick with one person. Kyle will understand."

"No, he won't."

"Trust me," Felicity said, her brilliant beam dimming down to a small smile. "Go get your dream man." Brigh's eyes widened at Felicity's phrasing and the air seemed to whoosh out of her when she winked.

"Remember the test we tried, but failed at?" Felicity asked. She didn't wait for a reply. "He's more of an Angel than a Spike. But he's alright in my book."

A smile forced Brigh's lips apart. She hugged Felicity and then went in search for Morpheus.

Literally, the man of her dreams.

31

MORPHEUS

After Morpheus's suggestion, Jerry, the DJ, put on a Journey song. Steve Perry's soul searching high voice flowed through Morpheus like a ghost. Cold, smooth, and penetrating his heart with a hard blast. Bob Marley's words, whispered with Brigh's tongue, slithered into his ears: the music may hit him, but he'd feel no pain. Maybe that was the appeal of music. Notes, chords, and vocals allowed you to float in place or dance without thought of anything else. So long as the instruments and the singer kept playing, peace would reign within everyone's hearts and chaos would remain a distant memory.

That's how he felt, anyway.

He watched his classmates look wonderingly at the large speakers positioned around the stage before settling into couplets and groups to sway in Perry's sweet melodic voice. The guitar solo hit Morpheus in the abdomen and spread through his veins like ecstasy. He felt like he could fly, felt like he could do anything. He wanted to dance, wanted the lyrics to become reality and submerge everyone in its harmony. He wanted—

"Morpheus?"

He turned slowly, the weightless feeling he'd had now slowly dissipating. A part of the ecstasy remained, warming his cheeks until he was smiling down at her. Under the roaming multicolored lights, she was a beauty to behold. Her golden dress brought out the strands of gold braided into her hair, brightening her emerald eyes. The idea of never being able to have her, to live lifetimes without her, made the smile quickly slide away.

Gazing into his eyes, she reached up and ran her pale fingers across his cheek until his jaw was cupped in her palm. Eyes closed, he nuzzled her fingers and wrapped his hand around hers. As though thrust back to his days of wanting her and not having the ability to physically contact her, the loneliness and desperation flared hot within him. He possessed a part of her soul, but without something tangible, he couldn't keep hold of her.

Now it was her who didn't seem real.

"What are you thinking?" she asked.

He opened his eyes. Brought their hands away from his face and nearly crushed her hand when she threaded their fingers. Laughing to conceal the sea of emotions swirling within him, he rubbed the back of his neck and looked her in the eyes.

"I was thinking how beautiful you look," he said slowly. "But you already knew that."

Brigh's smile warmed him. "I've been told that. But I didn't believe it till just now."

That feeling of not being able to breathe came over him so hard that he had to bend over. The concerned look that crossed her face made him smile, and once he got his heartbeat under control and air back in his lungs, he brought her hand up to his mouth and kissed each pale white knuckle.

"Morpheus," she said with a gasp. "I'm here with someone else."

"I don't care," was all he said, as he led her to the middle of the dance floor and wrapped his arms around her. She was trying her hardest not to smile and he found himself doing the same. But then he thought, *why should I deny my feelings? Why not show and share them with her so long as she feels the same?*

"Brianna," he whispered in her ear, slowly rocking them back and forth to the leisurely beat of the song. She rested her head on his chest, tilting her chin up so that her ear came closer to his mouth. He went against his better judgment and placed a chaste kiss on the lobe of her ear, then grinned lasciviously when he heard her gasp. Now that he had her in his arms, he wasn't sure what to do. He didn't want to over think. Hell, he didn't want to think at all.

"Be honest with me," he said into her ear. "Do you love me?"

"I told you I did."

He nodded his head. "I know. But I need to know, because..." He opened his mouth to form words, but didn't know where he was going with it. Why did he need to know? He wanted her. In every way a man could have a woman. He wanted her to be his and no one else's. He needed to know that she wanted and needed him just as badly as he did her.

"Why?" she exhaled. She'd pressed her palms against his shoulder blades, hugging him tightly as though she didn't want to let him go.

"I want you to be my girl." Many things had come to mind as soon as she'd broken his inner dialogue. But this response was the only thing he felt was the right thing to say.

She pulled away from his chest, gazing up into his eyes with her innocent beauty. How sweet her lips looked as she pulled them apart to say, "Please clarify before I assume you're saying what I think you're saying."

Morpheus puckered his lips to say something and stopped in understanding. "Sorry. Let me rephrase. I want you to be my gir*lfriend*."

"Thank you for that," she said with a grin. "I thought you were proposing, and doing a horrible job of it."

Morpheus felt himself blush. "Don't worry. I'm going to wait it out a year or two before I attack that question."

She laughed. Brought her hands around his sides and placed them on his chest. "I don't know what to say."

"Just be honest." *And say* yes, he thought.

Looking him in the eyes, she grasped his tie in her fist and tugged him lower until his lips met hers. Even with her heels on, she was still five inches shorter than him. But the difference didn't seem to matter as the kiss deepened and they explored each other's mouths with their tongues. Morpheus distantly thought about where they were and how inappropriate a place a school dance was to kiss Brigh in such a way. But as soon as her arms wrapped back around him, he forgot everything else and pulled her into a dip he'd seen in many romantic black and white movies.

She smiled against his lips and slowly pulled away.

Feeling as though he could run a mile or climb a mountain, he smiled lazily down at her. "I'm going to take that as a yes."

"You better," she said.

His heart soared within his chest. He felt like nothing could touch him. Nothing would surprise him. Everything he knew had changed, and the woman in his arms was his. He no longer felt silly in the tux. Instead, he thought himself handsome and gallant in front of this woman. And he had to admit, he hadn't thought she would say yes.

"I love you," she said.

"I—"

"Well, you do not look as much like a penguin as I do, if I say so myself."

Both Morpheus and Brigh looked to their left, pulling away from each other slightly to get a look at the loud male voice beside them. In a tux much like Morpheus's, he stood an inch shorter in height, but made up for it in the broadness of his shoulders.

The black jacket looked as though it might break at the seams.

"What?" Darius asked at the shocked expression Morpheus wore and the one of question on Brigh's face. "No welcome? Happy existence? Join our party?"

Brigh looked up at Morpheus. "Who's this?"

At the same moment Morpheus opened his mouth to explain, Felicity sauntered up to the group and put her arms around Darius's waist and arm. Confusion blossomed inside Morpheus when Darius returned Felicity's attention with his arm around her waist.

Felicity's smile could light a room. "Guys! Meet Darius. He just moved here from Sacramento. Isn't he *gorgeous*?"

The smile that came over Darius's face could only be described as the look a warrior got when he'd conquered a woman's heart, or at least her interest.

Morpheus was elated that his friend had ascended so quickly after him, but the shock of the fact just kept him staring at his friend until Brigh turned attention back to him.

"Is he the one you told me about?"

He knew what she meant. He'd once told her that both Felicity and Darius would make a perfect match. He hadn't known that his prediction would be so accurate.

All he could do in response was nod and listen to the girls talk about their beaus as Darius pulled Morpheus off to the side. Nothing had changed in his appearance. Eye and hair color had stayed exactly the same and so had his choice in clothing size.

"Try not to look petrified, mate," Darius said with a laugh. "I did not mean to scare you."

Morpheus shook his head and laughed. "You weren't what I was expecting. I thought her date had wizened up and come to fight me for her."

"If he has not already, he is an idiot."

"How long have you been here?"

"I came over last week."

Morpheus nodded in understanding. "I see you haven't lost your touch."

"And I see right through that wall you have there."

Morpheus's brows drew together. "What?"

Darius sighed. "Alphaeus told me what happened."

Morpheus wasn't surprised. Most likely half the populace knew about what had happened. "Don't sass me about it, please, Darius."

All joking and laughter melted from Darius's face. He put his hands in his pants pockets and looked uncomfortable. "I did not mean to tease. I only wanted to say that I am sorry."

Morpheus nodded. "Thank you. I don't even know how I'm going to tell Brianna."

Darius shrugged and Morpheus thought he heard thread snap. "My advice? Tell her soon. She will have longer to get over it."

"And longer to mourn," Morpheus added.

"Assuming she likes you that much."

Morpheus punched Darius in the shoulder. His friend laughed, grasping Morpheus in a tight hug. They pulled apart and went in search of Felicity and Brigh.

He knew he had to tell her. She deserved to know what she was getting herself into. But he didn't have the heart to tell her yet, especially not at prom. But he would eventually get up the courage to tell her he'd never die and that she'd age without him. He hoped she would take the new knowledge well.

Eventually.

32

BRIGH

She and Felicity were the belle's of the ball. Darius held on to Felicity like he knew if he let her go someone else might snap her up. But by the look on Felicity's flushed face, she didn't seem like she wanted to be anywhere else.

After a while of dancing, a group formed around the two couples, hooting and whistling as Morpheus and Darius swung the girls around, passing them back and forth to each other and continuing on as though they'd rehearsed such fine tuned dancing. Felicity and Brigh couldn't stop. laughing, Brigh's blush seeming to have been branded onto her face. Dancing with Darius, during the few minutes they'd switched partners, gave both of them insight into what had happened over the past year. Darius thundered through several questions without halting at the possible consequences his answers might bring, and Brigh was as honest as she thought Morpheus might want her to be. She grew to like Darius during their little chats and wished him and Felicity luck.

As the two were about to part, a hand tugged at Brigh's elbow, and when she looked up she saw Kyle. He looked a little sad and nervous as he came closer to her and Darius.

"May I have this dance?" Kyle asked, holding out his hand like the prince he was.

Brigh looked back to Darius for him to let her go, but his hands tightened around her waist. His eyes clouded with suspicion and anger, his lips lost to a deep frown as he regarded her response to the offer. The smile that came upon her face was genuine and gentle as she extricated herself from Darius's hands.

"It's okay," Brigh said. "Felicity and I have done this before."

Darius's eyes grew large and the anger seemed to rise. With an exasperated grunt, Darius left the two alone, obviously in pursuit of Felicity. The look of possession in his eyes worried Brigh a little, but thought the smothering of Darius and Felicity might do them both good.

When she turned back to face Kyle, he was closer than before. As if on reflex, she brought her hands up to his shoulders, curling her fingers around the roundness of them. She gave him a warm smile before placing her head on his chest. His heartbeat seemed irregular, but that was because of the tension she felt in him. He was obviously holding back whatever comments and criticisms to himself. She didn't want him to be angry or upset.

"Kyle, I—"

"Shh," he whispered in her ear.

She folded her lips together, the words bombarding into each other at their seal. She could feel them racing backward across her tongue, rolling around the back of her throat, and forcing themselves back at her lips. There were so many things she wanted to say, so many she thought she needed to. Maybe that's why he'd shushed her. Was it possible that he knew? Was he so insightful?

"He's watching us," Kyle said suddenly. Brigh didn't have to look up to see who he meant. She could feel Morpheus somewhere behind her, eyes locked on the two of them. "Don't worry. I'll give you back after this song's over."

At that she looked into his face. With his jaw tightened and lips in a straight line, Kyle looked like a man on the verge of murder. The tension in his hands only grew every second that passed and his body was now molded along hers as though they were one being. She didn't feel at all uncomfortable about Kyle's nearness, but the heat pouring into her back from her dream man unnerved her.

"I don't want to hurt you, Kyle," Brigh whispered. She didn't think he'd heard her because of the music, but he leaned down and glanced at her lips before looking her in the eyes.

"Then allow me," he said before claiming her lips.

An electric current soared up her back, gliding around her sides to come up and about her breasts. She felt herself lean into the kiss as his arms wrapped around her tighter. He kissed her with the ferocity of a dehydrated man, sucking on her tongue, clutching at her back so she, the pail of water, would not spill.

She enjoyed the kiss more than she thought she would and should. She'd made the decision about which her heart belonged to, but at the moment she didn't feel as confident. Kyle was stable. She knew him nearly inside and out, and knew that inconsistencies happened to him as often as a leap year. Morpheus, on the other hand, had too many variations that sometimes drove her over the edge or tested the boundaries of her sanity. His actions were spontaneous, his views and experiences unknown to her. In human years he'd barely begun to live, but in existence he surpassed her by one hundred years.

No matter how he felt or what he said, Morpheus had existed, but in such a highly sophisticated fashion that he felt unreal. He knew all the limits, but had breached them without conflictions or second thoughts, and had come out without consequence.

Kyle pulled away first, leaving her breathless and confused. His features were drawn into low dips of sadness and regret. She didn't understand the regret, and the sadness was something she didn't want to think about.

"I'll always love you, Breen," he said with a heartrending smile. "And I'll always be there to catch you before you fall. Remember that."

And then he was gone, and she was left in the middle of the dance floor, her heart bruised and breaking.

ᚱ

They'd left the dance before the last song, and were probably the first to leave. No matter how badly the next song had made her want to dance, she couldn't bring herself to move her legs and arms. Felicity had worried over her like the overprotective mother she didn't have, and Darius had pulled Morpheus to the side for a chat. In the end, no one had looked happy, but Felicity had tugged Darius to her with determination in her eyes, and they'd danced off into the crowd.

Brigh was impressed by Morpheus's choice of transportation, and even his gentlemanly nature as he held the passenger door open for her. What she didn't like was the incredibly stiff and awkward silence settling inside the car, fury evaporating off of him unattractively. She rolled down the window without asking and stuck her arm outside, cutting the air with outstretched fingers.

"Where would you like to go?" he asked. His voice was smooth and delivered with the delicate and carefully sculpted formality that he'd had since she'd met him. No amount of time saturated in her world would rid him of it.

"Turn left up ahead."

A second later the clicking noise of the turn signal kept time with her heartbeat, and they made their way into the woods. The natural world wrapped around them and the material fell away.

"How was it?" Morpheus broke the silence, but not the tension. His voice was laced heavily with scorn.

She didn't dignify his remark with so much as a glance in his direction. "How was what?"

In her peripheral, she caught him looking at her as though she had three heads. But he turned back to the road, grinding the steering wheel beneath his curled fingers. He let out a deep breath through his nose. "That must have been some kiss for you to not even remember it happening."

"I don't see how it's any of your business," Brigh said softly.

Morpheus hit the steering wheel. "God damnit, woman, of course it's my business. Or was my kiss nothing compared to his?"

Brigh suppressed a scream as she turned in her seat to face him. "You are not going to pull the jealous card on me."

He let go of the steering wheel for a second to raise them in surrender. "Call it what you wish, but I think I deserve a little pissing and moaning since you stuck your tongue down another man's throat after giving yourself to me."

Glaring at him, she yanked off her seatbelt and unlocked her door. "Stop the car."

"What?" he asked incredulously.

"Stop. The fucking. Car," she growled.

They both lurched forward as the car came to a sliding stop. Taking off her heels, Brigh pushed out of the car and, with the bottom of her dress bunched up around her knees, she made her way toward the grass mound she'd wanted to show him. She heard his door open and then slam shut, and a second later he was on her heels.

Directly behind her, keeping pace, she could smell his cologne, and through that the smell of pine needles and mud. "What is the matter?"

"I don't have time for jealous jerks, Morpheus. Either get over it or move on."

He was in front of her immediately, his hands wrapping around her arms to keep her still. The look on his face was of fear and confusion. Two expressions that were nothing new to his features, but their appearance made her stop nonetheless.

"I'm sorry," he began in a whisper. "I don't know how to do this yet."

"Didn't you have a century of practice at least watching people?"

He shook his head. "It's not the same. I'm trying, Brianna. I really am. It's just hard for me when you start kissing another man."

"I was dating that other man before you came along. I even came to the dance with him. The least I could do was let him kiss me."

He hung his head and closed his eyes. With a taut jaw he let go of her arms and took a step back. Silence stretched between them, and after a couple minutes, he still wouldn't meet her eyes. Though he looked miserable, his handsome façade and attire made her doubt herself. How was it that she'd made such a gorgeous man upset? Did she have the right? Or was he the one being childish?

"God," she gasped. "What the hell is going on? Why are we doing this? We're supposed to be enjoying prom— the fact that we're free from school in a few weeks. This isn't the end of the world."

"What if it is?"

"The kiss meant nothing," she murmured.

"Didn't seem that way from where I stood," he said just as softly.

Tears threatened her eyes as his words sunk in. She had done wrong by him. She'd given him a promise that had no words and broken it not twenty minutes after. But Kyle had also been wronged. A choice had needed to be made and she had. But there's always a price, no matter what.

The tears fell and she made no move to swipe them from her cheeks. "I'm such a horrible person."

"No." He looked at her then, seeming lost. "I forced you...I didn't give you a chance to decide."

"There's no contest."

He sighed, looking away. "Do not lie, please."

"Morpheus." She took the four steps to stand in front of him. Her palm slowly brought his face back to her, but his eyes wouldn't focus. She hated hurting him.

"Listen to me, Morpheus." He tried to look away, but both her hands kept him still. "I love Kyle, but not like I love you. You and I—we have something no one else can touch. I know you feel it too, otherwise we wouldn't be here. But you have to realize that I gave up a lot of things when you..."

"I understand."

The darkness within him was slowly seeping into her. Before she could second guess herself, she tightened her hold on his face and pulled him down to meet her lips. When he started to pull away, she grabbed tufts of his hair and held him in place, forcing his lips to open so she could release the sadness within. He'd taken in part of her soul, now it was her turn to take something of his.

MORPHEUS

He didn't know how to react to such a forward move from his innocent Brigh. He almost didn't recognize her. But that didn't mean such a surprise would be wasted. He held her so tightly that he was sure, with just a pinch more pressure, their atoms and molecules would merge and become one.

He lowered her to the warm grass, staring at the reflection of his face in her eyes. Kissing her forehead, his lips then travelled to tease the soft flesh of her neck, and when she gasped, he gently tugged at her skin with his teeth.

Brigh's hands found his hair, and she twirled his locks around her fingers. "I knew you'd not regret your ascension, you barmy fool."

He felt himself go pale in the warm wind as he pulled back to stare into her eyes. He hadn't noticed it before, but her hair held a very slight hint of red. Not like a natural strawberry blonde, but someone whose hair had been highlighted. "What did you say?" After a moment's pause: "Did you change your hair?"

Her brows met. "No, why?"

This change didn't sit well with him. The voice, the hair...they were too close to someone he once knew, someone neither of them wanted to remember. He didn't think it possible, but he couldn't ignore what was in front of him. Her voice had held that accent that couldn't easily be placed, and he knew her hair had been completely white blonde before this night instead of splattered with red. Had some of Narelle's essence mixed with Brigh's when the Elder's had banished her to the Hall of Damnation? He knew nothing about the Hall, except the fact that being's feared it. All he feared now were these changes, and wondered if they would stay minor or grow.

None of this would make any sense to her, and he didn't want to bring about panic, so he kept his lips sealed. He wasn't absolutely positive about the changes, but he wouldn't ignore them. For now, he'd pay close attention to details.

"No reason," he said with a nervous laugh.

THE END

I hope you enjoyed The Unfinished! Please leave a review on Amazon.com with your thoughts on the book. Reviews not only help other readers in their book search, but they also help me as a writer create stronger work for better books.

Let me know that you've left a review and I will add you to my list to receive a free e-book copy of any of my future books!

PLAYLIST

Many authors listen to music while they write to have background noise. Music, for me, works in a different way. Many songs have inspired scenes in my work, and how I feel during the song often dictates how the scene will work out. This book had many songs that inspired scenes, emotions, and more. I hope you enjoy these songs as much as I did while writing. Please remember to buy these songs, so the artists receive their due.

"The Poet and the Pendulum"	**Nightwish**
"Not Strong Enough"	**Apocalyptica Feat.Brent Smith**
"With or Without You"	**U2**
"She Don't Know Me"	**Bon Jovi**
"Faithfully"	**Journey**
"I Want to Know What Love Is"	**Foreigner**
"Second Chance"	**Shinedown**

Photo by Adam Geier

Tory Cameron is a University of Maryland, College Park graduate with her Bachelor of Arts degree in English Literature. Her poems, photographs, and short stories have been published in literary magazines and journals, as well as in The National Museum for Women in the Arts creative arts journal *Urban Inkslingers*. She's studied under authors such as Maxine Hong Kingston and Wanda Coleman in writing workshops, as well as having professionally edited eleven novels for published authors. She also co-created and co-starred in a short film for the Annapolis Film Festival; took three college courses at Cambridge University in Cambridge, England; and was given a creative writing award for Excellence in the Arts at The John F. Kennedy Center for the Performing Arts.

In addition, she's a voracious reader, crochets anything that has straight lines, is an animal and human rights activist, loves 60's-80's music, reads comic books, professionally pet sits for a living, and comes from a car racing family.

She currently travels back and forth between Tucson, Arizona and her hometown of Edgewater, Maryland. Most of the year she lives with her husband, a Siamese rat named Dwynn, and a rescued kitty named Phoenix, near a mountain in Tucson. This is her first novel.

Made in the USA
Middletown, DE
24 July 2021